PRAISE FOR KAIRA ROUDA

Praise for *Somebody's Home*

Listed as "Best Thrillers Coming in Spring 2022" by She Reads

"Whatever the opposite of family values is, Rouda seems intent on perfecting a genre that enshrines it."

—*Kirkus Reviews*

"Suspense and thriller readers will be on the edge of their seats for this novel that exposes the dark underbelly of human nature."

—*Library Journal*

"There are great characters moving the story along, that sweep away the reader in this story of families, revenge, and secrets."

—*The News and Sentinel*

"A truly unputdownable novel that had me gripped—and anxious—from the first sentence! Captivating, fast paced, and unsettling, *Somebody's Home* is astonishingly good. I gulped it down."

—Sally Hepworth, *New York Times* bestselling author of *The Good Sister*

"*Somebody's Home* kept me riveted from the first page to the last. A gripping psychological thriller you don't want to miss!"

—Lucinda Berry, bestselling author of *The Perfect Child*

"*Somebody's Home* starts like a hurricane out at sea: some wind, some waves, a sense of approaching danger. But the story moves fast, gains velocity, and suddenly you are turning the pages, unable to stop, heart in your throat, knowing that something terrible is going to happen and nothing will stop it. The threats come from all sides, and it's so hard to know who to trust. The characters are wonderful and complex; the setting feels like the house next door, which makes it all the more terrifying; and the ending nearly killed me. Kaira Rouda has written a terrific, gripping thriller."

—Luanne Rice, bestselling author of *The Shadow Box*

"With an intriguing cast of characters and a killer premise, *Somebody's Home* is a thriller worth staying up all night for. Fast paced and relentless, Kaira Rouda cranks up the tension with every turn of the page. With unexpected twists and jaw-dropping revelations, Rouda knows how to draw readers close and keep them entranced."

—Heather Gudenkauf, *New York Times* bestselling author of *The Overnight Guest*

"Privilege, social disenchantment, and extreme family tensions are the threads running through this tense novel. Kaira Rouda lets us into the lives of two families and what happens when their paths cross. Gripping and fast paced with an explosive conclusion!"

—Gilly Macmillan, *New York Times* bestselling author

"Taut with foreboding from the first page, Kaira Rouda's *Somebody's Home* is an unsettling portrait of an antisocial man, a master of the universe, and the women caught between them. The rotating points of view and incisive, clear writing are sure to keep you flipping the pages until you reach the shocking conclusion!"

—Katherine St. John, author of *The Siren*

"Trust your instincts and grab a copy of Kaira Rouda's *Somebody's Home*. In Rouda's latest thriller, a mother trusts her instincts when she knows the person on her property is threatening her family. But what if the threat is coming at her from all sides and more than one person is hiding a dark secret? A compulsive, fast read, *Somebody's Home* reveals what people will do to protect not only their homes but the families within those four walls. A captivating read."

—Georgina Cross, bestselling author of *The Stepdaughter*

Praise for *The Next Wife*

"Rouda hits the ground running and never stops . . . [*The Next Wife*] is so much fun that you'll be sorry to see it end with a final pair of zingers. The guiltiest of guilty pleasures."

—*Kirkus Reviews*

"This gripping psychological thriller from Rouda (*The Favorite Daughter*) offers a refreshing setup . . . Rouda keeps the reader guessing as the plot takes plenty of twists and turns. Suspense fans will get their money's worth."

— *Publishers Weekly*

"In *The Next Wife*, two women go ruthlessly head-to-head. Kaira Rouda knows how to create the perfect diabolical characters that we love to hate. Equally smart and savage, this is a lightning-fast read."

—Mary Kubica, *New York Times* bestselling author of *The Other Mrs.*

"Rouda's talent for making readers question everything and everyone shines through on every page of her propulsive new thriller, *The Next Wife*. Her narrators are sharp and unpredictable, each one with a tangle of secrets to unravel. *The Next Wife* will leave you tense and gasping, with a chilling twist you won't see coming."

—Julie Clark, *New York Times* bestselling author of *The Last Flight*

"One of the most insidious, compulsive books I've read recently. Kaira Rouda has a way of drawing you in with great characters, fast-paced writing, and a story that won't let you go. Brilliant, dark, and dazzling."
—Samantha Downing, *USA Today* bestselling author of *My Lovely Wife* and *He Started It*

"One man. Two wives. Kaira Rouda has masterfully created cunning twists and sharp narration that take you on an unexpected and delicious journey and will leave you with a gasp. Devious and fun, *The Next Wife* should be the next book you read!"
—Wendy Walker, bestselling author of *Don't Look for Me*

"I absolutely inhaled *The Next Wife*. Nail-biting suspense, dark humor, and family intrigue. I savored every page and now have the worst book hangover. Loved it!"
—Michele Campbell, internationally bestselling author of *The Wife Who Knew Too Much*

"No one writes deliciously devious narcissists like Kaira Rouda. *The Next Wife* showcases her remarkable talent for making unlikable characters alluring. With twisted egos, lavish wealth, and three women vying for power, this compelling, compulsive thriller is sharp, fun, and shocking. I was riveted by every word."
—Samantha M. Bailey, *USA Today* and #1 national bestselling author of *Woman on the Edge*

"Kaira Rouda has a gift for writing characters we love . . . to hate. Dark and devious, *The Next Wife* is a fast-paced, twisty thriller that will have you laughing, shaking your head, and gasping out loud right until the end. A perfect one-sitting read."
—Hannah Mary McKinnon, bestselling author of *Sister Dear* and *You Will Remember Me*

THE
WIDOW

OTHER TITLES BY KAIRA ROUDA

Suspense

All the Difference

Best Day Ever

The Favorite Daughter

The Next Wife

Somebody's Home

Women's Fiction

Here, Home, Hope

A Mother's Day: A Short Story

In the Mirror

The Goodbye Year

Romance

The Indigo Island Series

Weekend with the Tycoon

Her Forbidden Love

The Trouble with Christmas

The Billionaire's Bid

Nonfiction

Real You Incorporated: 8 Essentials for Women
Entrepreneurs

THE
WIDOW

KAIRA ROUDA

THOMAS & MERCER

Published by Thomas & Mercer, Seattle

www.apub.com

Amazon, the Amazon logo, and Thomas & Mercer are trademarks of Amazon.com, Inc., or its affiliates.

ISBN-13: 9781542039215
ISBN-10: 1542039215

Cover design by Damon Freeman

Printed in the United States of America

To the spouses, partners, and children of politicians. Thank you for your service and sacrifice—few will know how much you've given.

PART ONE

APRIL

LITTLE TIPS FOR NEW CONGRESSIONAL SPOUSES FROM MRS. ASHER, WIFE OF THE HONORABLE MARTIN ASHER (D-OH)

Welcome to Congress! I know, it's hard to believe you're here. You will be drinking from a fire hose these first few months, but I do want to get some items on your calendar. The very best events of the year are the Congressional Dialogues hosted by the Library of Congress. Any chance to get dressed up and be in the Jefferson Building is a recipe for success. Wear a special dress. Each member is allowed one guest, although senior members sometimes get extra seats. Go early and reserve seats for you and your hubby because the dinners are fabulous. Don't trust staff to do it for you, or you'll be in the very back of the room. Don't forget to wear your spouse pin!

JODY

Behind every successful man is a ruthless wife who made it all happen, or so they say.

My husband, Martin, seems to have forgotten that little truism. I may as well be a widow, what with the lack of attention he pays me these days. Sure, he's busy. He's always been busy. But this time it's different—this ignoring, this distractedness. It is something else entirely, and it's time it stops.

Fortunately, I've still got my looks, even if Martin doesn't notice anymore and hasn't bothered to look for me tonight here in the gilded halls of the Library of Congress. I smile as I check my reflection in the gold-framed mirror. Yes, I do look good. And he is decidedly not here waiting for me. We agreed to meet here at the first-floor entrance—him coming from his office in Rayburn and me from our townhome. In days past, he would've been here. But now, things are different. A strange tension has moved into the space between us, and it is pushing us apart.

I watch from my vantage point in the first-floor lobby as more members and their guests slip in through the side entrance under the stairs, a special entrance just for those of us with congressional pins. I touch my neck, the pearls holding the large gold-and-diamond pendant designating me as a spouse.

It's not the official pin issued to us at the beginning of every two-year term by the sergeant at arms. I have a collection of those—fifteen, to be exact—hanging from a bracelet on my wrist. The sixteenth pin, from this cycle, is in my jewelry box, ready to go when daytime events dictate.

The pin I wear tonight is by the famous jewelry designer Ann Hand. This one makes me look special, important. The other one—the official pin, with its small coin-like size and cheap metal backing—gives me rashes. I try to always wear the Ann Hand pin. My little way of standing out.

"Hello!" Mimi appears beside me in the mirror's reflection and squeezes my shoulders. Her shiny black hair, bangs and a bob, frames her face. She looks the same as when we met in law school more than two decades ago. "You look gorgeous tonight," she says.

Mimi is the one who looks gorgeous, bright-pink dress clinging to her thin frame, oversize breasts (implants, of course) straining the silky material.

She always has been the attention-getter in every room we share. Her Asian heritage made her exotic back in our law school days; her success since has made her even more stunning. But I have one advantage: she doesn't have a congressional-spouse pin. I smile and give her a peck on the cheek.

"I just love these events. Who are you with?" I ask. Mimi is a political animal, more connected than even we are, and that's saying a lot, since Martin has been in Congress for almost thirty years. Mimi and her husband, Spencer, run the Smith Institute, a well-regarded think tank.

"Congressman Labrond," Mimi says with a sigh. "It's hard to turn him down, even though he's a complete bore."

I smile and shake my head. "And because he's the chair of the Oversight Committee."

Mimi chuckles. "Oh, I hadn't even realized that."

She's lying. We both know it.

"Is Spencer here?" I ask, although historically speaking, her husband never attends social events, preferring books over people, research over reality.

"Of course not," Mimi says. "Where's Martin?"

"He was supposed to meet me here, at the entrance. Maybe he's running late?" I say. "Let's go on in."

We both turn and start up the worn stone steps that lead to the ornate Great Hall of the Jefferson Building, the sounds of a party—polite laughter and clinking glasses—drawing us closer. I glance at the mosaic of Minerva, the Roman goddess of wisdom, and hope for some. Beyond the Great Hall, down an elegant corridor, the open bar in the Members Room ensures the members of Congress are on time.

"Do you want to text Martin? Find out where he is?" Mimi asks.

"Likely holding court, charming staffers and guests with one of his old stories, if I had to guess," I tell her. Martin's endearing personality is larger than life. People are drawn to him, and he uses that magnetism to his advantage. I admire him for his relaxed acceptance of his place in the world, his innate look of power. He's risen through the ranks and is now chair of the House Foreign Relations Committee. Martin is undeniably handsome, with his midwestern square jaw, tall stature, and broad-shouldered physique, which looks good in a suit. Even at fifty-five, he still can command a room, especially around people who don't know him well and haven't heard all his stories.

We reach the main floor and the entrance to the members-only room. I nod to the library staffers monitoring the crowd. By now, I'm as familiar to them as my husband—one thing longevity in this town is good for.

"Welcome, Mrs. Asher!" says one of the young women who works for the library. Her name escapes me. "So glad you could join us!"

"Thank you," I say and paste on my campaign-wife smile. "I love these events. Wouldn't miss one."

I know better than to take a copy of the autographed hardcover sitting in a stack next to her. The books are for members only. Not spouses or guests. It's that way with a lot of things around here. My face hurts from the fake smile, so I allow it to slip away.

"Be sure to take a look at the artifacts in the Members Room before dinner," the helpful library worker adds. "They really bring the story to life."

Mimi thanks her and we make our way through the Great Hall of the most beautiful library in America to the Members Room, a stunning space with a view of the Capitol. It's a rectangular room, with eleven-foot walls of oak paneling, wood-carved arches over the doors, a beamed ceiling with paintings in the ceiling panels, and fireplaces at both ends. I remember my first time visiting this place, as a young wife after Martin's first congressional race. I was dazed and thrilled and overwhelmed. I expect to see a similar expression on a number of faces tonight.

Every cycle, the new spouses are invited to a luncheon in this very room, a place the general public cannot tour. Seasoned spouses welcome the new ones, tell them what to expect as best we can. We advise them to protect their calendar and their couples' time.

We try to warn them about what it's really like, but of course, nobody can. My shoulders tense as I think of all I've been through, all I've swallowed to keep Martin in his seat. I remember how naive I was back then, in the beginning, when he was first elected to Congress. That was a long time ago now.

"I see Martin," Mimi says, pointing toward a corner.

Yes, I see him too. He didn't wait for me. He's been here at the party. How dare he.

"He probably forgot your meeting spot. Let's get a drink before it gets impossible to reach the bar," Mimi suggests, pulling me through

6

the crowd of loud-talking, mostly male politicians, who likely have their second or third rounds in hand.

When we finally reach the front of the line, Mimi orders us each a glass of champagne.

"Thank you." I take the champagne flute before returning my attention to the back of Martin's head. I'm simmering with rage.

"I can't wait for the wedding this weekend. Charlotte will be a beautiful bride," Mimi says.

I take a deep breath. Yes, my daughter's wedding will be fabulous. It better be. It's cost us an arm and a leg, as they say.

Actually, it has cost much more than that.

"Charlotte is very excited," I say as we clink our champagne glasses together.

"That's what's important," Mimi replies.

I don't agree. What's important was for her to make an appropriate choice. At least someone from her own political persuasion. I urged her to take her time. But she's in love. I smile. I guess I can't fault her too much.

After all, I made the exact same mistake.

"Yes, there's nothing like young love." I meet Mimi's eyes.

"Like you and Martin back at Georgetown." Mimi winks, her dark eyes glistening in the golden light of the Members Room.

I smile at the memory. Law school classmates. I thought Martin Asher Jr. had come from a wealthy family. He thought a woman named Jody Prescott from Palm Beach had too. We were both wrong. You know what they say about assumptions.

"I guess we were just meant to be," I say and smooth my cocktail dress. The balls of my feet throb in my high heels. I knew better than to wear them, but sometimes fashion wins. I must admit, I struggle to keep up with the young spouses who appear like shiny new objects every two years. I also struggle to compete with the throng of newly minted graduates who are drawn to jobs on the Hill, swarming in every spring, as idealistic as the days are long.

And so young.

Mimi and I turn together and stare at my husband, whose head is bent toward the beautiful young woman standing in front of him. They're below a painting of the goddess of enlightenment. The woman touches my husband's arm as he turns away.

I know that woman.

The lights in the room blink off and back on. It's time for dinner. Martin looks my way, holds his hand up in a salute sort-of wave.

Beside me, Mimi says, "Nice of him to notice you. I don't like the optics of him with that young woman. She's one of his interns. They're standing too close. That's dangerous. And inappropriate."

"I don't know who she is," I say. I'm lying.

"Of course you don't. She's new. These politicians. They come in contact with so many people every day. And their young staffers—well, it's a revolving door," Mimi says. I happen to know she helps Martin fill those spots on occasion.

"Martin's harmless, you know that," I say.

"Right," Mimi says. She takes a sip of champagne. "Well, anyway, I don't know how these politicians keep anybody straight. Remembering all those names? Forget it." She shakes her head.

"Martin loves it. Always has. He has all kinds of tricks for recalling names. It's Martin's brand. It works for him," I say.

"Hello, ladies," Martin says. "Don't you look lovely tonight, Mimi."

"Oh, Martin, instead of flattering me, you should watch yourself, your behavior. You kept your wife waiting at the entrance," Mimi says, shaking her head. Then she smiles at me. "See you both this weekend." She disappears into the crowd to find the boring congressman she'll share dinner with.

"What's wrong with her?" Martin asks.

I can't find the right words, so I shrug. A dark voice in the back of my thoughts reminds me to hold on tight to him, no matter what. *He's the best you can get.* Thanks, Mom.

"Love the dress. Shall we?" Martin offers his arm to me.

And you thought chivalry was dead? It is—this is simply the pretense of caring. The actions of a man accustomed to the spotlight, playing his role, pretending his wife wasn't watching him looking cozy with a young intern: an intern who works in his office. Yes, I know exactly who she is. Sarah. New. Gorgeous. And apparently a big flirt. Just what we don't need.

I slip my arm through his and paste on my smile as we make our way out of the Members Room and into the beautiful corridor, Martin glad-handing and saying hi continuously. The flow of suits, and bipartisan goodwill of sorts, makes these evenings unique, no matter the featured author. The decor always matches the theme of the book, down to the era. Tonight, the ballroom is awash in suffragist banners, white table linens, and, as always, crystal and china to suit the theme. In this case, circa-1920s elegance.

"I'm assuming we're toward the front, if I know you," Martin says, squeezing my hand. I notice, just now, he looks gray, ashen. Despite his wide grin, he isn't feeling well.

"We're at the best table, right up front," I say. "Got here a little before the official time, but they all know me, so they let me in. Are you feeling OK? You don't look good. Do you need to tell me anything?"

Martin ignores my question as we arrive at our table. Because I could reserve only our two seats, it's anybody's guess who we'll be seated with. That's the point, the library staff tells us. Mix it up, make new friends. But we all know bipartisan friendship is a quaint notion from long ago.

I see our table is filled with representatives from our own political party. I take a deep breath, and as the other men stand, I slip into the seat Martin has pulled out for me. I say my hellos all around. Most of these men have been in Congress as long as Martin. The only exception is the couple across the table, who have the most unfortunate placement. Their backs will be to the program the entire night. They're young. They'll choose better next time.

I smile at the young spouse. Her eyes look glazed, from either too much wine during the cocktail hour or general anxiety at where she finds herself. Literally, the spotlight of the stage spills across her shoulders. Poor dear. In the headlight, so to speak.

I can't remember her name. I do remember a problem with appropriate attire, skirts too short, and a small-town accent. Oh well. She'll adapt or she won't last. I wish I could feel sorry for her, but I don't. She'll learn. Modesty and blending in work best here in DC—for the spouses, that is. There are no such rules for the members.

A waiter appears and pours red wine into the largest of the three crystal goblets in front of me. The other two are already poured, a white and what I believe is a rosé. I pick up the white, take a big sip, and try to forget about the young woman across the table. At least her husband seems solicitous, his arm wrapped around her shoulders as he tells some boring campaign-trail story.

"This will be another great night," Martin says loudly to the whole table, grabbing his glass of red. To me, he whispers, "We'll need to leave early, if that's OK. You're right. I don't feel well. And with the wedding coming up, I should take it easy."

"Sure," I answer, pushing away the anger. This is my favorite event. There is hardly anything fun left for us spouses these days. But that's OK. I will enjoy this lavish weekend—our only daughter's wedding— and all the festivities surrounding it.

"Thanks," Martin says. As the appetizers are served, he falls into a deep conversation with one of the representatives from Illinois. The man next to me is a bore, even worse than the congressman Mimi is stuck with. Talking to him would hardly be productive. Instead, I will pass the time waiting for the program to begin by remembering how far I've come, how much I've learned. On my own. Lesson number one as a political spouse: Don't expect anything. Not his time, not the team's thanks, and especially not a reliable calendar. Lesson number two: Nothing is a guarantee in this political life. Nothing.

I suppose I learned that lesson early. I couldn't count on my mom, and she was all I had. So I taught myself just about everything as a kid, without a lot of praise. I guess I was in training for this spouse role from a young age. I even taught myself to love, because my mom was incapable of it. And, for the most part, I've resisted my worst urges. I bet not many of the members of Congress seated at this table could say that.

I glance across the table at the young spouse. She's struggling over which utensil to use from the array at her disposal. I can't help myself as the stress of the past few years, the past few days, bursts from me in the form of an unseemly chuckle. I cover my mouth with my hand and decide I'd better excuse myself, get my wits about me. I push away from the table, laughter and tears mingling as I hurry toward the side exit.

Martin, wrapped up in his own conversation, doesn't seem to notice I'm gone. By the time I return to the table, the program has begun, conversation has stopped, all eyes and attention on the interviewer and the author onstage. Before dessert is served, Martin leans over and tells me it's time to go.

His driver waits for us on the street, idling between the Jefferson Building and the Capitol. There's nothing like the glow of these national treasures at night; it's enough to make you gasp in awe each time you see them, even after all these years. Martin pulls the door open for me and I slide in.

We ride the five short blocks home in silence. Perhaps neither of us trusts the words that might spill out. I turn and study my husband, the father of my daughter—the daughter who is getting married this weekend to a guy much like her dad.

Martin winces and turns toward the window. I know I should make him go to the doctor, but I won't. I know what is ailing him. Despite the fact the House physician is on call 24-7 for members—but not their spouses—Martin hardly uses his services.

I should care about his health. But right now, all I can see is Martin talking to that girl. Sarah. The girl slightly older than his daughter. A shudder runs down my spine. He needs to learn that this is forbidden. This is a serious threat. He needs to stay away from her, or he is going to ruin everything we've built. And all I know is I cannot let that happen. I won't. If he doesn't stop, his health will continue to suffer the consequences.

Our car rolls to a stop in front of our townhome, an elegant 1900s building we've fully restored with love and too much money. It's white with black shutters. It's the only thing black and white in our relationship these days. Most things between us are as gray as Martin's face.

I push open the car door because Martin doesn't appear to be moving, and I step outside.

"I'll be home in a little bit," he says.

"What? It's late. Come inside. You aren't feeling well," I say.

"I'll be home in a little while, Jody," he says. He leans across the back seat and pulls the door closed. They drive away, leaving me standing on the street alone.

How dare he? I stomp up the black metal steps to the front door and let myself in. I flick on the lights and pull out my cell phone. He's such an idiot, he really is. I watch as the dot representing Martin moves across Capitol Hill, stopping, as I knew it would, on H Street NW.

I walk over to our bar cart, pour myself a bourbon and one for Martin too. I drop onto the couch and kick off my heels. I will wait up for as long as it takes for him to come home. I will wait up no matter what he has done. No matter. I scroll through the endless TV stations, but I can't focus on anything. Finally, I turn to the local news. As the sportscaster begins his segment, Martin walks through the door. Game on.

"Come have a nightcap, Marty," I say, not looking his direction. I slip the Visine bottle into my pocket. I should have added more drops to his drink. I only added two. Four could kill him, and at this moment, I wish I *had* added four. I am beyond furious. His behavior is unacceptable.

"No, I'm going to bed," he says.

"It's not a request. You do remember everything we've worked for, don't you?" I ask, staring at the television.

I hear a sigh behind me. He takes the drink from my hand and finishes it in one gulp.

"You know, I'm certain you'd feel better if you stopped messing around with that young woman," I say. That's true. I'll stop if he does.

"Look, I can't take any more tonight, OK? The wedding has been enough. I'll talk to you tomorrow," he says. I hear the squeak of the third step as he makes his way upstairs.

I think of my mom, of all the times she walked away from me. I never do that to anyone, especially not someone I love. I've learned that much. I've always been there for Charlotte, for Martin. Always. I don't walk away from people, and no one should walk away from me.

Martin knows better, he really does. He knows what happens when he makes me mad.

LITTLE TIPS FOR NEW CONGRESSIONAL SPOUSES FROM MRS. ASHER, WIFE OF THE HONORABLE MARTIN ASHER (D-OH)

Use the extra official license plate! Put it on the dash of your car, and you can park anywhere in DC. Running errands is a breeze with the official plate. Don't let a staffer have it. Drive to his office and park in the garage under the building. Any spot not labeled is yours. Oh, and Rayburn is the most prestigious building. That's why my congressman has an office with a stunning Capitol view. Your spouse's lottery pick will determine where you start out. It will likely be a hole-in-the-wall, but everyone starts there. Good luck!

MARTIN

Rayburn House Office Building

My chest feels as if I'm trapped in a vise. I grab my water bottle and chug, hoping for relief. My office door swings open. No relief is in sight—just David, my chief of staff, the most efficient man in DC.

"Boss, we have a big problem," he says, closing the door behind him.

Although I know what he is going to say, I allow him to carry on. "What is it? I don't feel well."

"You're going to feel worse after you hear this. Seems this *Washington Times* reporter, a guy named Max Brown, is writing a piece about you." David sighs and drops into the chair in front of my desk.

"Why me? I'm boring," I answer and pull open my desk drawer. TUMS will help.

"You aren't boring, sir. He's writing a story about your ties to K Street and some of the major lobbying firms headquartered there. Seems he thinks you're being paid off by a firm, or several of them. It's ridiculous, I know, but he won't back down. Says he has proof," David says. He pushes his dark hair back in a move that is both annoying and familiar.

As I chew my TUMS—this one is cherry flavored and quite good—I take a moment to appreciate my surroundings. This is an office of stature. My walls are filled with awards and honors. There are framed photos of me with every president and most world leaders. Out my window, the Capitol dome glows in the morning sunshine. This is an office that tells anyone who enters that I am important.

"Ouch," I say before I can stop myself. I feel like I've just been stabbed in the gut.

"Sir, you need to see the physician," David says. "You look unwell."

"It's the wedding stress, that's all. It will be over on Sunday. Everything will go back to normal," I tell him. I look down at the floor, at the silk rug—a gift so valuable I couldn't take it home. Ethics and all.

"What do I tell the reporter?" David stands.

"Tell him my daughter is getting married this weekend. I will grant him an interview next week, when I have more time," I say. This wedding has drained all my savings, has stretched us to the limit. Jody is unable or unwilling to see it. And I am left holding all the unpaid bills. I have options, but nothing liquid. I let out a big sigh.

"I'll try to hold him off, sir," David says. "Are you sure I can't call the House physician for you?"

"I'm sure. Cancel all my afternoon appointments, please. Tell them I'm ill," I say. That isn't a lie. I am ill. But I have things to attend to.

"Of course," David says on his way out the door.

I stand and walk to the window. I pull out a new burner phone and place a call to the only person who can help me out of this immediate financial mess. He answers. I knew he would.

"Hey, I need more cash," I say.

"It's risky, as you know," he says.

"I don't have any other options," I say.

"Same amount?" he asks. I imagine him rolling his eyes, maybe even shaking his head. I'd promised not to ask for cash for a while. It was getting too dangerous. But here I am, begging.

"Double," I answer.

"Give me two hours," he says. "The reporter, he came here. He is watching me; he has some information."

"He has nothing. There's no way he knows anything. We've been too careful. And besides, I'm going to pay it all back. Don't worry," I say, then hang up.

I manage to take a deep breath before there's another viselike squeeze in my chest. Outside on the sidewalk below me, a line has formed to enter the building. Security screenings can back things up. There's so much to be on the lookout for.

Turns out, though, some threats can hide in plain sight.

LITTLE TIPS FOR NEW CONGRESSIONAL SPOUSES FROM MRS. ASHER, WIFE OF THE HONORABLE MARTIN ASHER (D-OH)

Get to know the Hill! It's such a fun walking city, especially in the daytime. At night, just keep your eyes open because, well, it is a big city with big-city problems. But seriously, during the day, Eastern Market is a treasure. Go there for fresh veggies, great deli goods. Shop all the surrounding boutiques. The weekend festivals and farmers market are excellent. Everything is better in the spring and fall, so if you're not living in DC full time, be sure to come to town then! Enjoy!

JODY

Au Bon Pain

My daughter selected this restaurant to meet because she likes the food and the speed of lunch. She likes to keep our alone time together brief. I would rather have met in the members' dining room over at the Capitol, where they have an elegant buffet as well as civilized table service. Her father could have popped by to say hi, perhaps, and I could have hobnobbed with the other members who happened to be dining there as well.

But Charlotte didn't want to deal with the security hassle and begged to meet here at this place. I get it. Adult kids of Congress members don't get to skirt the security line like spouses do. Not unless her dad is escorting her. But still, the members' dining room is much more my speed.

This is basically a glorified fast-food restaurant masquerading as a French bistro. The table hasn't been wiped properly, and my palm sticks to something icky. I pull out a wipe and sanitize myself. Another tip for spouses in this town of glad-handing: hand sanitizer and Lysol wipes are a must, pandemic or not.

Charlotte is late. As always. My beautiful, kind, intelligent daughter marches to the beat of her own drum—a slow, steady beat. She's my opposite. While I go through life darting about like a hummingbird, she's a graceful swan. We've made a certain truce with our differences. I think she knows I've always tried to do my best. She's what they consider "normal." Neurotypical. Martin insisted on testing her when she was in middle school. I'd assured him then she was as stable as her dad.

I brush a nonexistent crumb from the leg of my navy pants. It's one of my tips for new spouses: buy a sensible navy suit and low-heeled pumps—a uniform of sorts. I take a sip of tea and watch as a gaggle of four women walk into the restaurant. They all wear either red coats or red shirts. I gasp as I see one of the women is even wearing jeans. They spot me, unfortunately.

"Hello there, Jody," one of them says. She's the ringleader, I can tell. They are Republican spouses, but I don't know all their names. These women do not live here in DC but come in for weekends on occasion. It's odd, these separate lives they lead, but it must work for them. Their husbands often sleep in their offices to save money. I've told Martin for years there should be a rule against that. I mean, what constituent wants to come in and sit on a couch that doubles as your congressman's bed? Gross.

"Hello!" I smile and wave brightly. "What brings you all to town?"

I review the calendar of events in my head. I suppose it was last night's dinner? My question has elicited chuckles from the gaggle.

"Why, honey, your daughter's wedding rehearsal dinner," the ringleader says. "It's so fun to be included. Jim and I just can't wait."

I feel my face redden, the heat spread through my body. This doesn't make sense. None of them are invited to Charlotte's wedding. We don't even know them. I must act as though this is fine, as if I knew about this.

"Oh, of course," I say. I hide my face behind my teacup. They still surround me. I want to swat them like flies. I dismiss them with a wave of my hand. "See you tomorrow night."

The women saunter to a corner table opposite mine. I'm working hard to control my expression. I take a sip of tea. Charlotte will arrive any moment, and we will figure this out. Yes, that's what we'll do. Charlotte is practical, a problem solver of sorts. She'll explain why those women would be attending her wedding events. I take a deep breath and ponder her groom, JJ.

Charlotte is marrying a spoiled rich boy. Money is a plus, for sure—a plus Martin and I did not have. We had to start from scratch, get power the old-fashioned way. Charlotte will have a simpler road. It's much easier to push a boulder up a hill paved with gold instead of gravel. The boulder—Martin, in my case; JJ, in hers—must be pushed as well as supported.

Charlotte isn't ruthless, not yet, but she will become so. She is my daughter, after all. Otherwise, she'll be married to a rich loser, and that is the worst fate.

JJ is the only child of Jack and Margaret Dobbs of Grandville, Ohio. Jack and Martin went to the same high school, awkwardly enough, but were in different cliques, according to Martin. They hadn't seen or thought of each other for years. Fate has lumped us all together now.

I sense Charlotte enter the restaurant before I see her. Her smile is a cliché: she *does* light up the room. As she makes her way toward me, heads turn. Her hair is golden; her thin, five-foot-nine build makes strangers ask if she's a model. I do love her. I really do. I'm proud of myself for learning how.

"Mom! So sorry I'm late," Charlotte says, kissing me on the cheek and sliding into the chair across from me. "I hope you ordered for us?"

"I did, honey. How are you feeling? Any jitters?" I keep hoping she'll see the light. Marry someone better, more accomplished, less *Ohio*. I know, it's not a nice sentiment. I've learned to keep it to myself.

"No jitters! Just excited for this weekend, and the honeymoon, and for dinner tonight, of course," Charlotte says. Her engagement ring twinkles on her finger, dancing in the sunlight. It is gorgeous. It's twice the size of mine, not that I'm jealous, of course.

"Honey, I think we need to skip dinner tonight. Your dad isn't feeling well. He should rest up for the big weekend." I watch her smile fade. Truth be told, I should have paid more attention to Charlotte's future in-laws, but I've been so busy it slipped my mind. They are mid-westerners, so they'll be easy to manage.

Martin has a deep, visceral dislike of Jack Dobbs. His lips curl when he says Jack's name. It almost seems like a high school rivalry of sorts, although he says they didn't know each other well back then. Apparently, Jack was a rich bully, and Martin was a frequent target. A shy and skinny Martin who didn't stick up for himself. Of course now everything's changed. Jack still runs his family business, still lives in the same suburb of his youth, while Martin is a celebrity of sorts. Martin will never forget how Jack treated him then. Martin's made it a point to tell me we won't be friends with them now, either, which is absolutely fine with me. I have enough friends, and they are nobody. I do realize my daughter would rather have peace within the families. But as the song goes, "You can't always get what you want."

"Mom, you promised: one dinner with JJ's parents. Just to get to know each other a bit before the weekend," Charlotte says. Now her pretty mouth is pushed into a pout. I have a flashback to the beautiful, chubby toddler she once was.

"OK, fine. We'll go. For you," I answer. The Au Bon Pain employee brings our avocado toast to the table and delivers Charlotte's mint tea. I can pretend to like anyone for one dinner. I do it all the time. That's the spouse's job.

"I'm worried about Dad, too, but I know he can make it to a dinner," Charlotte says. "Do you know what's wrong? His voice sounded weak when I spoke to him on the phone. Last week, when I saw him for lunch, his skin was a weird color. Just unhealthy."

"Wedding jitters, maybe," I say and manage a chuckle. Of course it's not just the jitters, but that's my little secret. "I don't know what it is, Char. He's in the first year of his sixteenth term in Congress. He has achieved everything we dreamed of." That's a lie, but it's important to build up the husband to the children. I read that.

"Well, there has to be something," Charlotte says. Our eyes meet. "Anyway, I'm just worried about him, that's all."

"Well, OK, sure, he's under a lot of stress. And you know how he hates to part with his money." I smile but she doesn't.

"The wedding has to be stressing him out," she says. "That's probably it. The cost of everything. I hate to add more stress to his life. That job of his is already too much. But I don't know what to do."

"What do you mean? How could you possibly add more stress?" I ask. I touch her hand, but she pulls it away. "Charlotte. Do you know something I should know?"

My heart thumps.

"I just don't understand why Dad's team hasn't figured it out," she says. She's twirling a strand of hair around her pointer finger. She's hiding something. "I mean, I shouldn't be the one to tell him, or you."

"What do you know? What is it?" I ask the question and dread the answer. She doesn't know anything that I wouldn't know. Impossible.

"Someone is going to run for Dad's seat. They're announcing soon," Charlotte says, blue eyes blinking.

"Somebody always primaries us. It won't matter. The twelfth district is the Asher District," I say and begin to relax.

Across the table, Charlotte bites her lip. "This is different. It's a wealthy, connected Republican who thinks Dad has 'lost it.'" She makes air quotes, and as she does, the gaggle of Republican women laughs.

It's a coincidence. This is all nothing. If it were something, Martin would have known, and he certainly would have shared this with me.

"Don't worry about rumors, honey," I say.

"Mom, it's not a rumor. JJ told me everything. The man's name is Harold Kestler. He's announcing soon. Maybe this weekend. JJ's dad is friends with him. I think he's even a supporter. Excuse me, I'll be right back," Charlotte says. And much like a roadside bomber, she's dropped her news and exited for the bathroom before I can explode.

I pull out my phone and google *Harold Kestler for Congress*. And there it is. His website is under construction. More searches lead me to his filing papers and more websites under construction. I find out he's an entrepreneur, a self-made restaurant-chain owner. I find out he has an adorable wife and three elementary school–age kids.

I take a moment to purchase a few URLs on Squarespace before calling Martin. This is war.

LITTLE TIPS FOR NEW CONGRESSIONAL SPOUSES FROM MRS. ASHER, WIFE OF THE HONORABLE MARTIN ASHER (D-OH)

Your husband's time will be scheduled down to the minute. I'm not kidding. One of the most important features of his office will be the special clock mounted on the wall. It's not just any clock. On this one, there are six lights between the nine and two that coincide with the rings you'll hear coming from the clock. This is how things worked before texts. The clock tells your spouse when it's time to vote. If you know what the bells and lights mean, you'll know how voting is going. Of course, his chief of staff and legislative team will make sure he's on the House floor when he should be. This is one clock your scheduler cannot control. Everything else, they do.

You should be best friends with the scheduler, or at least pretend to be.

MARTIN

Rayburn House Office Building

Jody's call hasn't helped with the vise in my chest. As soon as we hang up, I google *Who the heck is Harold Kestler?* I discover I know him, sort of. He plays golf at my club in Columbus. He's younger, a successful guy who owns a restaurant chain that's growing across the country. One of his websites under construction is www.MartinAshersTimeIsUp.com.

He needs to stick to business. *His* business.

Or maybe he's right. Maybe my time is up. I stand and pace back and forth in front of my desk. It's been a good ride, this congressman gig. When I got the idea during my last year in law school, I thought it was a pipe dream. I still remember the moment I told Jody. We met during our first year at Georgetown Law. She was a stunner sitting in the front row. I could tell she was smart; she was always the first one to raise her hand when the professor asked a question. She had every answer correct. I loved how her blonde hair was pulled into a high ponytail, how it moved back and forth as she addressed the class. And her smile when our eyes locked made my heart bang in my chest. It was love at first sight, at least for me. Jody was the smartest student in our class. Beauty, brains, and—I found out—guts too. She was the whole package, everything I'd ever wanted. By the second year of law school, we were living together and planning our future.

The day I decided to make a run for Congress, I burst into the apartment—a dive that was all we could afford—and found Jody studying by the fireplace.

"Hey, what's up?" she asked, confused by the grin on my face, I suppose. Most of the last semester at school, I'd been complaining about my workload and clerking job. Grins were rare.

"I have an idea. The congressman representing Ohio's twelfth district is retiring. It's my hometown district. The guy has been there forever and wants to spend time with his grandkids. I want to move back home, with you, after we graduate and make a run for it," I blurted. "It's my dream, but I never imagined an opportunity would come up this soon."

Jody tilted her head, thinking. I knew the stories of her great-grandfather, the senator. I knew she was proud of her DAR lineage and her family's former political power. I knew she wanted that power back. But I didn't know if she'd believe in me.

"They'll rummage through your past. I hear from a reliable source you were quite the partier in college. They'll use that. They'll use whatever they can," she said.

"So what? Let them try. I'm not worried—not in the least. I'm the right guy for the district, I know it," I said.

"You'll need a partner," she said, grinning.

"I have one. You. You're a perfect political partner. You already look like the girl next door," I said. She did. And she knew it.

"We do make an attractive couple. Telegenic, I would guess, although I've never been on TV. I like it," she said. "Of course, we'll have to marry."

"Of course," I agreed. We'd discussed marrying, but now she was right. We needed to accelerate everything. I loved her. She was different from every other woman I'd dated in the past. Jody's own past was cloaked in mystery and, from what I could garner, sadness. That made me want to protect her, love her, even more.

I didn't know about her dark side until after we tied the knot. If I had known, I wonder, would I have married her? Probably—I was madly in love. Back then, in our tiny apartment, she smiled, stood up, and threw her arms around me.

"Let's do it, then. Together. If you're right and there will never be an opportunity like this again, not for years, we must do it," she said. "If you're up for the scrutiny, I'll stand by your side and smile."

"Heck yes," I told her. Back then, negative attacks were tame. I'd be accused of having no experience, of being too young. But I knew with Jody by my side, we'd wow them. "They need us representing them. We're young and attractive, full of energy and brains. We are the golden couple." The nickname our friends gave us during law school would stick and help our campaign. We even started to believe it.

"Sir!" David bursts into my office. "We have a challenger."

"I heard. From Mrs. Asher. Who heard it from our daughter. Why would she know before you? Before our district director or you, my chief of staff? Before anyone?" I am trying not to yell. I know I shouldn't, but I want to, I really do.

David ducks his head. "Look, sir, I'm not worried. I'd heard some rumblings about a well-financed opponent popping up, but nothing solid. Now we know. It's only April. We have months to gather oppositional research. He won't be a problem. All we need to do is keep clear of scandal, of trouble. No unforced errors."

I walk to the window, pretend to be viewing the dome, pretend to be contemplating my future. I've had such a good run. Who could have imagined this would turn into my life? Not I. Likely only Jody knew we'd make it here and stick. The moment I got the idea to run, she ran with it. She was the one with the vision for how our life together would unfold and that it would happen here, in DC. Without her support, her constant pushing, I likely would have ended up as a practicing lawyer at a midsize firm. I take a deep breath. She had bigger dreams too. Her only disappointment is I peaked early. No Senate seat, no presidential bid. But I like it here in the House.

It's easier to hide.

"What do you mean by 'trouble,' exactly?" I ask. I turn to face David, and he drops his eyes to the floor.

"Just that reporter, that's all," he says. He's mumbling.

"I'm not worried about him. You shouldn't be either. Go get the oppositional research started on good ole Harold," I say.

"Yes, sir," he says.

He's almost out the door when I add, "Send Sarah in."

I think I hear David sigh, but I could be imagining it.

I sit down at my desk and type in *Harold Kestler for Congress*. The website is a work in progress, but the guy has a finance committee, according to the filing papers. I scan the list of names and find Charlotte's husband-to-be's father at the top of the list. I slam my fist on my desk and stand up to pace. Of all the nerve.

Jack Dobbs is a piece of crap. Never worked a day in his life. While my friends and I partied like normal high school kids, Jack and his crew drove fancy sports cars and spent the weekends at second and third homes. What a poser. He's likely always been jealous of my rise to power. Sure, he has all the money, but money isn't the only thing that brings you happiness. You need power too.

Only one of us has a power position. I check my watch. I need to get going.

I hear a knock on the door. "Come in."

Sarah pokes her head through the door and flushes. She's so young, only a few years older than Charlotte. And gorgeous, with strawberry-blonde curls, huge brown eyes. But this has gotten too hot, too dangerous.

"Did you need something?" she asks.

As my stomach turns, I say, "Close the door, honey, and have a seat."

LITTLE TIPS FOR NEW CONGRESSIONAL SPOUSES FROM MRS. ASHER, WIFE OF THE HONORABLE MARTIN ASHER (D-OH)

I'm sure you're a bit worried about security, for you and your husband, and these days you should be. Rest assured, the Capitol, House, and Senate office buildings are secured. (Except for that one time when the Capitol wasn't, but let's not dwell on that.)

As a spouse, you are not required to go through the metal detector or to place your items through the X-ray machine. Just show the guard your pin. Based on recent events, these rules may change. It is one of the few perks we have left, so let's hope not. Oh, and please don't open any unusual-looking packages that may be sent to your home. They advise getting a PO box so there's another layer of security between you and a potential terrorist. I always felt bad putting the staff in jeopardy, so I just keep my eyes open. I've only had to call the Capitol Police once over a scary package. They whisked it away. Good luck!

JODY

Au Bon Pain

As I wait for Charlotte the bomb-dropper to return to our table, I think about the good old days when Martin first came to DC. When *we* came to DC. Where we would live was never a question; Ohio was never an option. We would move there, to Martin's hometown, only for his congressional campaign, and then we'd head back to DC, win or lose. I made that clear from the start.

"Mom, are you OK?" Charlotte sneaks up on me and takes her seat.

"I'm fine," I say. I am. No one can defeat Martin, no one.

"Sorry to drop this on you, but I just wanted you to know. And JJ's dad is involved in that Harold guy's campaign. I'm giving you a heads-up. But, please, I beg you, don't talk politics tonight at dinner."

I feel as if I've been punched in the stomach. My daughter is marrying the son of a guy who wants to ruin Martin's career. *End* Martin's career. How dare they? Charlotte is watching me, so I force a smile.

"Mom, I don't like the look on your face," she says.

"How long have you been sitting on this little piece of news? I know the Dobbses are Republicans, but I didn't expect this. Well, I guess I should have, shouldn't I? Aren't you insulted, Char?" I've kept my voice down and my tone calm. I cannot have the gaggle of spouses see me upset; no, that would not be acceptable. "Isn't it enough that you're knowingly marrying into a red family? And now this?"

"I don't know what to say," she says, then sniffs. I see a tear rolling down her cheek.

Now I feel something akin to remorse for making my daughter cry. I'll change the subject. The only thing Charlotte did was fall in love. This is all Jack Dobbs's doing, not hers. I will deal with him by shellacking his candidate. I take a deep breath and reach for Charlotte's hand.

"OK, stop crying. Let's focus on the lavish wedding we're hosting for our favorite daughter—the most beautiful and smart young woman in DC," I say. "How's that for a topic?"

Charlotte finds a tissue in her purse and dabs her eyes. The nosy ladies in the other corner would never know she was upset. That's my girl.

"You really have gone all out on this wedding, Mom. Thank you. It's a bit over the top," she says. "In a good way."

We are over budget and, according to Martin, one more wedding bill away from bankruptcy. He'll figure it out. He always does. I'm tired of his money woes and our fights. This is our only daughter's only wedding. It will be perfect. But back to the threat at hand.

"Yes, well, it's because we love you so much. And we want it to be perfect. Now, though, it could be a bit awkward. How well do your future in-laws know Harold? How closely tied are they? I saw Jack Dobbs's name on his website," I say.

"I shouldn't have told you. I knew you'd obsess over this. Don't worry. Dad will be fine, we all know that. That is his district—the voters love him there. I'm just sorry the Dobbses have ties to the guy, that's all," Charlotte says. She pours more tea as her diamond flashes at me.

"Look, I'm not obsessed. I'm just worried. He has a lot of money, and his backers do too," I say. "Dad *will* be fine." As long as he gets his act together. I remember the Visine in my purse as a cold chill rolls down my spine.

I think of Mimi's warning, my own intuition. Martin is making a mess of things. Across the table, Charlotte leans forward, a big grin on her face. Quite the change from a few moments ago, but I'll take a happy daughter over a tearful one any day.

"OK, now that the bad news is out of the way, how about some happy news?" Charlotte asks.

"Sure. Go for it. I know: You have something terribly embarrassing and borderline illegal on Harold Kestler?" I ask. "Tell me. Sex? Drugs? A gambling addiction? What is it?"

"Oh my gosh, Mom, it doesn't have anything to do with him," she says.

I try to keep the disappointment from showing. "OK, then, what is it?"

"It's a huge secret. Promise you'll keep it?" I don't like the strange look on her face.

"What now?" I ask, leaning forward, shaking my head. This appears to be the proverbial other shoe dropping.

"I'm pregnant," she whispers.

I feel the table shift, and my eyes drop to her stomach, hidden beneath the restaurant's wooden table. The old nursery rhyme runs through my head: *First comes love, then comes marriage, then comes baby in a baby carriage.* This is out of order.

"Mom?" Charlotte says.

I realize I haven't said a word, the thoughts ricocheting through my brain. She didn't look pregnant walking in. It must be early. The timing will be fine.

"A baby is a blessing," I manage. "Congratulations." I stand and close the gap between us, hugging her tightly around the shoulders. I've learned hugging is what people do to show affection, to demonstrate love. I also take the opportunity to notice her lap. No protruding belly, thank goodness.

I look around the restaurant. No one is watching us. I slip back into my seat.

"Mom, let's keep this between us for now. I'm going to surprise JJ on our honeymoon, probably the moment we arrive in Harbour Island. He'll be so excited," Charlotte says. "And Dad—well, he has enough on his plate. Promise?"

I want to protest, to tell her anything she tells me, she should tell her father or I will. But I don't. At the moment, Martin doesn't deserve such respect from either of us, and I like having this secret all to myself. I imagine my daughter stepping off a water taxi and splashing ashore. Telling her new husband the surprise. I imagine her barefoot and pregnant. Ha. Sounds romantic but still out of order. Oh well. This is one secret I will keep for sure.

"No one will know. No one should know. The focus should be on your wedding day," I say. "And it will be. No one will take that away from you. No one."

Especially not your dad or his upcoming campaign challenger, I don't add. *Especially not your dad and his looming scandal*, I don't add. It is going to be very hard to hide my anger this weekend. Every time I see Jack Dobbs, I'll see an enemy. Martin will feel the same. I tell myself to focus on the poorly timed baby growing inside my daughter's womb. Another Dobbs—just what the world needs.

I bite my lip and paste a smile on my face.

"So will you find out if it's a boy or a girl?" I ask my still-slim daughter. Her wedding dress will fit just fine, thank goodness. There is no time or money for another fitting, another dress. That much I know is true.

"I'm going to be surprised! I'll love the baby, boy or girl. What's the fun in knowing the future?" My daughter is so idealistic, so naive.

Knowing the future is everything. Planning. Preparing. Plotting. I would use every tool at my disposal, including when it came to my baby. I told you, we are very different women.

"So about tonight's dinner. Will the restaurant remove the steak knives from the table?" I ask.

"Mom, I really need you to behave. Promise?" Charlotte says. "I know it's going to be hard, especially with what I told you about JJ's dad. But I know you can do it. You're a politician too."

Whatever. I roll my eyes. "What should I wear tonight at dinner? Am I to wow your future in-laws or be subdued?"

"You can't help but wow. You know that."

Did I mention my daughter is almost perfect?

"Oh stop," I say.

"But, Mom, please be nice, OK? Don't bring up the campaign. I don't care what you wear. I just want you to behave."

LITTLE TIPS FOR NEW CONGRESSIONAL SPOUSES FROM MRS. ASHER, WIFE OF THE HONORABLE MARTIN ASHER (D-OH)

You must go on the Capitol dome tour. Trust me. The views from the top are astounding, and you'll never forget the history you learn on the way up. You can only do the climb with your spouse in attendance, so tell him it's at the top of your list. You'll thank me, I promise. Post pictures from the top so your constituents can take in the view too. Just don't promise you'll take them up there, because you can't—not without your spouse!

MARTIN

Rayburn House Office Building

Sarah sits across my desk from me, hands in her lap, brown eyes blinking. She's been on my team for only a couple of months. Mimi's recommendation, as I recall. Mimi should have known better.

"Look, Sarah, you are a lovely and talented young woman, and a fantastic intern for our office," I say. She rolls her eyes.

"What's going on?" she asks. Her crossed leg swings back and forth rapidly. I begin to tell her not to do that, but I catch myself.

"I've made a mistake here. Our flirting—*my* flirting—went too far," I say.

"Flirting?" she asks. She squints as if I'm shining a bright light her way. "I'd say it was more than flirting."

"No, sorry, it wasn't. I'm harmless, and well, sometimes, you know . . . I just get carried away," I say. My chest clamps up, and I search my desk drawer for a TUMS.

"I don't understand, Martin," Sarah says. Hairs perk up at the back of my neck at the way she says my name, the dark emphasis she places on it.

"Listen, you've been a great member of the team—you really have—but you need to go." I stand. "I will write you a recommendation, help you find another position."

"This is unbelievable. You must be kidding." Sarah pushes up from her chair and folds her arms across her chest. There's a knock on my door.

Sarah shakes her head, but she knows her place. I watch as she backs out of my office, all the while keeping her eyes locked on mine. She opens the office door and runs into my wife.

"Oh, excuse me, Mrs. Asher," Sarah says before hurrying away.

Jody doesn't say a word to Sarah. Instead, she raises her eyebrows and looks at me. She wears her favorite navy pantsuit, her spouse pin, and a scowl.

"Did you just get your hair done? It looks great," I say, dropping into my desk chair. I need another TUMS.

"No, I didn't. Nice try. What are you doing, Martin? Where did she come from?" Jody walks inside my office and gently shuts the door. I glance up at the vote clock, hoping for the bell-and-light summons. No such luck.

My attention lands on the stack of wedding-related bills. The ones I can't pay. Because of my wife. I can be indignant too.

"You're so far over budget on this wedding, that's what I'm doing. Sitting here, trying to figure out how to pay for all of this," I say. I stab my finger at the pile for effect. Right now, I'm drowning in bills and mistakes.

"Don't make this about me," Jody says, walking past my desk and taking a seat on the blue leather couch. For a moment, I have a fond memory of when we selected the pieces for my first office. We were new, so excited. After the lottery for new members, I secured a tiny office in the bowels of Cannon, but the space's lack of prestige didn't matter. We'd been elected. We'd won.

"Who decorates your office?" Jody asked at the time. It was a whirlwind, that first campaign, followed by a win, followed by a quick move to DC. We took one day to pick an apartment; the next, we found ourselves sitting in a meeting with the Architect of the Capitol, selecting curtains, carpet, and furniture for my office in DC. Oh, and then we had to set up my office in the district. It really was overwhelming.

"You do," I said with a smile, adding a big hug to smooth the way. I knew she'd love the decision-making process, actually; at least, that's what the more senior members had told me.

It turned out to be foolproof. They presented kits of sorts. These curtains match this carpet. We picked all blue. The Republicans in my class picked all red. Some guys picked gold, but I wasn't a fan. No matter your party, the furniture, like the couch Jody sits on now, was the same.

Jody runs her fingers along the seam of the couch. I doubt she's sharing the same memory.

"Remember when we decorated my first office?" I ask.

"Of course. We did make it look OK, for a hole-in-the-wall," she says. "Seems like so long ago—and then like yesterday."

I walk across the expensive carpet and take a seat on the couch across the coffee table from the identical one Jody is sitting on. "Look, I think I've worked out a way to pay for the remaining expenses of the wedding, but we need to watch ourselves. After this is over, we need to be low profile for a bit," I say.

"I'm on the First Lady's Luncheon committee. It's next month," she says.

Crap. It's her favorite social event of the season. The Congressional Club and Museum hosts the First Lady for a big luncheon at the Hilton. Thousands of people attend. And this year, she's on the committee, sitting at the head table just a few seats down from the honoree.

She loves all the social stuff in DC. I can't take that away from her. "Of course you need to do that," I say and feel my chest contract. Maybe, just maybe, we'll be fine.

"Of course I do," Jody says.

My phone pings. A text from David. The China story broke. And the reporter is back. What do I tell him?

40

I can't text what I want him to tell the reporter.

"What is it?" Jody asks, her anger dissipated by concern. "What's wrong?"

"Just a long, meandering piece about me and China came out in the *Washington Times*. It's boring and 'insider,' and no one will read it. The reporter—some Max guy—thinks I'm too close to China, the PRC. Like I'm an agent or something, of all things," I say. "I'll need to go handle it, though. Kill it, so to speak. No one cares about China; nobody will read a story about stuff like that. It's a ridiculous premise, anyway. Nobody has been tougher on China, in some respects."

Jody nods. "Agreed. You should point that out."

"I plan to. I haven't even talked to the jerk," I say. Of course, that lack of communication is my fault, not the reporter's. Being pro-China isn't a crime, I'll tell him. It's logical. They needed our help to survive and grow their economy, and I made sure they got it. If suddenly they are seen as a threat, that's not my fault. Things change.

Jody stands, hands on her hips.

"What?" I ask.

"That's not the story I'm worried about."

My chest-vise squeezes. "Don't worry about that guy running for my seat. Ohio twelfth is the Asher seat. Always will be, right?"

"Yes, it will be, dear, as long as you don't screw it up," Jody says. I watch her walk to the window, drawn to the view of the Capitol, as everyone who stands in this office is. I know I'm lucky, to have the view, to have this life, to have this wife.

"Everything will be fine. Let's focus on what matters. It's our daughter's big weekend," I say. "Look, honey, I've got to go. What time is dinner with the dreadful Dobbses tonight?"

"We'll walk over at six thirty," Jody says. She reaches for the doorknob closest to the window, the door that leads directly to my chief of staff's office. Even David barely uses that door. "Go figure things out.

Do what you must to kill the story. This weekend is about the best wedding in DC, the social event of the season. Not you. Understood?"

I take a breath. "Yes, of course."

Jody pulls the door open and closes it behind her. I take that as my cue to exit. In this lavish office of mine, I have a private entrance, my own bathroom, a room with a safe for important documents, and a closet. I could live in here if Jody ever left me. She wouldn't, of course. We're a team. We're in too deep.

I escape from my office and hurry down the hall. At the elevator bank, I press the button for the members-only elevator. I love that this elevator is only for me and my kind. No lobbyists, no constituents, no nosy staffers. I find peace inside it as I descend. I try not to think of Sarah, of the look on her face. She's young, she'll be fine. I'll call Mimi, have her find a new office for her. This will be Mimi's mess to clean up.

I check my watch. I'm late.

Little Tips for New Congressional Spouses from Mrs. Asher, Wife of the Honorable Martin Asher (D-OH)

Your relationship with the chief of staff is vital to your husband's success. The COS oversees the entire office staff, both in DC and the district office, and operations. He can make your life miserable if he wants. And, I suppose, vice versa is true. A happy member has a happy spouse. In my opinion, it's the COS's job to make that so. I've consoled too many distraught spouses, frustrated at being left out. Don't let that happen to you. And if it's happening, make it stop.

JODY

"What is it, Mrs. Asher?" David barely looks up from his desk, his deeply lined forehead glistening with sweat, before he drops his head back onto his fist. So dramatic. I do not like this man, and the feeling is mutual. He is a slob, his suits are always wrinkled, and his droll demeanor is completely joyless. He's like a dark cloud lurking in the corner, predicting trouble at every turn. His cup is always half-empty, and I'm tempted to put a dozen drops in the old coffee mug molding away on his desk. But I won't. Of course not. We pretend to get along for Martin's sake. Martin will not fire him, despite my urging for years.

Martin is loyal to a fault. David is an example of that weakness.

I may be another.

"Oh, David, so good to see you too," I say. I cross the small room and take a seat in the chair next to his desk. As I watch, he slides papers into the top drawer, hiding things from me. I really hate that.

"I'm busy. Can we chat another time?" he asks.

I don't like his tone. I don't like his face. I've been in his apartment. He lives like a pig. I wonder if I should tell him that? A rush of adrenaline flows through me at the memory of my little anonymous visit. I'm angry I didn't take more of a token, a remembrance. He has quite a campaign-button collection, likely valuable. Instead, I pocketed his favorite ugly tie. I'm sure he still misses it. I'm harmless, really, I am.

"I just want to remind you that I know everything that happens in this office. Everything. I'm the spouse. Don't forget that, David," I say.

David chuckles. It's annoying.

"I'm serious," I say.

"Oh, I know, Mrs. Asher. You've made that very clear over the years."

Someone knocks on the outside door. David yells, "Not now." But the office door opens anyway.

"Hey, I'm tired of waiting out there." A scruffy-looking man with long dark hair and a press badge stands in the doorway. "Your comms director never came back."

David sighs. "Yes, well, she's out sick. Sorry."

"Sure she is," the reporter says. He notices me. "Mrs. Asher? I'm Max Brown. I'm writing about your husband, his apparent ties to K Street, China, and others. Can I ask you a few questions?"

What is wrong with people? "How dare you barge in here without an invitation? Has no one taught you any manners? And no, you can't ask me any questions."

"Some of the money he's received through the years—well, you must know about it. His salary here on the Hill isn't enough to pay for your lifestyle," Max says. He's aiming his phone at me like I'm going to say something.

I'm not.

"OK, look, this is awkward, but I'm running another piece," Max says when I keep my silence. "I'm sorry to break this to you, but I am investigating your husband. His improper connections to China are just the start. I got a tip about your husband having an improper relationship with an intern, as well as improper use of his office budget. Maybe you want to comment on that?"

I stand up and walk to face him. I'm taller than he is, more powerful than he is.

"How dare you say something like that? Do you know our daughter is getting married this weekend? This is a celebration for our family. You and your innuendos, your lies, are not appreciated. I have no idea why you suddenly seem to have this vendetta against my husband. He is a beloved congressman."

"Yes, he has been on the Hill a long time," Max says. "Some would argue too long."

"What did you say?" I try hard not to sound shrill.

"Stay calm, Mrs. Asher," David says from behind me. It's about time he intervened. I'm sure he was enjoying this entire interaction, me on the defensive. "That's enough, Max. I told you, the congressman will meet with you early next week."

Max stares at me. "Next week is too late. I'm going to run the story. I'm sorry you'll have to find out things about your husband this way."

"I know everything about my husband. He is a true public servant. You have nothing," I say to him. "You are fake news."

"All right, both of you stop," David says. "I'll clear his calendar. Monday morning, he'll meet with you. All topics are on the table. Just let the man and his wife enjoy this weekend. That's all we ask. Don't ruin his only child's wedding with this crap. Come on. What's the harm in holding the story? It's Thursday. Give him the weekend in peace."

Max looks from me to David and back to me again. "I'm sorry, Mrs. Asher. I really am. Have a nice wedding," he says.

I push past him and walk through the constituent waiting area, nodding a hello to the newest intern manning the constituent desk, thankful it isn't Sarah. They all look like twelve-year-olds, those interns, younger every year. So ideological, so impressionable. Heck, the staffers are young, too, except David.

Except me.

I'm too old to be playing these games. And Martin, well, he knows better than to hide from the media. You need to control the story, be in front of the story. And at all costs, you need to avoid being the story.

As I walk down the stark hallway of Rayburn, I decide to call Mimi. She'll know what to do about this. My call rolls to voice mail. I leave a message. "Hey, call me when you can. It's about Martin. This reporter is trying to ruin him. I need your help."

Outside, the afternoon sun is warm, but inside I'm chilled. The China stuff won't stick. Everyone in Congress is lobbied by K Street—give me a break. Nobody really cares who takes money from whom. The public just expects it, anyway. All politicians are bought and paid for. It's the American way. I take a deep breath and hurry the five blocks home.

I need to let go of this for now. Martin says he's handling it. Just for this weekend, I'll focus on Charlotte. On her happiness. I will not focus on the baby, because it's out of turn. The baby will be celebrated when she returns from her honeymoon.

I have enough to juggle, enough social scandals to try to avoid. I am somebody here. I am a tenured senior spouse. I am respected.

And I will remain so, no matter what.

LITTLE TIPS FOR NEW CONGRESSIONAL SPOUSES FROM MRS. ASHER, WIFE OF THE HONORABLE MARTIN ASHER (D-OH)

Ethics, ethics, ethics. Those three words are key to your survival here in DC. You and your spouse will be held to the highest of ethical standards. This should be welcomed, of course. You will receive a briefing. If you have any specific questions, call the Office of Congressional Ethics. It's better safe than sorry. Bottom line is, you cannot take anything as a gift. Nothing. Those days are long over . . . the good old days, as I like to think of them. You should see all the wonderful gifts we were given back in the day. But you? Accept nothing.

MARTIN

The Asher Townhome

It's tempting to close the door to our bedroom and go to sleep. I feel awful. I look at myself in the mirror: I look terrible—eyes clouded, ringed by dark-red circles below. I suppose this is what it looks like to be rotting from within.

I'd like to blame so many people for this situation I'm in. But, in truth, it's all my fault.

My phone rings. It's Joe Roscoe. I want to decline the call, but I know I can't.

"Did you get the package?" he asks. His voice has a mob boss tone to it, now that I think of it. Roscoe & Partners is one of the biggest lobbying firms on K Street. You don't become that powerful without being equally ruthless. And he is.

"I did. Thanks," I say and avoid looking in the mirror. "I won't ask again. And I will pay you back. It's a loan."

"Right," Joe says. "Look. I know it's for Charlotte. She's lovely, deserves the best and all. Remember when she interned here?"

I hate that Joe knows my daughter, my family. I hate that I'm so beholden to him and to too many others like him. I hate just about everything right now.

"I remember. Look, Joe, there's going to be a *Washington Times* story out—probably tonight, online—about me. It's not going to be good," I say. "But don't worry. You won't be implicated in any way. The reporter is focused on China, for some reason."

"That better be the case," Joe says, more mob boss than ever. "No one cares about China. They should but they don't."

"I do. I want to keep them close, you know. That's all I've ever wanted. Friendly relations."

"Oh, cut the crap. That's not all you've wanted from them," Joe says. "I'll see you at the wedding. And, Marty, I better not be mentioned in the *Times* piece."

He hangs up and I drop into my favorite chair. Our bedroom has a giant window overlooking a grand old oak tree. The tree is so large its roots push up against the sidewalk, causing a bump next to our front gate. I don't want it fixed. I like the metaphor of the tree surviving, thriving and pushing against things trying to keep it down. I am the tree in some ways. No one ever thought I could overcome a questionable party animal past to become a congressman. No one believed in me but Jody, and she did for her own reasons.

We found a mutually beneficial life together. I would forgive her impulses, and she mine. It has worked well. I will never forget our first trip to Davos, where all the world leaders gather to talk and schmooze and connect. We were invited after my third term in Congress, when it became clear I would be a standout, a beacon of foreign relations. Jody had always dreamed of traveling to Switzerland, and both of us jumped at the chance to go on Congressional delegation trips, called CODELs, since I'd joined Congress. We've been on CODELs around the world, all for free. Davos was different, though. Next level.

As I delivered my remarks to a packed room of the most important men and women in the world, I spotted Jody in the crowd, hand over her heart, tears of pride streaming down her cheeks.

"We mustn't punish China for trying to join us as a leader in the international markets," I said. "Let's not push our own climate agenda down their throats, but rather work with them, help them to reach our levels of carbon emissions. We need to continue to help educate their population, grant the student visas. A more-educated Chinese population will make for a better future for all of us. The Chinese, I assure you, are more interested in economic growth than global domination. China's rise will be peaceful. We'll leave world domination to the USA."

The room erupted in applause. Jody jumped to her feet, as did her best friend, Mimi, by her side. After we'd all graduated law school, and Mimi and Spencer started their own think tank, Jody and I had questioned their sanity, much as they questioned our decision to move to Ohio and run for this congressional seat.

Turns out, we'd all made bold, spectacular choices. Mimi and Spencer's Smith Institute is one of the most respected in DC. And until this story drops, at least, Jody and I have been the toast of Washington. There is an end to everything, I suppose.

Sarah's angry face floats into my mind. I made a mistake there. One I must fix quickly. I pull out my phone and dial Mimi's number. Her voice mail picks up.

I leave a message. "It's Martin. We need to talk. Call me."

From downstairs, my wife yells, "Martin! Are you ready yet?"

No, dear, not at all.

"Give me ten minutes," I yell through the closed door. I really don't want to face Jack Dobbs, let alone have a meal with him. This I will do for my daughter. For appearances. I hope the goddamned story doesn't break tonight. I can only imagine the smug look on Jack's entitled face. He's always wanted to bring me down, I know it. I stand slowly, and the room seems to shift under my feet.

Everyone takes money from K Street. Vice President Acton openly told lobbyists if they wanted anything from his administration, they'd better pony up to his super PAC. If Max doesn't back down, I might have to tell him about some others I know. Maybe I can make a deal, although I'm certain a deal with the press is itself political suicide.

I pop a TUMS in my mouth as a wave of dread washes over me. I am worried that I may be precipitating my own political demise, that it may already be a done deal.

LITTLE TIPS FOR NEW CONGRESSIONAL SPOUSES FROM MRS. ASHER, WIFE OF THE HONORABLE MARTIN ASHER (D-OH)

The social calendar, from your perspective, may seem daunting at first. Just remember, you don't need to attend them all, but please mark your calendar for the First Lady's Luncheon in May and the White House Ball in December. If you don't attend anything else, these are the two you must. They are bipartisan festivities, and that's rare. The First Lady's Luncheon is a tradition that began in 1912 and brings together the spouses of the leaders of our government for one magical luncheon. Tickets always sell out. Mark your calendar now! And as for the White House Ball? Well, you better start shopping for that special ball gown. It is black tie, and the White House is decorated for Christmas. It's like floating through a fairy tale: you'll pinch yourself.

JODY

Martin is dragging us down.

Those are the only words that come to mind as I stand at the bottom of the stairs, yelling at him to hurry like he's a child late for school. I check my makeup in the foyer mirror. I think I still look acceptable—pretty, even—for fifty years old. I'm thin because I watch what I eat and ride my stationary bicycle. I'm wrinkle-free thanks to my discreet plastic surgeon, one of DC's most carefully kept secret weapons. And I'm the mother of the bride this weekend, a cause for celebration and wide society-page coverage. Tonight's outfit is just the beginning of the fabulous wardrobe the wedding planner helped me select. Vanessa LePlum is the talk of the town for good reason and worth the exorbitant price tag for her services, despite what Martin says.

I exhale a big sigh. We could have risen higher. I know we could have. Martin once wanted that: a Senate run or even, dare we say, a run for the White House itself. There was a time when the political operatives thought that for us. There was a time not so long ago when we were the new, shiny, beautiful couple, capable of anything. I swallow, pushing those memories aside. We peaked at the House of Representatives, and that must be fine. It *is* fine. It is everything now.

I hear Martin tromping down the stairs. I'm not going to worry about the reporter's silly story, not anymore. Scandals happen all the time in DC, especially among the members of the other party. This will blow over as fast as it popped up, like a summer storm. That's how these things work.

My phone pings as Martin joins me at the bottom of the stairs.

"You look lovely in pink, Jody," Martin says. I do appreciate his appreciation of my looks, even as he complains about the cost of maintaining them.

"Thank you," I say. I peck him on the cheek and turn to my phone. It's a Google Alert for Martin, and it's the story we tried to stop. "Congressman Faces Questions about Ties to K Street Lobbyists, Chinese Think Tanks," by Max Brown.

Martin meets my eye after I finish scanning the story. "It's thin. No sources on the record. And you, of course, didn't comment. It will be buried, page seven or deeper," I say. "There is nothing to be found here, right?"

Martin smiles and slips his arm around my shoulders. "Of course not, Jody. Everything is as it has always been. Aren't we late?"

I take a deep breath. "Yes, let's get going."

We walk down the black metal steps of the townhome side by side, Martin's arm slipped through mine. It's almost as if all is well, as if tonight is the start of a wonderful weekend of celebration. Almost. As we walk down our charming historic street—tulips bursting from gardens, new buds bursting from trees—I feel hopeful. Maybe the wedding weekend will be all I dreamed.

"Are you excited for the wedding? I know you've worked hard on everything," Martin asks.

I look up at him as we cross the street and enter Stanton Park, one of the prettiest in the city, in my opinion. The sunset paints the sky a bright pink and soft orange. I remember when we first moved to DC after Martin's win. I imagined we'd live in an apartment on

Capitol Hill for his first term. The Hill is the largest historic residential neighborhood in DC, stretching east in front of the US Capitol along wide avenues. More than 35,000 people live packed densely within the two square miles of the Hill, but I didn't imagine we'd be here very long. My plan was to quickly make our way to the DC neighborhood of Kalorama, where the rich and powerful all live: presidents, representatives, ambassadors. Even my great-grandfather, the senator, had lived in Kalorama, back when the Prescotts were "somebody," as my mom would lament. The elite neighborhood is filled with embassies, large mansions, and famous people. It's the DC power center.

I hired a young real estate agent, who set up a Sunday afternoon of property showings for Martin and me. He humored me, I suppose, just so I could learn the truth.

"This is the most beautiful home I've ever seen," I exclaimed as we parked in front of the first open house on our list. "Martin, isn't it beautiful?"

"How much?" Martin asked the real estate agent. Her answer left him shaking his head.

"We can stretch, honey, with your salary. And once the baby is a few years old, I'll go back to work at a law firm. We can do this," I said. I opened the car door and hurried toward the front door, painted a cheerful red. I remember it all like it was yesterday. Martin refused to come inside.

"I can't bear it, letting you down like this. But we can't afford this neighborhood," Martin said when I returned to the car.

I took a breath. "OK, Georgetown first?" I asked.

Martin turned to the Realtor and said, "Sorry for wasting your time. I think you should take us back to the Hill."

My face burned with shame the whole drive home. But instead of taking Martin's words to heart, I challenged myself to get creative.

Eventually, we were able to buy our townhome. It may not be where I'd imagined, but it was I who manifested it.

I remember Martin's question, his attempt to turn our conversation away from politics to the lighter subjects of me and our relationship, our family, and especially, the all-important wedding.

"I am excited, of course, and so is Charlotte." I swallow at the mention of her name, keeping my daughter's secret. "But I'll tell you one thing: tonight was not part of the plan. I'm still mad she talked us into it."

"She can talk us into anything, you know that," Martin says as he steps into the crosswalk. I yank his arm, pulling him back on the curb just in time to avoid being flattened by a speeding truck. "Wow, thanks."

Now he looks even worse. Ashen and shaky. "Martin, you may need a doctor. You aren't well," I say. The light turns green and we cross safely.

"I know. After the wedding. I'll handle everything after the wedding. Don't worry, Jody."

I shake my head as he gives my shoulder a squeeze. In the past, I was quick to forgive his flirtations, his mistakes. He'd bring flowers or surprise me with a Congressional delegation trip. He'd make things better between us again, and I'd move on. He always has been hard to stay mad at. It might be his twinkling blue eyes, his movie-star square jaw, or the way he holds my hand to tell me we are a team.

But this time is different. I'm still so furious I can't feel anything for him. Why doesn't he know by now that an intern, especially one who is almost Charlotte's age, is off-limits? Period. He is a fool, a laughing-stock, an embarrassment. I take a deep breath and try to push Sarah out of my mind.

Up ahead, I spot Charlotte and JJ standing on the sidewalk. I check the time. We are twenty minutes late. I give them a big wave and my political-spouse smile. I still wish Charlotte had picked a more suitable mate. JJ is a low-level staffer at the State Department. He's without drive or ambition. But I forget about maligning my son-in-law-to-be when I see my daughter's pursed lips. A frown looks so out of place on her sweet face.

"Mom, Dad, where have you been?" Charlotte is mad too. For good reason, I suppose.

"It's all right, Char," JJ says, trying without success to calm Charlotte down.

"It's my fault, honey," Martin says, surprisingly taking responsibility. He rubs his chest. He's a mess. "I hope your folks aren't too mad, son."

"No, they're fine. They know how busy you are, sir." JJ's deference seems genuine, but who knows these days? Who knows anything?

"Well, let's not keep them waiting any longer," I say and lead the way through the packed outdoor-dining courtyard and up the stairs. My favorite French restaurant is tucked inside a completely renovated town house, and it's the epitome of romance and power meals combined. We're near the Senate office buildings, and as we walk through the door, I hear a man call out to Martin. He excuses himself and heads toward the bar, where the man is seated.

The host appears. When I tell him the name on the reservation—a reservation that is coveted, especially for a party of six—the man bows and says, "Your guests are here. They were on time, n'est ce pas? Follow me."

He should watch his attitude. Of course our guests, the Dobbses, were here on time. What else do they have to do? As we follow the host up the stairs to the second floor, the red-room seating I requested, Charlotte grabs my hand.

"Mom, promise me you'll behave. For me?" she whispers.

"Why, darling, I'd do almost anything for you," I answer. And I have.

"Mom," she warns.

"As long as we don't talk politics, we should be fine," I tell her. "If Jack Dobbs goes there, well, I can't make any promises."

"And voilà!" the host says, sweeping his hand dramatically toward a couple seated at the corner table. "Your table is just there."

I take a moment to glance at Jack Dobbs. He returns the favor before the happy young couple notice.

Oh, game on.

LITTLE TIPS FOR NEW CONGRESSIONAL SPOUSES FROM MRS. ASHER, WIFE OF THE HONORABLE MARTIN ASHER (D-OH)

Etiquette is everything. If you weren't brought up in a formal household, it's time to teach yourself. Of course, I was one of the lucky ones, born with that proverbial silver spoon, but my heart goes out to a spouse or two each cycle who is caught off guard by her lack of breeding, overwhelmed by a formal dinner party or a ball. Don't let that be you! Resources abound, and once you join the Congressional Club and Museum, I'll be able to point you in the right direction. Come see me during orientation, and I'll show you the etiquette library. We'll get you fixed right up, or at least start rounding those rough edges.

MARTIN

Bistro Mon Cheri

Of course the guys at the bar are familiar: they're lobbyists. This is their Thursday-night gathering spot, as I'm well aware. I scan the group. Fortunately, Joe Roscoe is not here tonight. I've sent five calls from him to voice mail so far. As much as I'd love to know what's happening, I can't deal with him right now.

"Marty, have a seat. Tell us what's going down." A guy named Sid pats the stool next to him.

"Hey, Sid, good to see you. Just same old, same old," I say, shaking his hand.

"What do you think of the *Washington Times* article?" he asks.

"It's a bunch of crap, as you all know," I say. "Look, it's good to see you guys, but I'm having a family dinner, so I've got to get going."

"The wife still wants to eat with you?" a guy I don't recognize asks, smirking. I hate smirkers.

What does Jody have to do with the story? I wonder. "My wife isn't part of any of this. She's not in the story," I say. "See you guys later."

"She's not a part of the story that hit today, but she'll definitely be interested in the one that lands tonight," smirker guy says.

What is his name? I'm searching my brain. I am great with names, typically. This is not a typical day. And why would he know anything about an article that hasn't been published yet? "Have you been talking dirt about me to the reporter? What are you implying?"

"Let Martin go enjoy his meal," Sid says to the loser smirker. He turns to me and says, "Keep your head up, and keep your hands off your staff."

I swallow. "Don't even go there. I've been in this town longer than most of you. I'd never."

Smirker guy chuckles as I walk away. I slip a TUMS into my mouth as I reach the stairs.

"Good to see you, Congressman," a friendly-looking man sitting with two women calls to me.

I wave but don't go over to their table. I really need to get to dinner and then get home. And then call David. He warned me that the reporter wasn't finished, that he was planning another piece. I thought he agreed not to write anything until we meet on Monday. I can't imagine the reporter would run anything else about me without at least talking to me first. One story is enough. More than enough. I hurry up the stairs. I know where the table will be located—in the red room, as Jody calls it. The space is suffocating to me: heavy red velvet curtains, busy wallpaper, crystal chandeliers, booths barely big enough to sit comfortably. Jody tells me it's romantic, so we can "snuggle." We never do that, not anymore. Instead, I end up feeling trapped.

I stop in the hallway, reach in my pocket, and pull out my daily briefing. Every day, my scheduler hands me a sheet with the day's meetings, every person in them with a photo and a summary of their interests and requests. Included will be my talking points where needed, my policies where helpful. I'm lost without it.

I flip to the last page.

EVENT: DINNER

PURPOSE: Chance for parents to meet before the wedding

WHO: **Jack Dobbs.** Wealthy entrepreneur, restaurant business owner. Republican donor. You went to the same high school. Soon to be your daughter's father-in-law 😊 On website as campaign committee member for challenger **Harold Kestler**. Avoid politics for Charlotte's sake (Charlotte told me to add this).

SPOUSE: **Margaret.** Describes herself as an author. Library volunteer.

SON: **JJ.** Soon to be your son-in-law! State Department staffer.

I take a deep breath and try to settle my pounding heart. I am fine. We are fine. Sarah was a flirtation taken a bit too far, that's all. Nothing more.

I step from the hallway into the red room and sense the air shift. Diners stop their conversation, and a murmur rolls through the room. I am a celebrity of sorts, I suppose. But this type of response is atypical. Shit.

"Hey, Congressman," a woman says as I pass by her table. "Nice to see you. Ignore all the negative press. It means you're making waves, right?"

I pat her on the shoulder. Bless her. "Yes, exactly. Thank you. Enjoy your meal."

It's nice to have allies. It is. I look away from my supporter and toward the table in the corner of the room. Jack and Margaret Dobbs face my direction, and I see them watching me. Jody's back is to me. Charlotte and JJ sit together, practically in each other's lap. The empty chair between Jody and Charlotte is for me, unfortunately, directly in Jack's line of fire.

"Hello, everyone. Jack, Margaret, I apologize for being so late," I say and sit down because Jack Dobbs does not stand to shake my hand. Figures. He's a dick.

"Your wife has been busy trying to charm us, distracting us—beautifully, of course," Jack says. "Wine? We ordered a red."

"Thanks, no. I'll start with something else." I turn my head and a waiter appears. "Double scotch, on the rocks. No garnish."

Jody swats my leg under the table. A second later, my daughter does the same. I ignore both of them.

"Have you enjoyed your time in DC so far, Margaret?" I ask. Rule number one: make sure to acknowledge the spouse. I do.

"Yes, it has been so wonderful. The cherry blossoms, the monuments. It's a beautiful city. Every time I'm here, I wish I could stay longer," Margaret says. She's pretty, in a wholesome midwestern way. Dark-brown hair, straight and shiny. A blue dress that complements her dark-blue eyes. The rock on her ring finger must weigh a ton.

"I agree," Jody says. "It's almost like being in a European city."

"Almost," Margaret agrees.

There is an awkward silence, and then I remember my briefing. "So I hear you're an author? Would I know any of your work?" I ask.

Across the table, Margaret flushes. "Not yet. I'm working on my second novel. My first one, well, it was self-published. I—well, I'm querying agents now and . . ."

JJ jumps in. "My mom is so amazing. Talented. She put everything on the back burner for me, but I know she's going to be a bestselling author one day." JJ lifts his wineglass and toasts his mom.

I can't help but notice that this entire time, Jack has been staring at me. I return the favor. Jody, sandwiched between us, throws up her hands.

"So, JJ and Charlotte, we are all so proud of you two, so excited for your future," Jody says. She sounds like our wedding planner, Vanessa, the woman I send endless checks to—overly cheery and forced. "And Jack and Margaret, I hear you two have purchased the lucky couple a new home. Thank you. How generous."

What? Really? "I didn't know about this, Char," I say. It comes out fast, before I can stop it. Where is my drink?

"It's a bit of a fixer-upper," Margaret says.

"Mom, it's gorgeous. And the contractor already started on the renovation," JJ says. "It will be ready in six months. It's only a couple blocks from your townhome, Congressman Asher."

JJ is a nice guy, despite his dad. My daughter will be spoiled, I realize. I like that. Charlotte is a wonderful young woman. Smart, and an overachiever. She's worked her way up in Congresswoman Daniels's office and is a member of her legislative team, focusing on environmental issues. I wouldn't be surprised if she runs for office someday. I'd love that, actually. I take a deep breath as my cocktail arrives and allow myself to relax.

"Let's all toast to the happy couple and their new home," I say and raise my glass. Across the table, Jack leans forward and clinks my glass with his.

"Good to see you, Martin. It's been a minute since our mutual Golden Bear days of high school, but you don't seem to age at all. What's your secret?" Jack says.

"You need to get your eyesight checked," I say. "But thanks for the compliment. The years have treated you well too. Quite the successful business you've built."

"I've been lucky," Jack says with a smile. He turns to look at Charlotte. "Your daughter here is such a great gal. We are beyond thrilled to welcome her into our family."

"We feel the same about JJ," I say and take a deep breath. Maybe this little dinner will go smoothly.

"Everyone, please take a look at the menu. We should get our orders in and keep this an early night. We have a busy weekend," Jody says. She's great at keeping things moving: dinners, receptions, careers.

"Good idea," Jack says. He places his open menu on the table.

Beside him, Margaret holds the menu high, covering her face.

"What will you have?" Jody asks. A polite, innocent question.

"I'm still deciding, but I'm going to try something new," Jack says. "Sometimes it's good to make room for something fresh and new. Um, so what's with all the China stuff and all the other rumors, Marty?"

Beside me, Jody gasps. Charlotte turns to JJ. Margaret hides behind her menu, still.

"Dad," JJ says. "Not now. Not here."

"You know it doesn't look good," Jack says, grinning at me. "You've been in office, what, thirty years? That's plenty of time to get in a lot of trouble, isn't it?"

My chest tightens. I fight the urge to reach across the table and grab his neck.

LITTLE TIPS FOR NEW CONGRESSIONAL SPOUSES FROM MRS. ASHER, WIFE OF THE HONORABLE MARTIN ASHER (D-OH)

If you're living in DC, and I suggest you do, pop by the office and spend a little quality time reminding the entire team who the real boss is—in the nicest possible way, of course. Perhaps you'll remind them it's time to focus on the congressional art competition, for example, or tell them it is time to film one of the five public service announcements you can create with your spouse on nonelection years. Make sure your passion projects, your charities, get the time they deserve from his staff. Maybe review some résumés they've received and offer to help interview, especially for the scheduler position. It's in your best interest to be considered a vital member of the team, not just someone they use as a prop during campaign season.

JODY

Bistro Mon Cheri

Why isn't Martin speaking? Standing up for himself? I stare at my husband and watch as his face turns grayer.

Finally, he says, "This is not the time or place, Dobbs."

"You're right. I'm so sorry for this." Margaret sticks her menu in the air, and a waiter appears. "We'd like to order now."

"Oui, madame, what would you like?" the waiter asks.

As we place our orders, Jack and Martin continue to stare at each other, like kids trying to see who will blink first. It's ridiculous. I want to ask Jack what he thinks he knows about Martin. I'm aware of the rumors that have been swirling on the dark web for several years now: Martin is in China's back pocket, Martin has taken millions from think tanks and lobbyists, Martin is Putin's favorite. All sorts of ridiculous lies that never get picked up by the mainstream media. Not until Max Brown, that is. Nobody cares about whiffs of foreign influence, and everyone assumes there is corruption when money is involved in politics. It's just a fact. It's almost normal, these types of whispers. I don't care about any of those rumors, I really don't.

I only care about his attraction to his young intern. This is a first. And for that, he is paying a price. I eye Martin's drink and consider giving him another drop. Not here, though. That wouldn't be wise.

Once the waiter leaves the table, I kick into protective-spouse gear. "If you're referring to that ridiculous article in the *Times*, I assure you, nobody cares about it."

Jack smiles at me. "Ah, Mrs. Asher. The brains and the beauty behind Martin's successes. You've pushed him uphill as far as he'll go."

I can't help but appreciate the compliment. *Focus, Jody.* I say, "Martin will continue to represent Ohio's twelfth district until he decides otherwise. He's a fabulous congressman."

"I'm sure you've heard the news. My friend Harold Kestler has decided to run for the seat," Jack says.

"We've heard," Martin says. "I've had plenty of primary challengers over the years. This one is insignificant."

"This one is different. My man Kestler is going to win," Jack says. "He's building a huge war chest. He's from the district. He went to our high school five years after we graduated. Did you know that, Martin?"

"I didn't. Nor do I care," Martin says.

"Good old Grandville High. Marty was a party animal back then. Booze, drugs, and lots of girls. Still can't believe that didn't bring you down when you first ran," Jack says. "Anyway, Kestler's the real deal, not a carpetbagger who moved home temporarily to win a seat and move to DC for good."

Beside me, Martin stands up. "Time to go, Jody."

"Martin, sit down," I tell him. I glance at Charlotte. Tears stream down her face. "You're upsetting the kids."

"Stop being a jerk, Dad," JJ says to Jack.

"I need to go." Charlotte stands and hurries from the table, JJ close behind.

"Are you proud of yourself, Jack?" Margaret says.

"It had to be said. I mean, I needed to give them the heads-up about Kestler," Jack says. "It was the gentlemanly thing to do." He takes a sip of his wine. Beside me, Martin remains standing.

"You're something else, Dobbs. Always thought you were better than everyone. Spoiled, entitled shithead in high school, driving that ridiculous sports car, thinking you were above everyone else, and the same now," Martin says, his voice quiet but dark. "You have upset my daughter and ruined dinner, all because you're trying to get under my skin with that Kestler guy. We know all about him. You can't hide anything from me when it comes to my district."

"Good, then, you must know your time is up, don't you?" Jack leans forward and rests his hands on the table.

"You don't know anything about me, or DC, or how things work. Money isn't everything," Martin says.

Jack smiles. "It is, though. That and reputation. And you're just about to be ruined. You're rotten, Martin. You know it. I know it. And soon, everyone will know it. Bow out. Save yourself, your family, the pain."

I stand and reach for Martin's hand. There is no more room for civility here. I'm now convinced Jack is out to get Martin. "Let's go."

"Oh, stay for dinner, Mrs. Asher. You've already ordered," Jack says. "It would be a shame for that halibut to go to waste, oui?"

"I'm so sorry for this," Margaret says. "Stay for dinner. Please."

I give her my pity look, a look that says I can't believe she's married to that man. I say, "For some reason, I seem to have lost my appetite."

I take Martin's hand. He shakes with anger as I pull him away from the table.

"Don't give him the upper hand. Don't say another word," I tell him. "Smile."

We make it out of the red room and into the hall. I look at Martin's ashen face, and I wonder for a moment if maybe it *is* time to call it quits. Maybe it is time for Martin to step down, let someone else represent the district.

But that thought is gone as fast as it entered my brain. Never. We will not back down.

"What is he threatening you with, Martin? Is there more than just the China nonsense?" I whisper.

"I have no idea. You know they'll make things up. If it's a competitive race, all kinds of crap gets thrown at you," Martin says. "We've been lucky. We've never had a serious challenger. Don't worry. The *Times* will likely lose interest. The primary is almost a year away."

"You've never had a serious challenger because everyone considered you untouchable. That's because you were perfect at this job," I remind him. And he was, he really was. I don't understand why he had to ruin things. My phone lights up. The *New York Times* has picked up parts of Max's story. It's now officially in the national mainstream media: "Congressman Asher Has Ties to K Street." So what?

"What's going on?" Martin asks as he watches me read.

"Nothing, it's fine. Just more K Street nonsense, this time from the *New York Times*," I tell him.

"Is Roscoe mentioned?"

"No. No one specifically. Why?"

Martin ducks his head, bending close to my ear. "He left a voice mail for me. The feds paid him a visit today."

"Oh my God. The Roscoes cannot come to the wedding," I say. I make a mental note to tell the wedding planner to disinvite them. We cannot allow scandal in.

"Jody, there are more important things than the wedding," Martin snaps.

"Tell me what is happening."

Martin stares at me. For a moment, I see him as a young man: handsome, assured. "Let's go home. It's better to talk there."

We hurry down the stairs to the restaurant's lobby. I feel the stares without even looking at anyone. The maître d' appears.

"Is everything OK?" he asks.

"Yes, we—well, something came up and we need to go," Martin says as we head toward the front door. For a moment I feel guilty for not checking on Charlotte, but she has JJ. She will be fine. They've likely already left the restaurant. I need to get Martin out of here.

I look out the front door of the restaurant, and that's when I see them, just beyond the outdoor-dining area. Reporters. They wait like sharks, kept at bay by the wrought iron fence of the patio dining area. I try to tell myself they aren't here for Martin. Maybe there's someone else who has fallen from grace, earned their ravenous attention. I've seen it happen a million times. It's pack mentality, and they're looking for a kill.

"Congressman Asher!" a man yells. "Any comments about the *Times* story?"

I can't believe it. Martin is the prey. I turn around. We need to leave through the back door. "Martin, come this way. I'm calling the car to get us out of here."

Before we can get back inside, a man yells, "You know there's more coming out, Congressman. You can't hide."

Maybe not, I think. But right now, we can run.

LITTLE TIPS FOR NEW CONGRESSIONAL SPOUSES FROM MRS. ASHER, WIFE OF THE HONORABLE MARTIN ASHER (D-OH)

*As you no doubt have experienced, spouses are not allowed onto the House of Representatives floor during the swearing-in ceremony, although you will have a seat in the gallery, as you will for each House function. Some gallery seats are better than others, so as a freshman member, don't expect much. Sometimes your spouse will want to give **your** ticket to a donor. You don't need to let that happen. Watch out for that move during the president's State of the Union at the end of January. Your spouse gets only one golden ticket to this event, which brings together the Senate, Cabinet, and Supreme Court. This is your only chance to see the three branches of government at one event. Guard that ticket. (See notes about chief of staff and scheduler above.) Oh, and on another note, mobile phones are not allowed inside the gallery. You will be asked to check all devices and purses with the Capitol Police. That said, I once saw a sneaky spouse who had cut a hiding spot into her Bible, and she took all the photos she wanted during the swearing-in ceremony. I'm not condoning this by any means—just giving a little nod to ingenuity.*

MARTIN

Asher Townhome

I just need to get through this weekend, I remind myself as our black SUV speeds down East Capitol.

Nothing like hosting high-profile, high-attendance events during a media scandal. My consultants keep calling, David keeps texting, and Roscoe hasn't stopped either. They all want me to assure them everything will be fine. It will be, of course, one way or another. The fact is, I cannot undo anything I've done. I must simply ride out the storm, so to speak. Hold my head high.

Suddenly, my chest feels as if it has been crushed by a vise, and I lean into the side of the car.

I look over at Jody. It was a nice move she made, sneaking us out through the kitchen like we're famous celebrities. Or infamous, I suppose. Jody and I are quite a team, have been since we first met. I was older than most of my law school class; after undergrad, I worked on the Hill, solidified my dream of being elected one day. I knew I had to wait for the right opportunity. In the meantime, I also knew a law degree would boost my résumé, and so there I was. Sitting in the back row of the lecture hall, watching the most gorgeous girl I'd ever seen.

All through high school and most of my undergrad, I'd muddled through school, spending much more time at parties than in the classroom. But by the end of college, something had shifted. I didn't want to end up in a dead-end job like my dad. I didn't want my wife to be miserable and money strapped like my mom.

I wanted respect. To be taken seriously. I wanted to be a leader. So I'd changed starting junior year in college. I'd worked hard at school and at my internships on the Hill after graduation. I'd changed enough to get a great score on the LSAT and be accepted into Georgetown Law. And that's when Jody came into my life and completed the picture of my future. It really was love at first sight, as sappy as that sounds.

"Hi, I'm Martin Asher," I said to the beautiful blonde. I'd hurried to the front of the room after class.

"Jody Prescott," she answered, shaking my hand. We both felt it the moment we touched: the electricity, the spark that hooked us, connected us for life.

"Join me for a cup of coffee?" I asked, emboldened by the spark.

Coffee stretched into dinner and drinks. I'd won the housing lottery, moving in with a guy from the Hill whose parents had bought a Georgetown row house. Truth be told, I let Jody think I owned it. I may have exaggerated my pedigree, but she did the same. She was Palm Beach Jody to all of us at school. None of us knew she was on a scholarship, that she worked retail all summer to put together her perfect law school attire. We both were posers, not at all what we appeared. That was our superpower. Together we wanted to be more than what we'd come from. We wanted power and prestige. By our second date, we decided we would one day run this town.

As the driver pulls to a stop, we both scan the street in front of our home. The press is not waiting to ambush us here, thank God.

"What's the plan?" Jody asks as we climb out of the car.

I know she was biting her tongue the entire drive home. You can't trust anyone. Even loyal drivers have big ears and audio-recording devices.

"No plan. We carry on. Enjoy Charlotte's wedding, ignore the dreadful Dobbses as much as possible," I say, opening the front door.

"That's not what I'm talking about," Jody says, flipping on the living room lights and heading straight to the bar cart. "You know it. What did you do with the intern? I've heard the rumors, Martin. I saw you drooling over her at the Library of Congress dinner."

Jody pours herself a drink as I watch in cold silence. She drops onto the couch, stares in my direction.

I turn my back to her and make a cocktail. "Nothing happened. They are trying to ruin me. Jack Dobbs likely is behind it, or one of the RNC operatives. You know what they do, Jody. They'll try to make something out of nothing. It won't work," I say. I walk to the kitchen to get ice. While I'm there, I take a deep breath and glance out the back door. I'm tempted to walk out, hop in my car, and drive.

But I can't.

Jody paces the living room, her sensible shoes off, her cocktail glass empty. I pick it up from the table and make her another.

"Why are there talks about Sarah? Why did Mimi warn me about you and her?" Her hands are clenched in fists. "Why, Martin?"

"Sit, please," I say, handing her a fresh cocktail. I join her on the couch. "Look, I'll admit, my flirtation might have gone a bit overboard this time."

"What does that even mean?" Jody's blue eyes are ice.

"It means I was sloppy, that's all. There's been a lot of pressure, what with the wedding bills, and the scrutiny on China, and now Roscoe. I mean, it's a lot," I explain. I think about my phone call with Joe earlier today. Jody doesn't know the whole Roscoe story, about how Joe has been under investigation, about how the feds have been watching him. I know I'm not the only member of Congress he has a special arrangement with, but I also know our friendship is likely the oldest he has. We need each other. If the feds make a move, I won't be one of Joe's sacrificial offerings. No way. He's too smart for that. But how can I trust a guy like Joe if the feds close in? I hold my stomach as a wave of nausea sweeps over me.

No, Jody doesn't need to know about that. Not yet.

"Sloppy," Jody says. "The girl is only a few years older than our daughter."

"She's not a problem anymore, trust me," I say. "I'm starving. Let's order in, shall we?"

Jody stands. "Martin, you didn't fire her, did you?"

"Well, David will handle it all officially. I'll make sure she's placed in another office," I say, but a chill is spreading down my spine. It occurs to me I may have made a huge mistake. Again.

"Did you have cause for this termination?" Jody's voice is troubling, like I remember my mom's being so long ago. I don't need Jody going off the deep end like she can. I must avoid that at all costs.

"Of course," I say. I'm lying. I'm lying about so many things these days. "Italian sound good?"

My phone lights up with a call. David again.

"Answer that," Jody commands.

I do. "Hey, David, what's up?"

"Sir, Sarah tells me you fired her?" he says. "Just before a story is about to break that the two of you had some sort of relationship? And there's proof? Are you insane?"

I walk to the kitchen so Jody can't hear me. "Don't be ridiculous. I simply suggested it was time for her to move on, and it is, given the rumor mill. She doesn't need to be a part of this. It's all fake news. It's all the work of Harold Kestler and Jack Dobbs. They're trying to ruin me, force me not to run next cycle."

"Charlotte's fiancé's father is trying to ruin you?" David asks.

"Yes. He's friends with Kestler. You know he's supporting his campaign financially," I say.

"Yes, we know. It's all rather incestuous, isn't it? Strange, even for DC," David says. "We need to focus on the problem at hand: Sarah. Can I tell her that her job is secure?"

"Yes, yes, of course," I say, meeting Jody's eyes as she joins me in the kitchen.

"Good," David says. "Sir, I just got a call from Max Brown. He says Joe Roscoe is going to be arrested sometime soon. Max is on your calendar for Monday at eight a.m. I suggest we pull the team together, make a plan. This is getting hotter, gaining steam."

"I understand. Sunday, we'll meet. Sunday after all the wedding festivities," I say and clutch my stomach. What now, I wonder?

"OK, sure. We'll wait until Sunday," David says. "But, sir, keep a low profile until then. Please."

"Sure," I answer before hanging up. My wife has planned the biggest wedding Washington, DC, has seen this season. I'm sure a low profile is exactly what she wants.

I look at Jody. She shakes her head, walks back to the living room, and turns on the TV.

My phone buzzes with a call. It's Vice President Eugene Acton. I fight the urge to send him to voice mail. He is the last person I want to talk to, the last, but I force myself to answer the call.

LITTLE TIPS FOR NEW CONGRESSIONAL SPOUSES FROM MRS. ASHER, WIFE OF THE HONORABLE MARTIN ASHER (D-OH)

One of the most special things a spouse can do is invite constituents to the White House. Every time I do, I get butterflies in my stomach. You and up to six guests can take a self-guided tour. You'll need your guests' full names, social security numbers, and dates of birth to request a reservation. Work with your new best friend, the scheduler, to get this accomplished. When the special tour day arrives, remember: no purses, backpacks, or cameras are allowed—that includes even you. Phones are permitted. There will be a helpful Secret Service agent in each room to answer any questions. Writing this makes me want to walk through the People's House again right now. See? All the stress and sacrifice you make is worth it when you get to do something special like this, right?

JODY

Asher Townhome

I wake up with sun streaming through the window. It's late, I can feel it. Beside me, the bed is empty, the sheets cold. Martin is gone. Good riddance. Martin's sordid affair would eventually come to light—I knew that it would, I'd braced for it. But the exposé on his ties to lobbyists created this urgency. The reporter's spotlight on Martin illuminated everything he is up to, or surely would.

I picture Martin's ashen face, his constant chewing of antacids. I am both irate and beyond embarrassed by his actions and his appearance of late. His behavior is going to give me a heart attack, unless I use my special drops to take care of him first. Should I? Would it save us from all this? Martin, my sacrificial lamb.

But no. We need him this weekend. He is father of the bride. He is an important prop. It's sad and terrible timing, Max Brown's story, coming as it is on Charlotte's wedding weekend. The timing isn't Martin's fault, I decide.

I climb out of bed and make my way to the dresser and my phone, hoping no more Google results are pushed my way about Martin. Not today. The rehearsal dinner is tonight, and the wedding is tomorrow.

I unplug my phone and glance at my reflection. Who am I kidding? I'm not worried about Charlotte. I'm worried about how Martin's mistakes reflect on me, on everything I've accomplished socially. The older I get, the more jaded I've become. This wedding is a social event, an important one for the Ashers in DC. That's all. What's love got to do with anything inside the Beltway?

Tonight's rehearsal dinner, however, is out of my control. Whatever Jack Dobbs has planned, we will grin and bear it. I think of the gaggle of Republican spouses I saw yesterday at the restaurant, all of them in town for tonight's festivities. I wonder how many more there will be.

I dial Vanessa's number, and she answers immediately. I know she's pushed on her cat-eye glasses and is studying her event checklist, her full lips dripping with shiny red gloss.

"Hello, Vanessa," I say, my serious voice booming through the phone like a general's.

"Mrs. Asher! So exciting. Tomorrow is the big day!" she says. "Just spoke with Charlotte. She seems to be holding up well."

I should call Charlotte too. That would be a motherly thing to do. I make a note.

"Look, I need to make sure the wedding and reception are perfect. As such, there may be some last-minute seating changes for the reception," I say. I wonder how many "friends" will find Martin's press uncomfortable enough to cancel their attendance. I haven't heard from any so far, but if the coverage grows, I know it will happen.

"We are well equipped to handle last-minute changes. Happens at every wedding," Vanessa says.

"Please note the Roscoes will not be in attendance," I tell her.

"OK, I'll remove them from the seating chart. No problem," she says.

"Would you do me a favor, please? Call them, the Roscoes, and make sure they understand not to attend," I say.

"Of course, Mrs. Asher. Anything else?"

"Not at the moment," I say. "I just need to make it through the rehearsal dinner."

"Your outfit will be stunning. Perfect," Vanessa says. She would say that since she talked me into buying it. "And the venue—well, the Congressional Country Club in Maryland is elite. I'm still not sure how a couple from Ohio booked it, if the Dobbses are the country bumpkins you've described to me. It's quite a feat."

I feel my stomach twist into a knot and my jaw clench. I tell myself to relax. It's fine if they have tonight. Tomorrow is my day to shine. Or rather, Charlotte's. Charlotte's big day.

"Our event will be superior," I say. I need to hang up, get ready for the day.

"You know the Congressional is one of the top golf clubs in the world. So many presidents have been members. I think it's the number one country club in the US. Oh, and it has a ten-year waiting list. It costs hundreds of thousands of dollars to belong. It will be spectacular, if done properly."

Her comments leave me wishing we'd booked the stupid place for the wedding instead of the DAR Constitutional Hall. "Maybe we should have booked it?"

"No, ma'am, your venue is perfect. Of course, the wedding is the signature event, and it will be gorgeous. I'm not in the loop in this case, obviously, but for most rehearsal dinners, only a fraction of the guests are included. Is that the case with tonight?" Vanessa asks. "Most guests are only invited to attend the wedding. Your event is the event of the weekend. Trust me."

I don't trust anyone. Never have. I learned that at a young age. The minute you trust someone, they'll let you down. It's the way of the world. Trusting makes you weak. I prefer to pretend to trust while verifying everything. Verifying everything requires perfecting certain incognito sleuthing abilities, of course. That's how I've honed my lock-picking skills. I had a lot to verify through the years, with my daughter, my husband, certain friends. You'd be surprised what you find out, the truth you uncover, when you snoop around on the ones you love. I should have asked Charlotte for more details about the rehearsal dinner, like why that gaggle of women had been invited. Oh well. I'm prepared. I can handle anything.

I hurry to shower and get ready. Charlotte likely needs me after last night's dinner fiasco. She's not like me and will have taken everything to heart. And if that was any indication of how tonight will be, well, I tried to warn her, but she's in love. Poor girl.

My phone buzzes. It's Mimi.

"Hey, thanks for calling back," I say.

"No problem," Mimi says. "Look, the story with Martin and the money—it's not terrible. I think Roscoe will take the fall ultimately."

Thank goodness. As long as it's handled without implicating Martin, as long as it all goes away, it's fine with me. I say, "OK. Great. Good news."

"The troubling part is the intern," Mimi says.

"Yes, it is. *Has* been," I say. A thought pops into my head. "Did you place her in Martin's office?"

"You know I've helped Martin and his team with staffing through the years. I receive hundreds of quality résumés at the think tank," she says.

"But why would you send someone like Sarah to Martin's office?" I ask.

"She's smart, capable," Mimi says.

"Alluring, sexy, a distraction," I say. I feel my temper rising like a phoenix.

"It's not the young woman's fault she's attractive. This is a serious problem, but we shouldn't talk about that on this line. How is Charlotte doing? I meant to call her and check in. I'm a terrible godmother," Mimi says and adds a laugh for levity.

"Yes, please do check on her, thank you," I say. "And I'll see you and Spencer tonight, at the rehearsal dinner. We can talk there."

"Jody, now that the secret is out about Kestler's run, you know Jack Dobbs will try to use tonight's event to promote Howard Kestler's campaign somehow. I've warned Martin, of course. I want you both to stay calm, not let him throw you off if he pulls something," Mimi says.

"Sure, I can stay calm. Do you know anything in particular?" I can feel my pulse quicken at the thought of Jack Dobbs's plans.

"No. Just that I'd find a way to use tonight's event to my advantage—I mean, if *I* were Jack Dobbs and wanted to make Martin look bad," Mimi says.

"I need to get going. Do you happen to know where Martin is? He left early this morning, and I haven't heard from him." Martin and Mimi are as close as we are, maybe closer.

"Likely with David and his team. Figuring out a strategy to overcome all this. If the intern story drops, he's in real trouble," Mimi says. "Sex scandals eclipse all others in this town."

"He did not have sex with that young woman," I say. I don't know if I believe it, though.

"I hope not," Mimi says.

"But it doesn't matter, does it? The story is already out there. It's bubbling up; I can feel it," I say. "Max Brown is going to publish it, any minute. The good news is Martin is keeping her on staff, not firing her."

"Oh my God. He was considering firing her?"

"This all wouldn't have happened if you hadn't placed her there like some kind of honey trap," I say. I force myself not to yell. Martin needs Mimi on his side. I need Mimi on my side.

"You better hope he doesn't fire her," Mimi says.

"Actually, Mimi, Martin better hope he doesn't. I am not the one who has done anything wrong," I say. "I need this all to go away. This was supposed to be a special weekend."

Mimi chuckles and a chill runs down my spine. "Oh, don't worry. This weekend will be special, one way or another. That's a guarantee."

LITTLE TIPS FOR NEW CONGRESSIONAL SPOUSES FROM MRS. ASHER, WIFE OF THE HONORABLE MARTIN ASHER (D-OH)

The most wonderful part of your new role is the respect you will receive from the rest of the members of Congress. They all know how important the woman behind the man can be—they do. (Of course, these days, more and more men are spouses. It's a welcome change. I'll try to do a better job of giving gender-neutral tips. Old dog, new tricks and such.) I'll never forget the warm welcome reception the Democratic Spouses Forum had for our freshman-class spouses during my husband's first term. It was held in an elegant room called the Speaker's Room in the Capitol Building. The Speaker attended, and all of leadership. They thanked us spouses for our service and sacrifice. I was so touched. And, at the same time, a bit overwhelmed by it all. The real power belongs to the member, of course, but don't underestimate your own.

MARTIN

Asher Townhome

Jody greets me at the door. "Where have you been?"

"Had to meet with the team," I say, pushing past her to get inside. The entire walk home, I felt like I was being followed. Maybe I was.

"And what's the plan?" Jody asks, slamming the front door. "Is there a plan?"

"We're going to get through this weekend and then we'll go on the offensive," I say. I will not tell Jody about my meeting with the vice president; that will set her off. Turns out the darn reporter called the VP, said he knew I'd introduced him to Chinese party officials who donated to his campaign.

At the time he was grateful, I reminded him.

I look at Jody. "Nothing will ruin Charlotte's wedding day. Promise."

Jody bites her lip. "You know I've dreamed of Charlotte's wedding since she was a little girl," she says. "I can't believe there will be a shadow over it."

"Cut the crap, Jody," I say. "You haven't dreamed of this day at all. You don't even like JJ. And the event is a stage for you, not Charlotte. She could care less about all the pomp and circumstance you've created."

For a moment she pretends to be offended, but she can't help but smile.

"Maybe you're right, but I still can't believe the mess you've made," she says.

My chest squeezes. "I know. I'm sorry." I almost tell her. About everything I've done. The mistake I've made. I really do. But I can't.

"You need to get ready for the rehearsal dinner. The car comes in twenty minutes."

As the cloud of doom settles around my shoulders, I nod and turn toward the stairs but stop short. For the first time, I realize she's dressed up: hair and makeup done and clad in an expensive-looking navy dress. Her gold spouse pin glistens, held in place by a string of pearls. She is the epitome of the perfect congressional spouse. She has been my helper, my partner, a huge component of my success. And I'm the idiot mucking it all up.

"I can fix this," I say.

"I hope so," she answers.

"You look beautiful tonight."

"Thank you. Hurry," she answers.

I climb the stairs slowly, pausing halfway up to catch my breath. I'm unwell, yes, but what's more worrisome is Jody's calmness. I know she's seething, yet she's still speaking to me.

She will not be able to control or hide her rage much longer. That is her true nature. She will make me pay for the intern. I just have no idea what to expect, or when it will happen. But I know my wife. She will extract her revenge.

LITTLE TIPS FOR NEW CONGRESSIONAL SPOUSES FROM MRS. ASHER, WIFE OF THE HONORABLE MARTIN ASHER (D-OH)

You absolutely must join the Congressional Club and Museum! It's through that club, which is open to all spouses, that you'll get your big sister, a welcome basket, and a full day of training sessions to help you adjust. The club is the longest-running bipartisan congressional spouses club in DC. They've been meeting since 1911. You won't regret being a member. And just a note: you must be a member to attend the First Lady's Luncheon—you may not attend otherwise. More on that later!

MARTIN

The Congressional Country Club

I take a big sip of my drink as I look around at the crowd attending my daughter's rehearsal dinner. This feels off to me. I don't know many of the people here, and I also notice an astonishing number of folks from across the aisle. The days of bipartisan social gatherings are long gone in DC. Truth be told, we barely tolerate the other side.

Sure, I'm middle of the road, not a liberal by any means, but I am a Democrat. My daughter, as far as I know, is one too. And while I do see some familiar faces—a couple of my best friends who joined Congress at the same time I did—many of these people are strangers.

What the hell are they doing here at Charlotte's rehearsal dinner?

Jody appears at my side. "This is obscene. They are hand-making lobster risotto at that station over there, to order," she says. "And that's all caviar and vodka shots. How dare they? And they've stolen the hashtags. Those were for the wedding."

She hands me a white cocktail napkin sporting *#DobbsBigDay* and *#CharlottesWed* embossed in gold letters. Jody is fuming about the food, and I'm fuming about the guest list, which must be massive. All in all, we've been here ten minutes and I'm ready to go. I suspect she is too.

"Should we just leave?" I ask, knowing the answer.

"No," Jody hisses and then pastes on a smile. "Although I'd like to. Trust me. I talked to Mimi."

"As did I," I say. "I know. We are to remain calm and congressional no matter what Jack does. I don't think he'd have the nerve to ruin his son's big night over politics. He wouldn't."

"Why wouldn't he? No matter what he does, we will remain calm. We are good at smiling through painful events. I mean, think of all those boring conventions, sucking up to delegates, my God," Jody says.

We both see Margaret at the same time. She looks beautiful in a rose-colored dress, a sparkling diamond necklace, and earrings. I don't want to know how much her ensemble costs.

"Good evening," Margaret says, hugging Jody and then me. "I'm so sorry about last night. I don't know what got into Jack, really. Tonight will be different. It's for the kids."

I fight the urge to turn and run by locking eyes with Jody. That solved it. I'm frozen in place.

"Nice party you've got here," I manage.

"Thank you! So when the kids get here, we'll all proceed up to the head table. Sound good?" Margaret says. She is literally glowing.

"Where are the kids?" Jody asks. She's been searching for Charlotte since we arrived, and she has yet to answer either of our texts. "I haven't spoken to them since the rehearsal."

"All is well. Don't worry. It's a shame they didn't trust us, the parents, to be there, but after last night, you can't blame them. They told me the rehearsal was fine. They even made it here early, as I'd requested, so they can make their grand entrance. They're going to walk down the center of the room as soon as all the guests have arrived. It's so magical, isn't it?" Margaret smiles and we all look at what is the ritziest and most over-the-top party I've been to in a long time.

Giant floral arrangements burst from vases in every corner of the room: red roses and some sort of massive white flower I can't name. The tables are draped in gold silk. The napkins and plates are cream with a gold trim. Dozens of white roses fill huge vases on each table. I turn away from the dazzling decor and begin to watch the crowd again.

"Is the wedding party here?" Jody asks. "I haven't seen any of them yet."

"Oh, they're all here too. They'll be part of the processional. The wedding party, then our special couple, then the parents. Ooh, must scoot. Enjoy and I'll see you in the parade."

And with that, she disappears into the ever-growing crowd. Across the room, I see Mimi and Spencer Smith. Mimi and I lock eyes. She shakes her head, her face pinched in a frown. I know she's angry with me, and she's threatening to cut off our relationship. I need to talk to her.

"Martin, hey, how are you all doing?" a man says, touching my shoulder from behind. I turn around and blink as I come face-to-face with Congressman Johnson of Alabama. Why is he here? At my daughter's rehearsal dinner? He's as red as they come.

"Bo, good to see you. Why are you here, at my daughter's rehearsal dinner?" I glance at Jody to see if she's as confused as I am, but she's disappeared too. Fine. I'll get to the bottom of this myself. "I mean, the number of times we've been in the same room together when it's not for a vote is, let me see . . . none."

"Oh, Marty, I'm not here for your daughter. I'm here for good old Jack and his son," he says with a laugh. "Nice shindig, isn't it? Have you tried the caviar? It's the finest. That Jack . . . deep pockets. Good on him."

"Excuse me," I say and step away from Johnson. I need to get out of here. Where is Jody? I will find her, and we'll go talk to the Smiths together. Remind everyone of the good old days and how close we all are. As I scan the crowd, I see Mimi and Spencer. They're talking to Jack Dobbs, the traitors. What is happening here?

"Hey, Martin, nice party, huh?" It's the minority leader, Keith Crawford. What the hell? Is the Speaker of the House even here? I know we invited her to the wedding, but we have no idea if she'll appear. How did Jack get the minority leader to show up when I can't attract the Speaker?

Sweat is forming under my suit, running down my back, and I'm soaked under my arms. "Yes, great party." I pop an antacid and try to find Jody. A hand grips my shoulder.

"Marty, hey, can I speak to you?" It's Congressman Don Dean. He's one of my best friends, a representative from Minnesota, and a Democrat.

"Of course. Good to see you, buddy," I say, and it is.

"Come over here," he says and I follow him to the corner of the room, acknowledging all the good wishes of strangers and acquaintances on the way.

"You've been—" he says just as a bagpipe brigade walks into the room, making it impossible to speak.

I hold up my hand and Don nods.

Jody appears by my side and glares at me, yelling in my ear, "The procession is now! Come on."

My wife tugs my arm and I shrug at Don, who shakes his head as I plunge into the crowd with Jody. We make it to the center of the room in time to see Charlotte and JJ make their grand entrance. I smile and wave at my girl. She's so beautiful, so sure of herself. And they do look cute together. A power couple, even if JJ is a Republican. Even if my daughter is a Republican now too?

"Is Charlotte a Republican?" I yell in Jody's ear just as the bagpipes stop. Several people look my way as Jody, mortified, ignores me.

An announcer says, "Please welcome the future Mr. and Mrs. Jack Dobbs Jr.!"

The crowd goes wild. Jody again pulls my hand, and we stand in the middle of the crowd, our turn to be announced.

"Mother and father of the bride: the Honorable Martin Asher, representing Ohio's twelfth district, and Mrs. Jody Asher," the announcer says, and the audience claps politely as we walk to the head table. I settle Jody next to Charlotte after we both get a hug from our daughter and JJ, the Republican mole.

"And finally, our hosts and the stars of the show: Mr. and Mrs. Jack Dobbs of Columbus, Ohio—parents of the groom!"

Margaret seems to be floating toward me, her rosy dress as light as air, shining like a princess. Beside her, Jack preens for the crowd like he's a kingmaker or something. I'm stunned he knows this many folks in DC. It doesn't make any sense. From all the background digging my team did on the Dobbs family, they never indicated he was politically involved. I would never have guessed that Dobbs Industries needed to lobby, that he would have this many connections, made all these donations. Apparently, I was wrong. My team was wrong. They told me he was what he seemed: a rich jerk from the district. Somebody activated him politically. And that somebody must be Harold Kestler. Their shared cause: the desire to bring me down. A high school hatred, Jack's and mine, that just never went away.

I scan the audience and spot Mimi taking her seat at a front-row table. Somehow, even when the Dobbses are in charge, she gets what she wants. Who am I kidding . . . she always gets who and what she wants. Mimi is on her phone. In the next moment, my phone vibrates in my pocket. I'm certain Mimi has sent me a text. I pull out my phone. I'm right.

You're going down. It starts tonight.

I text back: ?

I stare at my phone.

I text: What are you talking about?

Mimi doesn't answer and won't make eye contact with me. Margaret arrives at the table, Jack on her heels, and we all stand. When I sit again, Jody is putting on a show, being the happy mother of the bride while I can tell she's seething on the inside. Her right finger taps the head table like a woodpecker looking for bugs to kill. I place my hand over hers to stop the tapping, and she pulls it away, giving me a frosty look before pasting the smile back onto her face.

I lean over, whisper to Jody, "Mimi says something is happening tonight."

Jody shakes her head. "Ignore her. She's trying to boss you around, as usual. And during your own daughter's wedding weekend. Really unacceptable."

It is, but it's my fault. I got greedy, and needy. That's weak. Mimi told me as much. I don't know what is about to happen, or what Mimi knows, but I do know my stomach is on fire. I look down the head table at Jody, our daughter, JJ, Jack, and Margaret. We appear to be one happy family, I bet. I remind myself to breathe as sweat trickles down my back.

Jack remains standing and looks as if he'll be the master of ceremonies. A man hands him a cordless microphone, and the guests begin tapping the sides of their glasses as a hush comes over the crowd. Now, from this perspective, I realize there must be almost four hundred people here, more than the number invited to tomorrow night's wedding and reception.

"Thank you all for coming to what is a beautiful evening at a fabulous venue to celebrate the love of these two wonderful young people. I hope you're all enjoying the food and drinks. But pace yourselves. There's so much more on the way." Jack pauses to wait for the applause to subside. "My wife, Margaret, is the one who put all of this together tonight to celebrate our son, JJ, and his bride, Charlotte. Thank you, honey, for everything you did to create this moment."

Margaret stands and waves as the crowd collectively says, "Ah," and points behind us. I turn in time to see *#DobbsBigDay* lit up on the wall. Another round of applause zips through the huge room. I watch as Margaret floats back into her seat. I wonder if she is enjoying this show tonight? The spectacle Jack is creating?

Jack is back on the microphone. "I promise not to yammer all evening, but I do have one more quick announcement. I know it's not typical to make rehearsal dinners political, I know that. I also know, though, that my son is marrying into a political family, and I have recently become active in the circus myself. Hadn't even given politics much thought until JJ got engaged to Charlotte."

My jaw clenches as I force a bigger smile. What is he doing? He wouldn't announce Kestler's candidacy here? No. It would be tacky, tasteless. He'd look like an asshole. I swallow. He *is* an asshole.

Jack says, "I'd like to take this opportunity to announce that after careful thought and deliberation, I have decided to back Harold Kestler in his run for Ohio's twelfth congressional seat. I mean no disrespect to the Ashers—none whatsoever. We thank Martin for his years of service. Harold, can you come on up here?"

I lean forward and look down the table, and all I see are shocked faces on the kids, on Margaret, and especially on Jody as she clutches her spouse pin hanging from her neck.

He just did it. Not only is he announcing a man's congressional run, for my seat, at my daughter's rehearsal dinner, he has invited the candidate here. I lock eyes with my buddy Don and he nods. This is what he was trying to warn me about. This is what Mimi was texting about. My primary challenger is here, at my daughter's rehearsal dinner. I shake my head before I can stop myself.

"And I know it may be awkward, especially for some of us up here at the head table, especially since we are welcoming an Asher into our family, but yes, Harold is running for Martin's seat. I'm a patriot, speaking up for the good of the district despite knowing it will cause friction between all of us up here. I firmly believe it is time to flip the district red, back to where it belongs, and my good friend Harold's the man to do it. This isn't personal, it's politics. But enough of that. Harold, why don't you come on up and offer a toast to the young couple? They're a shining example of how red and blue can even love each other, don't you agree?" Jack says, playing to the crowd, ignoring me. "Say a few words, Harold."

As Jack hands Harold the microphone, my stomach lurches and I fight the urge to say something, do something. I'm trapped here. Jody puts her hand on my knee and hisses, "Calm down. Now."

Harold is speaking. He's tall, with a booming voice and midwestern good looks. He is a younger version of me, I realize. To his credit, he looks uncomfortable standing in the spotlight at my expense. "Thank you, Jack, and everyone who came to support me and celebrate love tonight. This evening isn't about me, not at all. Martin and Jody, congratulations. JJ and Charlotte, I wish you years of happiness together. And Jack and Margaret, thank you for throwing one heck of a party. Cheers to love."

The crowd seems stunned as hundreds of red balloons drop from the ceiling, spilling over the tables and onto the floor, creating a crimson sea in the ballroom. This balloon drop belongs at a political convention, not a rehearsal dinner. It's tacky and tasteless, and all I can do as the balloons settle is sit up here on display like an idiot.

I manage to take a breath. Why didn't anyone on my staff know about this little surprise tonight? Why didn't we know Kestler was in the room? Why didn't Mimi warn me, tell me what she knew? It's almost as if she wanted me to be embarrassed here tonight. I don't understand everything at play here or who all the enemies are, but they are circling. They won't win.

My team is already busy digging through Harold Kestler's life, digging up whatever dirt there is, and I know there will be plenty to hit him on. Everybody's got something to exploit. I watch as Kestler walks back into the crowd and note he sits at one of the front tables, a table of honor.

At this moment I hate Jack Dobbs more than I ever have. At this moment I know I will do anything to keep my seat. I have a war chest. I will take him down. And I will ruin their reputations, both of them, in the process. It will be through surrogates, of course, but it will be done.

I spot David seated at a table toward the back and watch as he stands and sprints out of the room. I can tell from the expression on his face that he is as blindsided as I am.

The applause subsides, and Jack says, "Bon appétit. Dinner is served." As he finally shuts up and takes his seat, he makes sure to look my way.

He smiles. It takes everything in me not to walk over and punch him in the face.

Jody pushes away from the table. Charlotte starts to stand up, but JJ takes her hand, urging her to sit.

"No, both of you, stay here, please," I say. "We cannot let them see us upset." I nod to the crowd, some watching the head table, some already enjoying their first course. I spot several members of the DC media in attendance.

Charlotte blinks and sits back down as JJ wraps his arm around her shoulders. Jody pastes a smile on her face and pulls her chair back to the table.

We are Ashers. We are strong. At least we will appear to be.

"Eat," I whisper and manage to stab a piece of lettuce and shove it in my mouth.

I cannot believe this week. My honor and ethics have been assaulted in the press, and now everyone finds out I'm being primaried at my own daughter's wedding rehearsal dinner. I reach in my pocket and pop an antacid.

I will not give up without a fight. Jack does not know what he has started, but I do know how to finish it.

I'm a swamp creature. I'm proud of it. I lean forward and stare at Jack until he meets my eye. I smile.

LITTLE TIPS FOR NEW CONGRESSIONAL SPOUSES FROM MRS. ASHER, WIFE OF THE HONORABLE MARTIN ASHER (D-OH)

Don't make plans based on the published congressional calendar. Period. It will always change, no matter which party is in charge. And don't make travel plans for the days leading up to Christmas. Because even though it will appear they are off the week before, they won't be. I tell you this because I spent many years on vacation with only my daughter, my husband stuck with votes right up until Christmas Eve. Sorry to be the bearer of bad news here. I'll try to make my next tip more fun.

JODY

The Congressional Country Club

How could Martin have been so stupid? Why didn't he know about this? We should have expected something from Jack tonight, and we did. But we had no idea Harold Kestler would appear.

I blame David. I saw him scamper like a rat out of the room. He should be ashamed of himself. Martin's chief of staff should have known this was happening and stopped it.

And now, because we had no warning, Martin looks like a has-been in front of his friends, his family, and his enemies. I'm not going to sit here and take it. It's obscene. I lock eyes with Mimi, who sits with her husband at a table near the front. She appears to be as shocked as I am. But I'm not so sure I believe her act. There's something going on between Mimi and Martin, a fight or worse. I saw them glaring at each other. Martin told me about her threatening text. I don't know what it's all about, but certainly with her connections, she would have known about this announcement tonight by Harold Kestler. And yet she didn't warn us.

It's simply unacceptable. This just isn't how these things are done. I think I'm going to die. Up here, in front of everyone, I am just going to croak. Or, better yet, I'll kill Martin on my way down the table to kill

Jack. Yes, that's better. I'll off them both and lovely Margaret too. I wish I brought my eye drops with me. I could taint the water pitcher and take them all down—get the red out, so to speak. Well, not Charlotte of course. I drum my fingers on the table and lean forward to glare at Margaret.

Compared to her, and her amazing dress and jewels, I look like a washed-up conservative has-been. We've been played, Martin and I. This was not in the plans. But I paste on a big smile. So nice of Harold to wish Charlotte and JJ lots of love. So smart, too, so I'm stuck applauding his toast like an idiot. I cannot appear to be upset even as my blood boils. Jack allowed his friend Harold the opportunity to give the first toast to the happy couple.

They cannot beat us. They won't beat us. I clap, clap, clap. This is politics. I am a political animal. I can handle anything.

As for my husband, I'm not so sure. I see Martin's stunned expression—eyes wide, mouth open—and think perhaps I might not have to kill him after all. The stress might just do the job for me. He's troubled already and this shocking announcement during our daughter's rehearsal dinner could do him in. He'll just keel over. I touch his knee, tell him to breathe. After a beat, he's fine. He doesn't pass out or have a heart attack. After the reality of the situation hits, he leans back in his chair, a small smile on his face. I like that. He's calculating, figuring out how to get one step ahead. I like to see that fight in him.

And he'll need it because this campaign now will be a battle. Jack has unlimited resources, we all know that. But he also is backing a candidate who has baggage. Everyone does. Any little deviation from the perfect life, well . . . we'll find it and ruin your political aspirations.

It applies to Martin, too, of course. There's likely an oceanful of mud on him now.

They drag everyone through it, into it. The spouse. The kids. Next to me, Charlotte and JJ are deep in conversation while also attempting to smile. I taught her well.

"Mom, I'm so sorry about this," Charlotte says, her innocent young face a mess of worry. "This is all my fault. We should have eloped. I never should have trusted JJ to keep his dad in check. Nobody can. I'm so sorry."

Martin leans in. "There is no need for you to apologize for anything. The only one at fault is your future father-in-law. I'm fine. Your mom's fine. We've handled worse." Martin has a big smile glued to his face. "Don't let them see you worry, honey. I'll keep my seat. This is just some quest for attention. Look, you and JJ make a great couple, despite all this political nonsense. Let's focus on that, shall we?"

"I love you, Daddy," Charlotte says.

JJ leans forward. "So sorry about this."

Martin says, "We're fine, son."

He takes my hand and kisses me on the cheek. I know we should stop talking, here, now, with people watching us from the crowd. "It's going to be just fine, Jody. Nobody knows what's really involved in this job, not until you're here. Not even you realized, remember? We all learned so much," Martin says and pats my hand. "We should eat. Act like nothing is wrong."

"I've lost my appetite. But I'll try," I say to Martin as Charlotte tries a bite of her salad—some exotic dish that I didn't hear the description of because I've been a little too distracted by Jack's antics.

"Jody, please, eat. Pretend to eat, at least. Put a smile on your face," Martin says and grins at me. "Pretend like we knew he was going to announce. We are not surprised, just amused that he selected this particular venue. Jack is tacky and tasteless. We are not worried at all, because we are going to annihilate his man in the election. This little stunt will completely backfire."

That confidence makes me smile. I pick up my fork and force a piece of lettuce into my mouth. I lean forward and meet JJ's gaze. "I'm sorry," he mouths, as if he didn't know this was happening either.

Could that be possible? Could this have been Jack's little secret, not even telling his own son? He better not have known about this. If he knew and didn't warn Charlotte, well, that's not a very loving move for a groom, is it?

I take a deep breath and mouth, "OK," with a shrug, and JJ turns back to his salad.

That's when Mimi and I lock eyes again. She nods in the direction of the exit nearest me. We need to talk. I need to find out what she knows, what she's hiding.

I want to throw something at Jack. So much so that I imagine it: hurling my dinner knife down the table until it pierces his dark heart.

But I can't, of course I can't. I'll simply bide my time. Revenge is a dish best served cold, I recall. And I can wait with the best of them. I can wait, sometimes a lifetime.

The waiters swoop around us, gathering my salad plate and depositing a main dish overflowing with fish, chicken, and steak, or something that looks like all three things. I'm going to be sick. How much did they spend on this night?

And then, before I can escape, he does it again. Jack taps his wineglass and the room quiets.

"I know, I know. I promised not to make this special night about politics, but I need to recognize the minority leader. Keith, stand up and wave to everyone. Keith, thanks for being here tonight."

A round of muffled applause scatters through the room.

"OK, back to toasting the lovely young couple. The reason we're all here tonight. Did you guys know Martin and I went to the same high school? Same class," Jack says. "Never imagined he'd be a congressman, not if you knew him then."

I lean forward and see Margaret pull on Jack's sleeve.

"Oops, here I am talking again. Well, anyway, a toast to the happy couple. To Charlotte and JJ. May you have a happy, honest, and honorable marriage. May you trust each other and have that trust rewarded. And, selfishly, may you have lots of grandkids for me to spoil. Cheers!"

That's it. I cannot take another moment of this. "He's got to be stopped. I won't allow him to humiliate my family like this," I say and push away from the table.

"Jody, wait," Martin says and somehow grabs my wrist.

"Let go of me, Martin," I say, and he does. I walk to the end of the head table and stare at Jack, who is now sitting and enjoying a bite of steak. I lean in close to his ear. "This is an embarrassing spectacle that will reflect poorly on you, your so-called candidate, and your family forever. Mark my words. Forever is a long time." I turn my back on him, find the steps down from the head table, and take my time walking to the exit, saying hello to people I know in the crowd. I make it to the restroom and am relieved to find it empty.

I hear the swoosh of the door. Mimi is here. The sight of my friend almost brings me to tears. Almost. I remind myself she isn't a friend, not any longer. Maybe we never were. This is politics. I need to know what she knows, but I need to have her think I am still a friend, still dependent on her and her pretend benevolence.

"What do we do?" I ask.

"We remain calm. You remain calm. We knew this guy was a candidate, and we know he's got big money backers. But Martin is an incumbent; he has a war chest and will easily raise more," Mimi says. "They see Martin as wounded, weak, for once. The Republicans are so tacky. Cannot believe they pulled this off here, of all places. Inappropriate, but they don't care about decorum anymore. It's only about winning."

"Yes, but they've become quite good at winning, no matter how," I say, nodding.

"Martin should be fine," Mimi says. "As long as things stay as they are, as long as nothing else comes to light."

She's referring to the intern. To Sarah. Martin's incumbency and huge war chest will not matter if that story comes out. If it's proved to be true, Martin is done. No one could save him, not even if I wanted to. My stomach turns.

"Martin looks desperate up there at the head table, desperate and ill. He looks like a man filled with secrets and guilt," Mimi says, applying red lipstick. She looks at me in the mirror. "You should know there are candidates lining up."

"What do you mean 'candidates lining up'?" I ask, my heart thumping in my chest. "You mean Democrats? No, this is the Asher seat."

"He cannot afford another scandal. He cannot get more bad press. If he does, he's toast," she says. "You and I both know it. And we also both know there's more to come."

The door swishes and an older woman enters the room. We cannot talk here any longer.

"No, there's nothing else," I say and walk out the door. But is it already too late, I wonder? I walk, smiling, through the ballroom, confident and poised, and take my seat next to Martin and Charlotte and grin at the crowd. "Did I miss anything?"

Charlotte shakes her head. "JJ didn't know his dad was doing this. I promise. He confronted his dad last night, and Jack promised to behave himself. He betrayed all of us."

"We believe you," Martin says.

I am not sure if I do. We sit and smile back at the crowd, pretend to eat our meals, and finally, somehow, it's time for dessert.

"Let's go," Martin says, tossing his napkin on top of some fancy dish that has a C & J monogram entwined in gold on top. "We've put up with enough."

"She could come with us," I say as I stand up, looking to Charlotte.

"You know she can't," Martin says and he bends to kiss her cheek. "We'll see you tomorrow, honey."

Charlotte nods, seemingly still in shock. JJ waves in our direction and wraps his arm around our daughter. At least he will take care of her, shield her from some of this.

Martin clasps my hand, and we walk through the ballroom, smiling and waving, accepting accolades and shouts of "Don't worry, Asher," from supporters until we're out of the clubhouse.

"The car should be here any minute," Martin says. "I cannot believe this."

"Tomorrow is a new day. Tomorrow is our time to shine. Jack outplayed us tonight, that's all. But it's over. He's revealed his plan, so we pivot accordingly. Harold is a nobody. He can't beat you. Your constituents love you."

I watch Martin. He's worried about something, and it's not just Jack and his proxy, Harold.

"Congressman Asher, can I have a word? It's Jordan Bard from *Politico*." A young man in a suit has followed us out. "Did you know about Harold Kestler's challenge before tonight? Did you know your new in-laws are backing him?"

I watch Martin's face as he calculates what to say.

"Off the record?" Martin asks.

"If you must," the reporter says.

"We heard there would be a challenger in the primary. I had no idea he'd actually show up at my daughter's wedding rehearsal dinner. But it doesn't matter. I'll win by a landslide," Martin says as our car pulls up.

"Sir, any comment on the Roscoe investigation? I hear you have big ties to the firm?" the reporter asks.

"No comment. If you'll excuse us. Special day tomorrow," Martin says.

"Ah, yes, the wedding. I'll be there, sir. Good night," the reporter says, slipping away from us as Martin opens the car door and helps me inside. I stare at his face, ghost white and lined with stress. At least the reporter didn't ask about the intern.

I reach for Martin's hand and pat it reassuringly. "Let's not worry about anything else tonight. Tomorrow will be spectacular, and this night will be forgotten. Promise." I close my eyes. I cannot wait for tomorrow.

The Ashers will regain control. At least, this one will. Even if the reporters cover tonight, it will make Harold and his lackey Jack look bad and uncouth. Tacky and tasteless. The wedding story will replace the lobbyist money story. And then the intern story, if it comes out, will trump them all. But not before the wedding, I say, issuing a silent prayer to the media gods. I lean back against the cold leather seat for the long ride home.

Certainly nothing else can happen this weekend.

My phone lights up with a text. From Mimi. He slept with her, didn't he?

In any other situation, this type of question would never be asked of the wife. But in politics, it's a dog-eat-dog world. Whoever has the scoop, the dirt, wins.

Of course not, I type. Who knows if I'm lying? Martin does. I look at Martin's face. His eyes are shut; he appears to be asleep, but I know he is not. Like a toddler, he is trying to hide from me by closing his eyes. I shake my head and stare at my husband.

What has he done?

What does Mimi know?

And more troubling, after all these years, is this question: Is Mimi the one who is trying to bring Martin down?

LITTLE TIPS FOR NEW CONGRESSIONAL SPOUSES FROM MRS. ASHER, WIFE OF THE HONORABLE MARTIN ASHER (D-OH)

Here's a fun tip! The August recess is almost a month long! Yay! You'll have your husband to yourself, and if you're lucky, you'll be invited on fabulous Congressional delegation trips called CODELs. These overseas trips are all first class, I'm telling you. We've been on fact-finding trips to Fiji, the Bahamas, Switzerland, and Portugal. Paris was spectacular. A doctor travels with you to care for any needs that arise, and you'll fly in a military aircraft—the safest in the skies. These trips include special itineraries for spouses, shopping trips, and educational sightseeing tours too. The embassy staff wherever you are headed takes care of all the arrangements. During these excursions, I've met lifelong friends and visited many wonders of the world. It's truly one of the most special spouse perks. The press doesn't like spouses traveling with our members, despite the fact we are traveling at no extra cost to taxpayers. So I'd keep social media posting to a minimum. Some places, they'll take your phones and give you secure ones just so you don't get compromised. Very "spy novel" feeling.

If you aren't invited on a CODEL, well, you and your honey should make a point to go on a vacation. It's really your only big break.

MARTIN

Town Car

The ride home seems to take much longer than the drive to that ridiculous event, but I know it's all due to the added stress of Harold's announcement. As if I didn't have enough on my plate. The good news is there is a glass privacy divider between us and the driver. I have plenty of time and freedom from eavesdroppers to yell at my team, and so I do. Beginning with David.

"How the hell can we be blindsided like this? They used a rehearsal dinner to infiltrate and sabotage our happy celebrations. It's my daughter's flipping wedding weekend."

"It could backfire on them, sir," David says. "I mean, the press could point out that Jack and Harold used a Democratic congressman's daughter's wedding for a Republican political spectacle. Voters won't like that, sir."

"I hope you're right. I know I didn't love it!" I am yelling, so I turn toward the window. Jody hates it when I yell. "He's already been named a fucking top gun! I just googled him, and there he is."

"I know. They really pulled everything together quickly, but it's in such poor taste, sir," David says. "It's in all the trade press. *Politico* has a front-page scoop on it, complete with photos of the lavish event. Your face, Jody's—well, of course you weren't happy. Let's just say that's clear from the photograph they're running. People will feel sorry for you. They'll see what a bastard Jack is. Harold by association."

"I hope so. I hope they feel for us. In the meantime, make sure this never happens again," I say.

"Already started the opposition research. We'll ruin him, sir. But, sir, the Roscoe problem," David says.

I glance over at Jody. "I'm not at liberty to discuss that now."

"Fine, but sir, we need to," David says.

"Look, the wedding is tomorrow. My daughter, for some unknown reason, has decided to marry a dickhead's son. Unless I can change her mind about the love of her life, we'll be forced to talk about everything on Sunday," I say and rummage in my jacket for an antacid.

"Per that, sir, remember your daughter has exposure, too, with the firm, sir. As you know, she worked at Roscoe & Partners," David says. "And she couriered some things, could be—"

"Stop right there. Don't go any further. She interned there, but that was a couple years ago. We will discuss this on Sunday," I say, then hang up on him. Charlotte will not be a part of this story.

"Tell me what's happening," Jody says, her tone grave. "What did David accuse Charlotte of doing?"

"Nothing, I'm sure it's nothing. Just gossip," I say, stifling a burp. God, I feel sick. The drop and pickup yesterday will be the last. I make that promise to myself. I've flown too close to the flame. Charlotte was never involved in any of this. She is innocent. My chest tightens.

I'm tempted to call my campaign consultants, especially Mark, whom I trust implicitly on all these things, but I see Jody's face and decide I best speak with her first.

"What do you think the chances are that Charlotte will call the whole thing off? I mean, the timing, the situation, the whole thing has gone to shit," I say before chewing on my antacid. For all these reasons and many more, this wedding should not go on, not like this. Maybe not ever.

"No one—no politics, no personal grudges, nothing—will stop the wedding tomorrow. We will not stand in Charlotte's way. She's in love. It's like Romeo and Juliet or something. But our two warring families won't stop this wedding, because it is what she wants. I've given my all to planning this, Martin. It will happen tomorrow, do you understand? Or else there will be consequences." Jody's face is tight, fury in her voice. And something else I don't often hear. A threat.

"Are you threatening me?" I ask as a knife stabs my side. Damn stomach ulcer is getting worse. Everything is getting worse.

Jody brushes her hands, wipes imaginary crumbs from her dress—a habit of hers when she's angry and thinking. "Of course not, dear. I'm just stating the fact. The show will go on. It must, and it will. For all our sakes. A canceled wedding wouldn't look good for you. Besides, you've already paid for it all."

My heart drops. "Do you realize what's happening? Jack is backing Harold Kestler for a run to take my seat. He may be behind these false rumors about me having some sort of affair. He's stirring the pot with the K Street stuff. I know he is. Have you even talked to Charlotte? She must be mad too. I mean, she loves me; she understands politics," I say. "I'm going to call her. Let's talk to her." I pull out my phone and punch in Charlotte's number.

"It's not going to change anything. Charlotte loves JJ," Jody says.

"I'm the one paying for the goddamn thing," I say to Jody. "Char, hi. Can you talk?" I ask once my daughter answers. "Look, I'd understand if you want to postpone the wedding. It's going to be a circus tomorrow."

"Dad, you know we can't do that. JJ and I are in love, and I've chosen to forgive his dad for the mess he's made the last two nights. JJ is all that matters to me, and he didn't do anything wrong. You see that, right? Mom and I have worked so hard to make tomorrow very special. We'll beef up security, make it a politics-free night somehow. JJ is talking to his dad now. He can make him behave, he thinks," Charlotte says. She sounds tired and bummed out. "I'm worried about you, though, Dad. You didn't look good tonight, like you weren't feeling well. And I know that whole announcement had to be hard to watch."

"I'm fine, honey. If you're sure you still want the wedding to proceed, I'll be there," I say.

I feel Jody's stare. I turn to face her and shrug.

She grabs my phone. "Charlotte. The wedding will be the talk of the town, for all the good reasons. You and JJ are the perfect couple. See you tomorrow. Love you."

Instead of handing me my phone back, Jody pushes the button for the window. Before I can stop her, she flings my phone out the window. Just as we're driving on the bridge crossing the Potomac. Oh my God.

In addition to always being in charge, my wife does have impeccable timing and a strong throwing arm.

"Fuck you, Martin," she says. "I don't like your schemes. I don't like how you're acting. How dare you try to get Charlotte to call off the wedding? How dare you ignore my wishes? This is my weekend."

Silly me. I thought this was our daughter's weekend, *her* wedding, and I was just the patsy suckered into paying for it all somehow. "It's Charlotte's weekend. And JJ's," I add, feeling in my suit pocket for my phone before remembering it's gone. Damn her. "I guess I'm all yours. No distractions. What exactly did you want to talk about?" Despite my calm demeanor, I'm seething. I want my phone. I'm wondering how I can get David to deliver a new one to me tonight. Thank goodness we still have an old-fashioned landline at the town house.

"I want to talk about tomorrow. We need to be in sync. Like Jack and Margaret were tonight. We need to have a united front. And especially for you, you must look like a leader. You must be congressional at all times. One or two drinks at the most. Am I clear?" she says.

From the front seat, the driver's eyes meet mine in the rearview mirror. I'm not sure if he noticed the phone hurtling out the window. He must have. I shake my head and roll my eyes up.

"Yes, you are more than clear. I will pretend to be the perfect husband, father, and congressman tomorrow. I will act scandal-free." I know I can pretend to be that for a day.

I've had a lot of practice pretending. Eventually, though, people see through the facade of perfection. That's when the trouble begins. I'd say, given the present circumstances, trouble is here. There is nowhere left to hide.

LITTLE TIPS FOR NEW CONGRESSIONAL SPOUSES FROM MRS. ASHER, WIFE OF THE HONORABLE MARTIN ASHER (D-OH)

Sometimes it can be a lonely place, being a congressional spouse. Your husband works long hours and then has evening commitments too. And before you know it, he'll be running for reelection. Two years is a very short time. Everyone always asks you how your spouse is doing, how he's holding up under the stress and strain. As you likely learned during the campaign, if your spouse happens to be by your side, all the attention is on them. I've been to many dinners where I didn't get asked one question, so focused were the others at the table on my husband and his opinions. Of course he is the interesting one and the one in power, but if you're like me, you have a brain too. You're not just an accessory on his arm.

It's hard. And nobody tells you this. If you feel lonely, reach out to another spouse. She'll understand. She might be the only one who can.

JODY

Asher Townhome

At least I finally have Martin's undivided attention. Without his phone, he's like a little kid, fidgeting in his seat, biting his lip, anxious. He can't escape, virtually or otherwise. I stare at him and realize I've begun to have a little doubt. My mind flashes back to his quick departure from the townhome yesterday morning, his ever-growing ulcer, his haggard appearance.

I think of how he assures me the news story is no big deal but seems distraught, as if it could bring him down. *Us* down. Martin stares at me, eyes dark, unflinching. Do I even know who he really is anymore? Who he has become?

"Don't pretend to be anything," I say to his ridiculous promise. "Why don't you just be truthful?"

He stares at me. Fine. We will hash out his troubles on Sunday. For now, I will focus on the glorious joys of the wedding day.

Martin says, "Can I use your phone? Now."

It's not a request. It's a command. I've provoked him enough.

"Fine." I stick it in his outstretched hand. "I don't know what you think David can do about it at midnight on a Friday night, but knock yourself out."

Martin pivots in his seat so he's facing the window, but he keeps the phone on speaker and I hear David pick up. "What's wrong, Mrs. Asher?"

"It's me. I've lost my phone," Martin says.

"This could be bad, sir. Where did you last see it?" David asks.

"In Jody's hand when she flung it out of the car and into the Potomac."

David takes a beat to respond. "Well, at least no one will ever find it in that filthy sludge. We have a backup of all your emails and contacts but not your texts or phone calls. I'll grab you a new phone first thing in the morning and load what I can."

Martin turns and stares at me. At last, he realizes what I've done.

"You're welcome," I say. He smiles.

He puts the phone on mute and says, "The cell company will have records of everything, you know. The cops can get access if they try, so you haven't really solved the problem."

"I've bought you some time, though, haven't I?" I ask. "And it felt really great."

He nods. Takes the phone off mute. "Sounds good, David. Just bring it with you to the wedding. I'll get it from you there."

After he hangs up, he hands me my phone. "Maybe it will be good to be phone-free for a bit. A clean slate in the morning. No texts. No past. It's good."

He squeezes my hand as the car stops in front of our townhome.

"Have a good night," the driver says, opening Martin's door. "You too, ma'am. Nice arm."

I smile and take his hand as he helps me out. "Ah, thanks for noticing."

I have many secret talents, and Martin knows about most of them. I'm different, and that's a blessing. I'm not crazy. I've learned to exist inside society's bounds. I'm smart—street smart. It's the difference that allows me to be one step ahead, always. *Literally and figuratively,* I note as I begin to walk up the steep metal steps of home. I don't know all of what Martin has done, but I'm now certain he's guilty of something. And he likely put it in a text message to someone. I know there were messages to her, to Sarah, because I read them.

"I need you to understand something," I say, slipping the key into the lock and staring at my husband. "I've overlooked a lot and stayed by your side, and it has all been worth it because it led us here. You must win reelection. My life is here, in DC. The wedding must be perfect, and perfectly congressional. And all that nonsense with Roscoe & Partners? That needs to go away. Do you understand me?"

I step in the door and hurry to the alarm pad.

"I'll try. Believe me. I want what you want. As for Roscoe, these types of investigations take months, sometimes years. It won't go anywhere for a while, but it will go away. There's nothing there." He takes a breath and meets my eye. "It will go away. Joe would never implicate me."

"Because you haven't done anything wrong?" I say, flipping on the light to the stairs.

"Because he won't," Martin says, but he breaks eye contact and begins trudging up the stairs.

All I can think as I kick off my heels is that we're in trouble if we're at the mercy of somebody's silence. This is Washington, DC. Trust no one.

I turn on the television to the late local news. I'm hoping, beyond hope, that none of tonight's events are covered. I didn't see a news camera, but we left early. The anchor says, "Joe Roscoe, founder of one of K Street's most successful firms, was taken into custody tonight." The screen is filled with images of Martin's disgraced friend being escorted out the front door of his stately office. "We'll update this story with more details as they become available."

Behind me, Martin stops halfway up the stairs. He's staring at the television. "This can't be happening."

"You said the investigation would take months," I say, not bothering to look at my husband.

118

"I was wrong. Damn it," Martin says. "They had him in handcuffs. Poor Joe."

My phone pings with a text. It's from David. For Martin. It reads: Please, tell Martin do not comment on Roscoe. Talk to no one. I'll have a new phone first thing in the a.m. I'll pick him up at 8 a.m.

"David says not to talk to the press and he'll be here at eight in the morning," I say. I stand up and turn to face Martin. "What now?"

"We focus on the wedding, and on Sunday, we fight back," Martin says. As I watch him climb the stairs, I wonder what ammunition we have to fight back with.

"How?" I yell after him, but he doesn't answer.

Little Tips for New Congressional Spouses from Mrs. Asher, Wife of the Honorable Martin Asher (D-OH)

I think I better stop writing tips for now, as I might make you melancholic. Apologies. There really is much to love, many one-of-a-kind experiences to be had. It's just a bit thankless and a bit frustrating at times, that's all. Don't let it get you down. Keep your own interests, stay in touch with friends. Take care of yourself.

MARTIN

Asher Townhome

As usual, I can't sleep. I lie here, in bed, reviewing my life. It's funny: perception versus reality. Most people in DC think Jody and I are blue bloods with lots of family, generational money. Heck, she's a Prescott from Palm Beach, and I'm an Asher from Ohio, descended from a long line of Revolutionary War generals, state senators, and even a US congressman long ago.

But the truth is, we've worked hard to rise to this level. It's tough to feel it all slipping away.

I think back to when we met Mimi and Spencer, back in law school. Mimi was scrappy, like Jody and me, but she was smart too. She went after Spencer for his trust fund, and it has worked out well for her. I push away the look on her face at the rehearsal dinner, the displeasure she has with me over Sarah even after I promised her nothing had happened.

I hate lying to Mimi. She has played an important role in my success—more than Joe Roscoe, more than Jody would ever suspect. The disappointment, and anger, on Mimi's face spells trouble for everything I've built. She does not believe my innocence with the Sarah situation. I shove these thoughts aside for now.

I turn back to my laptop and the breaking news story. Joe Roscoe was arrested. Nothing else matters. Roscoe & Partners is one of the most-respected lobbying firms on K Street. They've been in business for two generations. Joe's dad, Moe, started the place. If Joe is guilty of what they're charging him with, embezzling millions from a nonprofit and directing the money to illegal lobbying activities with lawmakers, the scrutiny could be a problem for all of us. According to this article, Roscoe could make a deal, turn government witness, and testify against six unnamed lawmakers.

Preposterous. He'd never do that. They're just trying to scare him. If he talks, he'll ruin his business forever.

My heart squeezes and I reach for a TUMS from my bedside table. Today is my daughter's wedding. An event I've looked forward to even as I've gone broke trying to pay for it. I look at the clock beside my bed. It's four a.m.

As a congressman, I've learned to live by time—increments of it, that is. Ten minutes here, five there. I wouldn't have imagined it before I got here. The time. The schedule. The pace. It's exhausting and strangely exhilarating at the same time. It's like a drug, a feeling of power, of being able to help people. "I can make a difference," this job tells me. "Keep going. Next session, you will see. Next session you'll make even more of a difference. Don't stop. Raise money. Sign on to legislation. Let them see you in the district. Smile in the parades, kiss the babies."

And then a constituent walks through my office door. Someone who, somehow, connected with me and my office and was helped. And helped a lot. And they come into my office and thank me, with tearful eyes, because without me they wouldn't have lived, voted, worked, had housing, had food, had a voice, had a pet, had an academy appointment. You name it. And then their time is up, and I'm off to the next thing.

That's how it was. But now, I'm just waiting for the other shoe to drop.

I can't lose this job.

That's all I can think about seeing my friend Joe in handcuffs on the news.

I won't lose this job. Without it, I'm nobody. I'm nothing at all. Morning can't come soon enough. I need to talk to David.

I try to figure out how to get out of the mess I'm in.

David already suspects I've been compromised. But that's natural— staffers are cynics. I should tell him to follow my example. You must be what you want others to be. Who am I kidding? I fell off my high horse after my freshman term here. The system makes it so easy to mess up, so easy to ethically be in the gray zone without even trying. A gift here, a dinner there. The rules seem arbitrary, temptations abound, and it's hard to stay on course.

I suppose, actually, life makes that so. At every turn, you can decide to honor your commitments or not. You can decide to be true to your word or not. Jody and I have always lived above our means since arriving in DC. We wanted the best, for ourselves and our daughter. And I figured out ways to make the best happen: the best schools for Charlotte, the best vacations for our family, the best tickets to the best events in town.

I thought I was a hero. I guess that's how I've always seen myself.

If only I hadn't started to believe I was invincible.

I grab the side of the bed as a wave of sickness sweeps through me, and I pray I don't vomit.

I hope they don't come for me with handcuffs like they did Joe. I wouldn't survive it.

Little Tips for New Congressional Spouses from Mrs. Asher, Wife of the Honorable Martin Asher (D-OH)

Unlike your spouse's travel back and forth to the district, your tickets cannot be paid for with government funds—even though we know how much work you do to support him and help him serve his district. (See tip above on this.) If you choose to live in the district, or partially in DC and in the district, travel will become one of your challenges, especially if you're from the West Coast. You have three choices for how to pay for those plane tickets: with your own money; with your spouse's frequent-flier miles; or, if helping on the campaign, with campaign funds. Just be careful with all this . . . ethics will be watching.

JODY

Asher Townhome

Have I wasted my life on this man? *With* this man?

Those are the first thoughts that pop into my mind as I take in Martin's empty side of the bed. I had terrible nightmares about him being arrested, about him being censured and removed from Congress. I don't even know how that works, but I don't want to know. I remember a congressman who was kicked out for flying his pet rabbit across the country, among other things. I will not have our family be turned into a spectacle for people to gawk at or be the focus of lurid news stories. It will not, cannot, happen.

My phone rings. Who would be calling this early on a Saturday—the Saturday of my daughter's wedding?

"Hello?" I answer. I use my spam-caller voice, hoping to scare them off.

"Jody, hello. It's so nice to hear your voice," a woman says. "This is Amanda Jones. We sat together the other night at the Library of Congress dinner."

The woman who doesn't know how to use utensils. "Yes, of course. What can I help you with?"

"Well, I'm so sorry to say my husband and I won't be able to attend the wedding today. Brett's seat is in a swing district, so we need to 'fly under the radar,' to use an airplane term. Ha!"

She's a nervous nincompoop. "Oh, is that so? I'm not sure I understand."

"Well, your husband's race has become quite the talk of the town, and the news media has a lot of things about him taking bribes and maybe other stuff with an intern. Oh, I need to go." She stops talking, as if someone has muzzled her.

"My husband is innocent. My daughter will be a beautiful bride," I say before I hang up.

My phone rings again. It's Ambassador Viola from Chile. "Hello, my friend. How are you this beautiful morning?"

"I'm so good, Jody. But I'm calling because I cannot make Charlotte's wedding today. I'm so sorry. I hope she'll enjoy my gift, though. Have a wonderful ceremony," she says.

"But, Viola, why?" I ask before realizing she has already hung up.

I take a deep breath before throwing my phone across the room.

I hope my daughter isn't receiving calls like this from her friends. I hope her friends are loyal and true. Some of this could be my fault, of course. I'm not one for making and keeping friends—not once I've moved past them. No, I am bad about remembering the little people who've helped along the way.

I walk to the corner of the bedroom and retrieve my phone, which is ringing once again. This time I'm happy to answer.

"Charlotte, darling, are you excited for the big day?" I ask.

"Mom, you sound funny, like you're faking it. Don't. It will be lovely. We've planned a great event," Charlotte says. "It must be overwhelming for you, with all the Dad stuff."

My little empath. She's just so very opposite of me. She never lies, never acts impulsively; she plans ahead, always gets her work done; and she's never engaged in any criminal behavior, not even shoplifting. She's risk averse and never manipulates people. And she always feels too much for others, putting herself last. She'd never throw her phone across the room—or her husband's out the window, for that matter. We've joked about it over the years, how she could be so normal when she has me for a mom and a workaholic congressman for a dad. I want to be in control, and she just wants to get along.

"I'm doing just great. I cannot wait for this evening. The Ashers will be the talk of the town," I say and imagine a glowing society-page article with a color photo.

"I think Dad already is," Charlotte says. "Anyway, I'm glad you're happy."

"You and your bridesmaids need to meet at the venue at three for-ty-five sharp," I remind her.

"Would you like to join us?" Charlotte asks.

How sweet. I can't imagine anything I'd rather do less. "Oh, that's so kind, Charlotte. You girls go ahead. I'll need to take care of Dad, make sure he gets where he's supposed to be on time. He's a little scat-tered," I say, glad to have come up with a quick lie. I'm good at that.

"Please do take care of him. He must be under so much stress," she says.

"I am too," I say. "You wouldn't believe the phone calls, the press nonsense. It's exhausting."

"Mom, practice your sympathy, OK?" Charlotte says. "Dad needs your support."

That makes me smile. I do have sympathy and empathy "games" to practice. My therapist provided them. I've learned not to smile or laugh when people are being hurt on a TV show, and I've learned to try to feel sad when someone else is crying. This life I've lived as a political spouse has been great practice for honing my skills, socially speaking. When someone bores me, I know how to say the right words to get away from them. When someone important takes my hand, I know how to charm him to make sure he will help Martin in the future. I know how to work a room for favors and how to seem completely engaged in listening to a speech I've heard a million times. I'm really not there—that's my secret. While Martin drones on about something, I'll imagine sneaking into that fancy purse left casually at a supporter's feet. And sometimes I do more than imagine. You have to make all this a game, you see. A game you must win. It's daunting sometimes, but I've become a pro. I know how to keep myself amused.

As for Martin, he doesn't deserve any of my energy. Not until he fixes what he's done.

"You know I will handle your father. See you soon," I say. "Love you, Charlotte."

"Thanks for trying your best, Mom," Charlotte says.

Five voice mails have been left for me during my brief chat with my daughter. I know they are all guests backing out of the wedding, the weenies. I forward each message to Vanessa without listening.

And then I call her. "Look, I'm sending you an ever-growing list of people who suddenly can't make it to the wedding. I need you to revise the seating appropriately."

"Yes, Mrs. Asher. Will do. As you know, the food is already being prepped, so there won't be a refund. Would you like to donate the extra meals to a particular charity?"

Her words provoke a fit of rage I cannot tamp down. "No, throw them away," I say, then hang up.

I head downstairs to make coffee, and I stop at the front door for today's paper. I flip through the pages quickly, looking for anything about Martin or last night. And I find it. The byline is Max Brown. The headline reads: "Congressman Asher's Continued Challenges: Candidate Announces Run at Congressman's Daughter's Wedding Celebration—and the Candidate Is Endorsed by Daughter's New Father-In-Law." The photo is of the head table, all of us watching as Harold Kestler is lauded by Jack Dobbs. I don't read the story. I know what happened. I throw the paper across the room and head to the kitchen.

Right about now, a woman would call her best friend.

For a moment, I wish I had one. But then I shake off the sentiment.

Focus, Jody. Emotion makes you weak, you know that. And just about now you need all the strength you can muster.

Today's the day. *My* day.

Little Tips for New Congressional Spouses from Mrs. Asher, Wife of the Honorable Martin Asher (D-OH)

No matter what, never let them see you sweat. Just don't. Literally and figuratively. Campaigns are terrible these days. They will attack your husband, lie about him, spread rumors—anything to destroy him and his reputation. It's the politics of personal destruction. Don't let them ruin you in the process. Only cry in private.

MARTIN

Asher Townhome

As I walk inside our house, I remind myself I've decided to wait until Sunday to tell Jody the extent of the bad news. She's already on edge with the society-page coverage of the shit show last night at the Congressional Country Club—of all places—and I'm afraid what my news would do to her.

I take an antacid and wonder briefly if they will interact adversely with my new blood pressure medicine David brought from the House physician, but decide not to care. I need both to make it through the wedding.

Jody rushes down the stairs and halts in front of me. I walk past her and take a seat in my favorite chair in the living room, feet up on the ottoman, laptop on my lap. I pretend to be engrossed by my screen, but she clears her throat.

She says, "We will talk Sunday. Today we focus on the wedding."

I feel her staring at me before I look at her. "What's wrong now?" I ask, dreading the answer.

"Why were you gone so long this morning?" she asks.

"I told you. Official side-staff meeting, followed by campaign-side strategy meeting with all the consultants," I say. I don't add the meeting at the attorney's office. I don't tell her that my attorneys think the feds have solid evidence. No, now is not the time for that.

"Are they worried?" she asks.

For a moment I think she means my attorneys, but she means the campaign staff. About Harold Kestler. About his ridiculous campaign. "No, not really. I mean, our district loves us."

Jody tips her head to the side. I note she's wearing oversize sweatpants and a baggy T-shirt. She is not her typical model of congressional spousehood. "Do voters love us, or do they like bright, shiny objects? Change and all of that?" She sighs. "Look at who gets elected nowadays. Nothing matters."

"Money does. That's the only thing that worries me. Money matters most," I say before covering up a burp. My stomach is an acid-filled pool ready to erupt at any moment.

"You have great supporters. Plenty of cash on hand," Jody says, demonstrating her knowledge of my campaign finances. I didn't know she was paying attention. "What? Don't look surprised. I need to know where we stand. This is my life, too, all of this. DC is my world too. We can't lose it. We won't."

I take a deep breath. "I'm doing my best not to."

"I always thought it would be some young liberal woman taking you down. Not this. Not a white man, a rich jerk from our very suburb. Not your future in-laws, for heaven's sake. This isn't the way it was supposed to end. So don't let it," Jody says. Her phone rings in her hand.

"Go ahead, answer," I say.

"No need to answer. I'm sure it's another cancellation. I wonder what the reason will be this time? A spring cold. An urgent meeting. I've heard all the excuses. It's rude, that's what it is." Jody plops down on the couch, and my heart breaks a little for her.

"Canceling because of me? Because of what?" I ask, even though I know the answer.

"Because of the news from last night's event. Because of Joe Roscoe's arrest. But mostly, it's because of the fiery spotlight on you. Ambassadors and other dignitaries shy away from this sort of debacle, and apparently my so-called friends do too," Jody says, dropping her head.

This is all my fault. "I'm sorry, honey."

She looks at me. "I know. Tell me the truth: Should I be worried about the Roscoe thing or about anything or anyone else?" Jody asks. "I mean, our stars are rising—shooting, even. Right, Martin?"

You know what they say about shooting stars: they burn up upon entering the earth's atmosphere. Maybe we've gone as far as we should. If I hadn't flirted with Sarah, maybe we'd be fine. Maybe we still will be? Maybe it's time to—

"Martin?"

"Tomorrow, we'll talk. Today is your day. The wedding will be spectacular, honey. It will be your crowning achievement in DC. I just hate to see you so sad on your big day," I say. I mean that. After all we've spent, all we've squandered on this event, Jody should at least have this day. "Let's just focus on the wedding and enjoy ourselves tonight. You deserve it."

Jody begins crying. Big, wet tears streak her cheeks. I realize I've never seen her cry before. "Thank you. That's the sweetest thing you've ever said to me. I love you."

"I love you too," I say, despite the fact I know that in about two days' time, if my attorneys can hold things off, she'll likely hate me.

My new phone, dropped off this morning by a staffer, lights up with a text from David via WhatsApp. Encrypted. Subpoena coming today. Phone calls, emails, texts.

And then I remember: Jody already knows what's coming. She's just hanging on to the illusion for one more day.

"How can I help you get ready? You should stop crying; it will make your eyes puffy for the pictures," I say, ignoring David's text.

"You're right," she says, then sniffs. "I'll go get some ice."

"Allow me," I say as I hurry to the kitchen. I pull open the freezer drawer and fight the urge to pour myself a scotch on the rocks.

I realize this might be one of the last acts of kindness I'll be able to do for Jody.

If I can't get in front of all these scandals, she'll leave me—I'm certain of it. And I wouldn't blame her, not a bit.

Little Tips for New Congressional Spouses from Mrs. Asher, Wife of the Honorable Martin Asher (D-OH)

You'll want to be the face of constituent services, both in DC and in your district. Yours can be the softer touch, a balance and helpmate for all your spouse's hard work. Give tours of major attractions in DC. In the district, volunteer at charities close to your heart; help support the Congressional Art Competition for high school kids, for example. Your constituents will love you. You are an extension of your husband and his deeds. You are tied together, wrapped in the American flag. A team. Your fates joined together for life.

JODY

Asher Townhome

The sequined aqua dress pools on the floor and, as I spin, fits my curves with perfection. It is worth every dollar we spent on it, worth everything we had to do to buy it.

I stare at my reflection and force a smile. I'm wearing something blue, my exquisite designer dress, and something borrowed. I touch my ears; the large diamond studs belonged to one of my law school buddies. She thought she'd lost them.

I know, I'm not the bride, but as the mother of the bride, I'm the next most-important member of the wedding party. I will hold my head high tonight. I will leave it to Martin to take the blame and the shame, as he should.

My phone buzzes with an alert. Vice President Acton has been implicated in one of the China schemes. There will be an investigation.

Martin is involved. He must be. I stare at my reflection in the mirror and force myself not to cry again. It's so out of character. There is no time for a pity party, not today. It's time to go. I force a smile on my face and glide down the stairs. Martin smiles when I arrive downstairs.

"Gorgeous," he says.

"The vice president too?" I ask.

His face turns white. "How did you know?"

I hold up my phone. "News alert."

"Let's go to the wedding, shall we?" he asks, not meeting my eyes.

"You involved the vice president?" I ask, knowing the answer.

"Not now," Martin says.

"You're brilliant," I tell him as relief washes over me. "A bigger fish is just what we needed here. Bravo!"

LITTLE TIPS FOR NEW CONGRESSIONAL SPOUSES FROM MRS. ASHER, WIFE OF THE HONORABLE MARTIN ASHER (D-OH)

Here's a happy thought to start your day: once you get to know Washington, DC, you'll fall in love. You won't ever want to leave.

MARTIN

DAR Constitution Hall

We sit in impossibly small gold-backed chairs pushed together so tightly I feel as if my shoulder is crushing the lovely woman to my left. I pivot sideways again to give her a break. Beside me, Jody pats my leg. Her way of telling me to sit still. It must be eight hundred degrees outside, and we're in the sun, lined up in rows of tiny chairs, crunched together, waiting for this thing to start.

Jody has a bead of sweat rolling down her forehead. I know she must hate that. I reach into my tux and pull out a handkerchief. She needs to stop that river before it reaches her dress. The thing must have cost a fortune. It's light blue and shimmery. When I first saw her, I thought she looked like a beautiful mermaid.

Now she looks like a mermaid who needs to slip into a cool pool.

"Here," I whisper, handing her my handkerchief.

"Thanks. Where is the wedding party? What is taking so long?" she whispers. "I am going to kill Vanessa. It's her job to keep things on schedule. We walked down the aisle almost ten minutes ago."

I shrug and look around. Since we're basically seated outside near the street, we've heard many drive-by honks of congratulations and some unruly tourists on the sidewalk. And still no wedding party, despite the fact the ceremony was to begin at six thirty and it's almost six forty-five. I guess I can't blame them for staying inside and enjoying the air-conditioning. I wouldn't want to come out here either. I glance up and see the orchestra, if that's what you call five sweaty guys looking bored and holding string instruments. One of them puts his violin under his chin, and the others snap to attention. A good sign.

How the heck can it feel like August outside when it's only April? The air is thick with humidity, like we suddenly plunged into a greenhouse, the entire city, overnight. Yesterday evening wasn't like this. The Dobbses had perfect weather for the now-infamous rehearsal dinner. Of course this evening is a weather shit show. I pull at my collar, slipping my tie away from my neck. I feel like I'm being watched. And I am.

I look to my right and spot one of them. Federal agents stand out like sore thumbs, even here in Capitol City. I resist the urge to give them the finger. Why can't they just leave us alone for one more day? On *this* day, my daughter's big event. I just need one more night of peace. But it's not going to happen. David warned me they'd be here. He unfortunately was right again. I feel like I'm trapped in a spiderweb with no way out.

As the music begins, some sweet and soothing string melody, my stomach lurches. I stare straight ahead and tell myself to calm down. If I look to my left, Jody will give me the stink eye. Beyond her, across the aisle, I'll have to see Jack the joke and beautiful Margaret, shimmering in a champagne dress and a diamond necklace that is worth more than our townhome, not that I noticed. To my right, the tourists and the feds. I look straight ahead and am relieved when the bridesmaids finally begin appearing at the front like pale-pink illusions. Wilting, beautiful illusions.

The groomsmen file in from the side, and suddenly a minister appears. We all stand, and Charlotte and JJ glide down the aisle together. I wasn't upset when she ditched the idea of the father giving away his daughter. I know it's tradition, but it is rather arcane. The way I feel, and with all the negative attention, it's for the best.

My daughter is so beautiful.

The cameras click and the videographer rolls as they reach the front row. Charlotte walks over to us and kisses first her mom and then me on the cheek. Before I can stop them, tears roll down my cheeks.

"I love you, Charlotte," I say.

"Love you more, Daddy," she says.

The minister says, "Please join your groom."

Charlotte floats to the front and takes JJ's hand. She looks like a princess.

And before I realize it, it's over. Charlotte and JJ kiss, and we all jump to our feet and applaud, relieved to be free of these tiny chairs, the unrelenting sun, and the unbearable humidity. I clap like everyone else, and then I feel Jody's grip on my forearm. I know we are to exit somehow, get photos taken somewhere, and then grandly appear at the reception. I know all this, but I'm not sure how it works. I'm not sure I'll survive it all the way I feel.

"Follow me," Jody says.

And I do as I'm told, like a guy whose wife wears the pants. As we make our way down the aisle, everyone else remains standing where they are. The folks on the edge, on the aisle seats, check us out head to toe—Jody more than me because who hasn't seen a tux before. I know Jack and Margaret are following us in this little procession, so I take my time, keep my shadow on them. I smile. Wave. Even shake a couple of hands. I'm Martin Asher—Congressman Martin Asher, the Honorable Mr. Asher, Esquire—and I don't have a care in the world.

"Lovely wedding," a woman I don't know says as we pass by. "Almost as beautiful as last night."

Beside me, Jody stiffens. I squeeze her hand. "We're only getting started, madam. We'll see you inside," I say to the horrible guest. If my staff were near me, I'd have her escorted out.

Besides, she's on the groom's side.

She's probably a Republican.

LITTLE TIPS FOR NEW CONGRESSIONAL SPOUSES FROM MRS. ASHER, WIFE OF THE HONORABLE MARTIN ASHER (D-OH)

Good luck. It's a tough job, but I know you can do it. Hold your head high, and don't forget the family Bible for the swearing-in ceremony. Phone cutout optional. Ha!

JODY

The evening moves forward in a haze of happiness and alcohol-fueled cheer. The guests have murmured their delight at the class of the venue, the elegance of the decor, the wonder of the petite and elegant appetizers and French-wine display. Mini gazpacho soups garnished with huge prawns pass by on silver trays. The fresh raw oyster bar in the corner looks to be a big hit.

I help myself to a tuna-tartare cone as a server passes by and pop it into my mouth. Fabulous. Everything is fabulous. Yes, even as my makeup melted, the show went on, and so far everyone seems pleased. They'll forget the heat. I see smiles on the guests' faces as they pop prosciutto-wrapped persimmons with goat cheese into their mouths and nosh on biscuits topped with chipotle sauce. There's something for everyone; I made sure of it. People are happy.

I head out to the terrace, where a full bar has enticed guests. From where I stand, the White House glows like a wedding cake in the darkness. To think I imagined Martin would be president. I thought we could go that far.

Mimi swoops into view. "Wonderful reception, Jody. Everything is just perfect." She gives me a big hug and holds on, whispering, "Except Martin. He has created a huge mess."

I pull away from her embrace. "We're not talking about that tonight. This is Charlotte's night. Tomorrow, we fight back."

Mimi smiles. "It's too bad, really. We've had such a good run together, all of us."

"What are you talking about? Nothing is over; everything is the same. We just have a challenger. Big deal," I say.

"I really don't think you get it. I really don't," Mimi says and folds her arms across her chest. "He's done."

We stand together for another moment, and I ponder how we got here. Mimi is, I suppose, the closest thing to a best friend I have ever had. But maybe her notion of friendship has always been a lot like mine? Convenience, mutual benefit. Maybe that's what drew us together, and maybe that's what is now pushing us apart. She doesn't think we're useful anymore.

"You're wrong. Martin is a survivor. Don't bet against him," I say.

"Oh, Jody, I already have," Mimi says. "Excuse me. I need to find Spencer. You know how he hates parties."

"What did you say?" I ask. My mouth is dry, so I take a big sip of champagne before I grab her arm. "Look, I'll make sure Martin is staying out of trouble. I will. Promise."

Mimi shakes her head. "It's too late for that. He's crossed a line. There will be an ethics investigation and more. But, yes, enjoy tonight. It's so special. Excuse me." Mimi squeezes my hand before plunging into the crowd.

I float back into the main hall and look around. I know I'm in shock. When Mimi said it was too late, she meant it. I don't see Martin, but I do find Charlotte, glowing and making the rounds. I take a breath.

I must focus on this night that I've worked so hard on, that I've spent so much money to host. There are so many happy memories for Charlotte and me tonight, so many more photo moments. Dinner will be served, and it will be extraordinary. There will be toasts. There will be the cake cutting. And my favorite part: the bouquet toss from the balcony. After that, it's just dancing and whatever into the night. It will all be so lovely.

That's when I spot him. The reporter. Max Brown. He is here, at the reception. Who let him in? There was to be security. I search the room for Vanessa. When I don't see her, I decide to handle him myself.

I make my way across the ballroom, smiling and nodding at guests. Before I can reach the other side, Max has disappeared.

"Jody! Hey, how you doing?" It's Jack, the jerk. Beside him Margaret looks stunning in an exquisite dress and gigantic diamonds.

"I'm fine. Excuse me," I say, then turn away.

Somehow Charlotte and JJ appear at my side. "Mom, let me escort you to your seat," Charlotte says.

"Dad, Mom, come with me," JJ says. It's then I realize they're being the buffer between us.

"Thank you, Charlotte," I say, relieved. "Honey, we should find your dad. Dinner is about to be served."

"You're right. I saw him out this way," Charlotte says. She leads us through a glass door and out onto a smaller balcony. It's quiet here, the band and crowd noises muffled by the heavy doors.

There are only two other people here, huddled together in the dark corner.

"Dad?" Charlotte says.

Martin turns around. Beside him is Sarah, his intern.

"What are you doing?" I ask. I'm astonished to see her here, shocked to see my husband alone out here with her, at his daughter's wedding. My mouth goes dry. I watch as Sarah puts her hands on her hips and glares at me.

"We're talking, not that it's really any of your business," Sarah says. "We have things to figure out."

"You aren't invited here, to my daughter's wedding. You should leave," I say.

"Martin has been avoiding me. I knew where to find him tonight. So I came," Sarah says. She is acting as though she is the one in power. Her light-pink cocktail dress shimmers in the dim light. She looks irritatingly beautiful.

"You need to go. Now," I say. I sound scary.

"Mom, calm down," Charlotte says. I hear the quiver in her voice. She's angry. And it shouldn't be at me. "Dad, it's time for dinner. I need you inside."

"I'll be right there. I need to finish—" But whatever he needs to finish will remain a mystery. With a puzzled look, Martin drops to the ground, clutching his stomach, unable to break his own fall.

Beside me, Charlotte screams.

Sarah yells, "Call nine-one-one!"

I rush to where he's collapsed and kneel by his side. He's trying to speak.

I lean over, close to him. My husband, he can't leave me. Not this way. "Martin!"

"Safe," he murmurs.

"Yes, you're safe," I say.

"Open safe," he whispers.

"I understand. Martin, hold on." I cradle his head in my hands, and I feel him die, his face contorted in pain and anguish.

PART TWO

MAY

A Guide for New Members of Congress from Mimi Smith of the Smith Institute

A campaign for Congress can be all encompassing. Make sure your family is on board. The campaign and the job itself require a big sacrifice by the ones you love. If you should win, you will be married to your job. You will have little time for anyone or anything else. Are you up for this? Is your spouse?

JODY

It still doesn't seem real. I can't believe Martin is gone. I sit at his desk, holding his favorite pen, signing thank-you notes. Avalanches of well-wishers have sent florists' shops' worth of flowers to his office, which we've promptly dispatched to hospitals across Capitol Hill.

I've kept a single arrangement, elegant white lilies in a crystal vase, that adorns his desk. Many of Martin's constituents have donated to the American Heart Association too. We will make sure portable defibrillators are installed in public spaces throughout DC. We tell people Martin might be alive today if he'd had the heart attack anywhere in the Capitol complex. No one needs to know that Martin actually died of a gastric hemorrhage, the poor man, and that there was nothing doctors could do to save him. The cloak of privacy afforded to Congress members means the attending physician could sign the death certificate noting the much more common and civilized cardiac arrest as the cause of death. And I've asked for that to be done.

There was no need for an autopsy, and thankfully all the official paperwork a sudden death requires is complete. As a precaution, I did get rid of several vials of Visine. It's not good to use the drops too often or for too long, I read. Your eyes can have an adverse reaction. And that's if you're using it for the approved purpose. The dose I gave Martin each time he came home from seeing the intern simply made him feel bad, as he should have. I'm relieved, I suppose, that I am not the one to blame for his death. Poor Martin.

I'm startled by a knock on the door. Ever since I watched my husband die at my daughter's reception a month ago, I'm easily spooked.

"Come in," I answer, swiveling in Martin's massive leather chair to face whoever needs me.

"Mrs. Asher," David says, bowing a little. "I know this is a difficult time, and I've been putting off a conversation we need to have. But we must. We need to talk about Congressman Asher's successor. The party needs to have some sort of approval from you to commence the search. I'm sorry. I know it feels too soon, but there is the work of the people to be done."

Ah yes, blame it on the people when we both know it's the party.

"Come in, David," I say, standing and leading him to the sitting area of the office. We both know there will be a special election to fill the remainder of Martin's term through next January third. The regular election for the next two-year term will take place next November. The governor, nice man, told me he'd picked June twelfth for the special election. Wanted to know if I was OK with it. Said we needed to move on, for the good of Ohio. Continuity and all.

"Well, he is a Republican, so he's probably anxious to get Harold Kestler in this seat," David says.

"Over my dead body. I have a much better idea. I've given this a lot of thought these past few weeks. The people of Ohio need the torch passed to someone with the ability to reach across the aisle, someone who cares about good-paying jobs and lowering taxes. Someone who cares about infrastructure and climate change, don't you agree?" I ask.

"Yes, sure," David says.

"I knew you'd see it my way," I say. I'm so excited about my decision, and I can't wait to see his face. "And I've decided that someone is me!"

David only stares at me, and then he blinks.

"David? Isn't it great? I'm running for Martin's seat. I'm the perfect candidate."

David's forehead pleats, and he shakes his head. He looks both stunned and annoyed. "Mrs. Asher, I'm not sure that's what our party has in mind. There's a young woman, a state representative named Margaret Boyce. There's also a woman entrepreneur by the name of Frankie Dawson who is quite impressive. The party wants you to support one of these other candidates. I'd urge you to throw the Asher name behind Dawson."

I walk to the window, taking in the view of the Capitol glowing in the morning sunshine. I turn around and face David.

"Are you familiar with the Widow's Mandate?" I ask.

"No, what is it?" David asks.

"It's just a nickname for what has become an accepted practice of widows taking on their husbands' vacant seats," I say.

"I don't think that's a thing anymore, Mrs. Asher," he says.

"It's completely precedent. Forty-seven widows have been elected or appointed to fill congressional vacancies. Do you remember when Sonny Bono died in that ski accident? His wife, Mary, ran and won. I will do the same," I say.

For a few days after Martin died, when all the world was shocked and I was, too, I didn't care about his seat. But then, as the shock wore off, I thought of Harold and Jack. I thought of what Martin would want me to do. So I googled and discovered there was a practice of appointing spouses to fill the remainder of a senator's term if he died in office. On the House side, special elections are called when a congressman dies. Quite often, spouses run and win those special elections.

"Ma'am, the party has a candidate. You should take some time to rest, mourn your husband," David says.

"Don't you dare tell me what to do. I've been an important public servant to this district for more than thirty years, as long as Martin has been. This is my life. My lifestyle. I'm not going back to practicing law to support myself. That ship has sailed."

"Mrs. Asher, look, I know you're under a lot of stress. This has been tremendously upsetting, to all of us," David says.

There is nothing else I want to do. No other job interests me. I want this one. And I will get it, earn it. The people will love me, like they loved Martin. I've been watching and I know just how to convince them. Besides, I need to stay on the inside to figure out what Martin was up to and who was dead set on killing his political career. I need to protect myself and Charlotte. Our future is tied to this seat and to salvaging Martin's reputation. I must stay in power to accomplish anything around here. I meet the gaze of the chief of staff.

"I'm running in the special election to keep the Asher congressional seat. Will you and the staff join my team?"

David leans back on the couch, arms crossed at his chest. "The Speaker is considering backing Dawson. The moderates are considering a candidate too. There's too much bad press about Martin. You know the feds were closing in on his relationship with Roscoe. And China. And Sarah. It was a mess. You know I've been a loyal staffer, Mrs. Asher. I'd do anything for him, may he rest in peace."

"But not for me," I say. I pick up one of Martin's signing pens and twirl it in my fingers. Loyalty is such a finicky thing. "Even though I am his wife, the love of his life."

"I need to think," David says. He walks to the office door. "I just don't see you winning."

"Well, you better think fast because there isn't much time. And while you're thinking, send Sarah in," I say. When I arrived at the office today, unannounced, the entire staff greeted me with pleasantries and tears. They've been off for the past few weeks, but now we're all back together, one big happy family. Well, except Martin. When I arrived I saw everyone but the young woman who'd been trying to ruin our future. Of course she's around here somewhere, hiding from me, the little rat.

"Sarah didn't show up today," David says.

"Knock, knock," Mimi says, sweeping into the room and wrapping me in a big hug. I can't help but hear the music for the Wicked Witch of the West. I wonder what she wants now. "Are Charlotte and JJ happily off on their honeymoon? That was quite a large funeral you had for Martin. Everyone was there. Charlotte gave such a wonderful eulogy for her dad, even after what she witnessed."

I nod and push away the memory of Martin's death and focus on the standing-room-only crowd at the funeral. "It was a nice service. I'm glad the kids are off enjoying themselves."

"Maybe you should go on a vacation, Jody. Take a break. Get some sunshine?" Mimi says.

I need to tell Mimi my decision. I need to have her support. I wonder if, now that Martin and his misdeeds are behind us, we can come to some sort of understanding. She could be of immense help to me. If she chooses to be. "Come in, take a seat. David, that will be all."

Mimi sits on one of the blue leather couches, and I join her. I take a deep breath and wonder whether I can actually do it—run for Martin's seat. I've been tossing the idea around for a week, pondering the possibility, then second-guessing myself. Last night, I looked in the mirror and decided the woman staring back at me would make a great congresswoman, despite my ulterior motives. Maybe I would be a welcome noncontroversial Asher? Will everyone think the idea is as crazy as David does?

"How are you holding up?" Mimi asks. "You've been through quite a shock."

"Honestly, I feel so guilty," I tell her. "I should have forced him to see a doctor. I knew he was sick, but he kept pushing it off, told me he'd get checked out after the wedding. I just thought it was an ulcer." I can't get the shocked look on Martin's face as he died in front of me out of my head. Shock, pain . . . and he was trying to tell me something. That I'd be safe? Or look in the safe?

"Jody, let's get you out of here," Mimi says. "Let me take you home."

I look around Martin's office, and I am surrounded by him, his presence, his success, his power. And now, his absence. I never imagined this would hurt so much. I never imagined I could feel this much emptiness. I've never felt this before. I must have truly loved him.

I remember Mimi. I remember I need her.

"This feels like home, though—this office, this place," I say. I walk back over to the window and take in the beautiful Capitol. "I can't give this up."

"What do you want to do?" Mimi asks. She joins me at the window, a twinkle in her eye. "Are you going to run for his seat?"

I'm surprised Mimi would ask me this. Surprised and pleased. "It's the Widow's Mandate, isn't it?" I ask. "It's my duty to serve out the remainder of his term."

"Like Sonny Bono's wife," Mimi says.

"There are so many others," I say. "It's what Martin would want. We were a team."

"Yes, but Martin had a lot of baggage. They can tie you to the money, the bad press, China. You also will be running against your daughter's father-in-law's candidate, but I think we can use that to our advantage. There's a lot of sympathy for widows, especially widows who were blindsided during their daughter's wedding weekend. I can see the headline: 'Grieving Widow Must Fight Her Own In-Law in Run to Save Her Husband's Congressional Seat.' Something like that."

"Our constituents back home don't care about any of the accusations against Martin, not now that he is gone. They love the Ashers, they loved Martin, and they love me. They reelected us sixteen times. *Us.*"

"That they did," Mimi says.

"I'm assuming the Kestler campaign can't tie me to the affair with the intern, right?" I ask, smiling. I flash back to Sarah's shocked face, her wide brown eyes as she watched Martin die in my arms. I hope she feels responsible for some of this, as she should.

"Of course not. I mean, what does she have to do with you?" Mimi asks.

"Nothing, nothing at all," I say. "Martin was the love of my life. That is all that matters."

"You know, she was a referral from me. I had to look far and wide for someone with her particular skill set," Mimi says. "Such a shame, really. I think, in different circumstances, you would have enjoyed getting to know each other."

As if. And what are the particular skill sets Mimi was looking for? Sexual predators? I stare at my friend, looking for answers, but she smiles at me and I look away. My mind leaps back to the night of the reception—Sarah and Martin huddled together, Martin dropping to the ground. His face. I shake my head. Martin trusted Mimi's candidates. Something else about Sarah is nagging at the corner of my mind, but I push it away.

"I haven't talked to her, but someone on my staff will. She will need a new job, if you can place her somewhere, anywhere, immediately. She didn't show up for work today. Very unprofessional, but hopefully she's already moved on. For now I'd like to focus on my future," I say, although it has been tempting to focus on little Sarah. Maybe pay a visit to her apartment on the Hill. No, Jody, focus. I smile at Mimi. "Keep your enemies close" is one of my favorite sayings. "Will you help me?"

"Haven't I always?" Mimi asks.

Well, no, not lately. In fact, you were trying to ruin Martin. But now, here I am. The perfect solution for retaining the Asher seat. A known commodity. She must understand that too.

"Thank you," I say. "We must work quickly to build a team and block any potential challengers."

"That will take some finessing," Mimi says.

I take a deep breath. I know I will win this special election. I've studied the stories of other widows, in particular, the story of Jean Spencer Ashbrook of Ohio, who completed her husband's final term in office. Jean was in office from June to January. She didn't have the option to run for another term. The district was eliminated.

But our district won't be going anywhere. It's the Ashers' district. I will continue Martin's work with the dignity his legacy deserves, and polish up that legacy in the process.

"Shall we call the Speaker?" I ask.

Mimi looks at me. "Sure. Why not?"

And just like that, we're on the same team again. Or so it would appear.

A Guide for New Members of Congress from Mimi Smith of the Smith Institute

Do you know your district? Or are you moving into it to run for the seat? People do that all the time. If the latter, it's fine, but you must get to know the people. Genuinely. The more you can relate to the people, the more likely they are to vote for you. It's that simple. Do your homework—spend your time wisely.

MIMI

This is a surprising, but interesting, turn of events. As we sit in Martin's very masculine, award-laden office, I evaluate Jody's surprise announcement. Martin's disappointing and now-much-publicized poor behavior aside, an Asher in the twelfth district has been very good for my business.

"Let's get your story down first. You'll definitely win some sympathy votes," I say, seeing Jody Asher clearly. She has a commanding presence and is still attractive in her middle age. We'll need to work on her stump speech, but she definitely has experience on the campaign trail. I think she could hold this seat. "And it's great you're up to speed on all the pending legislation. I know you said you read everything."

"I do. I mean, some of the bills, at least. I know I can win this seat, keep this seat, with your help," Jody says.

She seems capable, I suppose. She's not going to make waves. It's not in her nature. I've observed her in action in DC: desperate to get along with everyone, desperate to be accepted. She's polished her looks, her demeanor, over the years, of course. She doesn't *seem* desperate for power—she simply is. But most people will underestimate her, of that I'm certain. We will win with sympathy votes and name recognition.

Jody will win, but she will not be the new darling of the House. She's much too old for that, which is perfect. I need a stable under-the-radar Congress member to work with—just like Martin was, until he blew it. I wonder how much she knows of Martin's dealings, of his complicated web of support. I decide it's not important. The same people will support Mrs. Asher. I will see to that. She will become Martin's proxy, a rubber stamp for all he's done. It will now continue, uninterrupted and controversy-free. I like it.

The path of least resistance and fewest surprises is what my supporters are looking for. From a young age, I was taught this lesson. No surprises. No drama. Just results, always results. My parents were pleased the party saw my potential so early and so clearly. And they have been amply rewarded for their devotion to the party and mine. I return my focus to Jody and her campaign.

"I do believe you can win. First things first: we need to inform the powers that be," I say. "I'll make a list of everyone you should call, in addition to the party leadership, of course."

Jody walks to Martin's desk and takes a seat. She looks like a natural.

"I always loved this desk," Jody says and swivels her chair. "I decorated this entire office, top to bottom."

"Oh, I know you did. You did a great job, my friend." I take it all in: Martin's awards, his self-aggrandizing photos with world leaders. I look down at the expensive rug beneath my feet. Jody didn't select *everything* in this office—I happen to know that for a fact. Some things are priceless gifts from foreign clients. It's in both our interests that she keeps this seat and this office.

"I'd suggest we hang on to it, then," I tell her. "Have David come in. Tell him to set up calls with the leadership, beginning in the next hour. Try to reach the Speaker first, but if her staff stonewalls you, move on. They can't stop you."

Although they will more than likely *try* to stop her. I'm certain Martin had fallen out of favor by the end, as he had with me. Even without his multiple scandals coming to light, most self-imposed, the notion of another entitled old white guy, or woman, holding on to office for decades isn't popular. But too bad.

"I won't back down. Don't worry," Jody says. She picks up Martin's phone, pushes a button. "David, can you join us? Bring Jason."

"The scheduler? Do you like him?" I ask. I'm well aware of the tension between entitled congressional wives and their husbands' staff. Jody complains nonstop of being left out. The tug-of-war between the two is legendary. I confess I find it amusing.

"Not particularly. He has ignored me lately, stopped forwarding invitations to social events, and has basically tried to cut me out, but I'm not sure if it's because of David's influence or if he did it on his own," Jody says. "Schedulers should know the spouse is the most important part of the team, not to be underestimated. I guess he'll find that out now."

I laugh as the two men walk in.

Jody says, "David, I've decided I will run for this seat, and I will win."

David looks at Jason, who looks at the floor. I shake my head. I do not abide insubordination from staff.

"Jason, I need to talk to the Speaker as soon as possible," Jody says. To his credit, he nods and leaves the room.

I like witnessing Jody's take-charge attitude. I must admit, I only envisioned her as Martin's spouse. Effective, somewhat boring, focused on minutiae like social events and embassy parties. I find all that an annoying, but necessary, part of the job. Jody was right to focus on those things. And she was very good at it. I should have appreciated all she did, applauded her social achievements more. Well, I'm here now to help her and I will. She'll be much more than a spouse, much more than an appendage of Martin.

I notice David and Jody are in a sort of staring contest.

"What is going on?" I ask.

"I just don't think this is a good idea, Mrs. Asher. The candidate they want to run for the seat is superb, a perfect fit for the district. Young family, accomplished tech start-up CEO, passionate women's rights advocate. She literally checks every box, and she's loaded. You know how the DCCC loves self-funded candidates," David says. "You could back her, be part of her welcome to DC. Face it, the Widow's Mandate is an old-fashioned notion, as dated as the concepts of chivalry and honor. It was only meant to provide a placeholder until a suitable candidate was found. But we have one now."

How dare he? "Are you interviewing for this other candidate's campaign?" I ask, standing up. "It's Frankie Dawson, correct?"

David's face turns a satisfying color of pink. Truth be told, we were backing Frankie Dawson, too, until Jody offered this new "Widow's Mandate" twist. It's best to stick with a known commodity in this seat, until it's run its course, that is. I doubt she'll last long in the job. It's exhausting, and I don't know if Jody fully appreciates the workload involved, even though she watched Martin closely. It does take work. I'll help her, though. Help smooth the transition, help make the right introductions.

"Wow, Mimi is right," Jody says. I give her a kind nod and a smile. Her focus turns to her husband's chief of staff. "You're a traitor, David. I can't believe it."

"I am not. Martin is dead. I was loyal to him. You know that," he says, his voice shaking with emotion.

Jody says, "You're fired."

That was rash. But it isn't my place to say anything to her, not yet. I do agree the man has to go, but there are more subtle ways of accomplishing it. That's my worry about Jody Asher: she's conned everyone with her spouse act. But I know her. I've known her for decades. She's smart and cunning. Unlike Martin, I really don't think she cares about people. Something's off with Jody's personality and has been since we met, but I can't put my finger on it. Like now, firing David. That's impulsive. Those types of things can and will be used against her.

I need to coach Jody, tell her she needs to step into a new persona. She needs to care about people. That's the whole point of public service. It will be fine. She can do it. No matter what, she's better than a man who slept with his intern, among other things. The financial crimes would have faded with time. The affair? What a fool.

He had to go down, one way or another. He just made it so very easy at the end. What a tragedy, but also what a way to shut down the stories. There's no one digging anything up on Martin anymore. Like him, it's all buried now.

David hasn't left the room. "You can't just fire me. I need time to find a job. I've worked for your family for more than fifteen years."

Jody stands and points to the door. "My family values loyalty, and you've just proven you have none. Leave. Now."

I tap my fingernail on the desk. She glances my way. "There are procedures," I say. "Rules, process. It's the government."

"Fine. Just get out of my office, would you?" Jody's frustration spills through the room like a pungent perfume.

"Fine," David says and walks to the door.

Jason pops his head in the room. "Madam Speaker's office is on line one for you, Mrs. Asher."

Jody picks up the phone and puts it on speaker.

The Speaker of the House comes on the line. "Jody, I'm again so sorry for your loss. Martin was a good representative and a long-serving public servant. He will be missed, of course. And you held a lovely funeral service, just lovely. So, anyway, I understand you're interested in running in the special election, is that right?" Her voice is calm.

I watch as Jody takes a deep breath. I nod.

"Yes, Madam Speaker. I've given this a lot of thought, and I think I'm a natural to continue in Martin's footsteps, to honor his legacy," she says. "The district loves us. And I know I can continue doing good for the people of Ohio."

"I am sure you understand your election is not a given," the Speaker says. "It will require hard work and significant resources. The governor has set the special election for June. That gives you just over a month."

"I understand. I am the only one who can fend off Harold Kestler. I have the Asher name recognition, and I'm known and well liked in the district. All I need is your support and for you to clear the field. Please." Jody adds the word as an afterthought. There is no humility here, I note. Seeing Jody in this role was never something I expected. I will work with her to soften her up, make her understand all the players involved. Surely someone who has conquered the spouse world will be a fast learner.

We both stare at the telephone on Martin's desk, waiting for the Speaker's response.

"The problem is, Martin was quite, shall I say, compromised before his death."

"No, that was all a bad rumor. It was nothing," Jody says.

The Speaker chuckles. "Well, I guess we'll never know. And, while he did do wonderful things for the district, the Asher name is a bit tarnished now."

"That's why I need a chance to make it shine again. For Martin. For his memory," Jody says.

"We have a very well-qualified candidate, a young woman ready to jump in," the Speaker says.

"I know. I heard. Can she please just wait her turn? Please, for my family, just let me finish his term?"

There is silence on the other end of the phone. Jody looks at me, and I smile encouragingly. She's said it all correctly. All we can do is wait for the Speaker.

"OK, Jody. Yes, you are right. It is the Ashers' term to finish. Martin did win his last election," the Speaker says. "OK, Jody. Are sure you want to do this?"

"I am. Thank you. I'll make you proud. I'll keep this seat," Jody says.

"See that you do," the Speaker says.

Jody hangs up. She looks my way. "Game on."

A Guide for New Members of Congress from Mimi Smith of the Smith Institute

There are only 435 members of the House of Representatives and only 100 senators. Only about 12,000 people have ever served as a member of Congress. It is an honor to get there, to serve there. And if you happen to be elected, do not screw it up.

JODY

"I need to clean house," I tell Mimi. I settle back into Martin's desk chair. There are several staff members I'd like to dispense with in addition to David. Sarah is at the top of the list for obvious reasons. "Who do I call to get help with that?"

Mimi stands and begins pacing back and forth. "You're focused on the wrong thing here. You need to move to your district. Immediately. These people need to continue to hold down the fort, so to speak. Same with the district staff. Use them to keep Martin's efforts and legislation alive."

Of course she's right. I need to keep the staff intact, responding to constituents. And as much as I hate the thought of moving to Ohio, I will do it. She's right about that too. Mimi is more of an asset to me than a liability. As much as I don't trust her, I need her help. And I need to find out why Martin was so beholden to her, why she would put Sarah under his nose to ruin him.

"You know so much. Will you help me? Be my campaign manager? I know that's a lot to ask, with all of your commitments with the think tank," I say. "I don't know if I can do this without you. Please?"

Mimi smiles. "It would be fun. To run a campaign. Just for this special election, for less than two months, I can do it. Sure. I'm in."

"Thank you." I'm certain this is the right move. I'm also certain I don't have any other options. Right now, I need Mimi.

"All right, let's get going. You can have three staff people on the campaign, pulling from the official office-staff side," Mimi says. "But in this case, I think we'll need to bring new people on board. The good news is Sarah's ethics complaint is dead in the water with Martin's death. Oh, sorry—bad analogy."

My stomach twists as Martin's death stare pops into my head. "Please, if you'll handle staffing, that would be great. I know we have a considerable war chest built up."

"Of course. And, yes, you do. Money won't be a problem. I should go start making some calls. Remember, campaign calls cannot be made from government offices," Mimi says. "Let's leave for Ohio in the next couple of days?"

I think about that, about picking up and heading to the district alone. Not as the spouse of the candidate but as the candidate. I remind myself I can do this.

"Sure. Give me a day." I have a few things to finish up here, and then I'll be ready. I hope.

"OK, I'm off," Mimi says. She seems almost as excited as I am. "This will be fun!"

Fun isn't the word I'd use for campaigns. After she leaves, I pull out the suitcase I brought with me this morning. I wheel it into the walk-in closet Martin used to stash his entertainment supplies: alcohol, crystal glasses, a bucket for ice. I see the safe and open it with the code we use for everything in our lives: our birthdays, mine first.

Inside, I find what I'm looking for—folders Martin had told me were in here for years and some folders I wasn't expecting. The manila envelope with my name on it, written in Martin's choppy cursive, I expected. I tuck it into the suitcase along with the other contents of the safe. I see his collection of congressional pins, one for every term, displayed in a velvet case, and I hold the box to my chest before I put the collection inside the suitcase. I'll go through everything later. I zip the bag quickly, lock the safe, and hurry out of the closet. I tuck the suitcase back under my desk.

I push the button on my phone and summon David.

"What now?" he asks from across the office.

"Call a staff meeting. Ten minutes," I say.

He nods. The next thing I know, I'm rallying the troops. Everyone seems to be on their best behavior at the moment. I'm sure David has warned them of my wrath.

"You've done some great work for Martin. I'd like that to continue once I'm elected to finish his term. So, in the meantime, please keep the correspondence going. Keep the office running as usual. Look, I'd like to keep this team together. I hope you'll stay on board in honor of Martin and his memory." I'm lying. I'll get rid of most of them after the special election. But that's for me to know and them to find out.

Jason raises his hand. "What should I do about the official schedule?"

"Well, nothing for now, as the congressman is dead. When I return from the district victorious, you will be working with me," I say. "Won't it be nice to work together directly, finally, Jason?" I don't add *as you should have been all along*. I'll deal with replacing him later. Mimi is right: I need to use the proper procedures. Staffers talk. I want to be known as the widow, a sympathetic, kind boss. I smile.

"Yes, Mrs. Asher," he says.

That's the deference I deserve. For a moment, I imagine the power of returning to this office as an elected member of Congress. It makes me almost giddy. As the staff files out the door, David stops.

"Mrs. Asher?" he says. "I'm assuming you'd like Sarah replaced."

"If we're allowed to do something about her, yes," I answer. "Did you know something was going on between her and my husband?"

"No, I didn't even suspect it. Not until it was news," he says. I think I believe him, but I'm not sure. "I can place her with a nonprofit. A women's rights group has a great job open."

"Yes, that sounds perfect. A young woman who sleeps with a married congressman should be promoted to a better position. She was the victim, of course," I say. I like to tell myself that Martin cracked under pressure, that he'd never cheated on me before. That this, this was a onetime thing, a sloppy, desperate act. He was crying out for help, in a terrible way. He should have turned to me. That young woman should never have been allowed into our lives, and Mimi knows it. It's her fault. And also mine. I should have been watching more closely, like I typically do. I was caught up in the wedding planning and missed what was happening right under my nose.

David smirks.

"Is that all?" I ask. He bows and heads out the door.

I take one last look around Martin's office. So many photos, awards, framed mementos of a long career. I make a mental note of the ones Charlotte may like to keep, but thinking now about Martin's affair has stirred the anger in me and killed the grief. I decide most of this stuff will belong to the trash can. It will be nice to start with freshly painted walls, open space for my own achievements.

I reach under the desk and grab the suitcase. I roll it behind me as I head out the back door of Martin's office. In no time, I'm riding the members-only elevator to the basement parking garage. The elevator stops on the first floor, and I stand tall, shoulders back. The doors close again. No one else joined me in this special elevator, but if they had, would they have challenged the right of a grieving widow of a deceased member to use this elevator?

They wouldn't dare.

A GUIDE FOR NEW MEMBERS OF CONGRESS FROM MIMI SMITH OF THE SMITH INSTITUTE

Hire the best, most experienced chief of staff you can find and afford. This is the single most important person on your team. Period. The position is as important as your campaign manager was, but they are different animals. The campaign manager is a street fighter, a person who will play dirty and do anything to win. A person who doesn't follow the rules, who is ruthless. None of those qualities will serve you in a chief of staff. A chief is a rules follower, a Beltway insider who knows his way around. Hire a Hill rat to lead your DC office.

MIMI

The Kalorama Smith Estate

The call with Frankie Dawson went as expected: terribly. As much as I tried to explain pulling my support, she simply wouldn't hear it. The folly of youth, I suppose. I promised her congressional terms are short. There is only a year and a half left in Martin's term, and you never know how things will go. Jody might hate being a member of Congress. She might just want to finish her husband's term and then ride off into the sunset. Then the seat would be Frankie's to win.

"You said this was my seat," Frankie whined into the phone. "I have everything ready. You approved my campaign logo. I can win."

"Things change. Mrs. Asher wants to run, and the party is backing Mrs. Asher, for now, despite her husband's wrongdoings. And if they are willing to do so," I said, "then I am too."

She wouldn't listen to reason, so I hung up. Very unsatisfying.

Another unsatisfying development: there are simply no suitable houses to rent in Ohio's twelfth district, not for the few weeks of the campaign. Nothing that compares to this modest eight-thousand-square-foot abode Spencer and I call home. Ha.

I look around my spectacular office, with floor-to-ceiling windows overlooking Kalorama's most famous park on one side and floor-to-ceiling bookshelves behind me. Our entire home is decorated in muted grays, whites, and creams. There are no bright colors, nothing out of place in my office or the rest of our home. We hate disorder here and in the world.

No, there is nothing like this available for rent in Columbus. Nothing close.

My husband drifts into my office. He's sweating from a run around the neighborhood. He stays in the doorway, as he has been trained to do. We both value our privacy and our personal space. It's an arrangement that has suited us well since we met in law school. I am proud of him. Spencer has become known as an expert in all things congressional, a calm and reasonable force in DC, a sought-after and well-paid counselor. Of course, the money isn't an issue. He was loaded when we married, which definitely added to my fondness for him. He tilts his head and takes in the scene.

"What?" I say. "I'm busy here."

"You're gorgeous when you're scheming. Are you sure you want to run a congressional campaign?" he asks. His long, skinny legs are birdlike, delicate, like his neck. Spencer is an introvert, a policy wonk, a strategist. He could no more consider running a campaign than being a candidate himself. He chuckles at my tips for congressional hopefuls, can't believe I've written a guidebook. It sells well every two years, and some of the hopefuls actually get elected. When we meet on the Hill, they thank me. I'm the first name they turned to for information about this crazy job. They sort of owe me—me *and* my guidebook. So who is laughing all the way to the bank? We both have our own skills; that's what makes us so perfect together. I wrote the book because I love being behind the scenes, manipulating outcomes. You might say I was born for this.

"You know I was unofficially running several campaigns last cycle, dear," I say.

"Yes, but with this one, your name—*our* name—will be publicly associated with it," he says.

Of course I've thought this all through. "I literally wrote the book on congressional campaigns. And we already are associated with the Ashers. Have been since law school, basically. This move is what a friend would do. I'm helping a grieving widow polish her husband's legacy. No one can find fault with that," I tell him.

"It's politics. Someone will. Hopefully not our clients."

"Our clients want one thing: votes to go their way. With this Asher continuity, I can guarantee them that, more so than with a new candidate like Frankie Dawson. Who knows what she'd actually do once in office?" I say, although she was well vetted. More than Jody Asher, that's for sure. We play the long game for our clients. We keep the Asher seat first, and then we turn to Dawson. I'm certain I will get Frankie in line. I just need to explain to her how to play the long game. I will make her understand once she gets over the initial disappointment. She'll learn.

"Jody Asher is a 'vapid, selfish social climber,' someone once told me," Spencer says, using air quotes like a goofball. We both know that someone was me. I just see the darker side that the society ladies don't see. I'm sure she'll keep the darkness off the campaign trail too. "I hope you know what you're doing, dear."

"You just worry about your things, and I'll worry about mine," I tell him. It's our refrain, the way we manage to stay in business together without killing each other. "You can come visit me in Ohio."

"Oh, that's a good one," he says.

I blow him a kiss as he drifts out the door. For a minute, I think about Martin. We had a good run, the two of us. He was the face, and I was his connector. By the time we attended our law school class reunion at the Four Seasons in Georgetown, Spencer and I had a thriving think tank and Martin had been in Congress for three terms. And they'd just had Charlotte, which should have made Jody completely happy. I made a point to stay in touch after we all graduated, and once I heard he was running for Congress, I watched his career closely.

Martin was on top of the world, but Jody wasn't.

"Mimi, can you help us with Charlotte?" Martin asked when he and I found ourselves alone at the bar in the corner of the ballroom. Spencer had drifted off, as usual, and Jody was working the crowd.

"That's funny. I don't have kids, you know that," I answered. I loved my little goddaughter, all my little goddaughters, of course, but I wasn't the babysitting kind.

"I need to get her placed at one of the schools. Get her on the waiting list, if you know what I'm saying," Martin whispered. The child wasn't old enough to speak, but in DC, it was already time to pave her way.

"Ah yes, of course," I answered. "I'm on it. Sidwell Friends, I'm assuming? Starting in pre-K?"

Martin nodded.

"That'll be a steep price tag, assuming I can swing it," I said. "Forty-five thousand dollars a year for preschool. And there are only twenty spots. You'll be competing with, well, everyone. From what I hear, less than seven percent of the applicants are admitted."

How did I know all those stats? Jody had already called me on this very subject a few days before.

"We can't afford it, not on my salary. I don't know what Jody's thinking," Martin said. "Thanks anyway."

"Let me make some calls, Martin," I said. "There are scholarships of sorts available."

I smile as I think back to the day they found out Charlotte was admitted, to the wonder in Jody's voice and the worry in Martin's. That's when we decided his backstory needed to include family money. The Ashers had to have deep pockets, what with his long ancestry in America.

Martin simply sighed and kept his mouth shut. I let him know at the time there would be plenty of ways to pay me back. And there were. We reached an agreement the day Charlotte was accepted to the best preschool in DC. We were a great team, until he got sloppy. Until his good-old-boy, flirtatious style actually became who he was.

Until the stupid reporter Max Brown started digging. Once that happened, we were finished with Martin, actually. The Roscoe thing was dumb, and desperate, and the Sarah dalliance—well, that was unacceptable on many levels. I hoped Sarah would become a useful ally inside Martin's office, that we would grow close and share information. But she crossed a line. And so did Martin.

I had to forward the photo my trackers took to the reporter. I mean, if I had the information, if Martin was that stupid, who knows who else had it. Besides, this affair took the focus off the real purpose of our working relationship. He was compromised and no longer an asset. Don't get me wrong—I wasn't happy about this. I loved Martin like a brother. We shared so many laughs, so many good times. I will help Jody polish his image because he was a good man. He just did a few bad things, as far as society is concerned. His legacy shouldn't be doomed because of stupid missteps.

His suffering, grieving, and highly sympathetic—when she wants to be—wife is the answer to our problems.

Jody is clean. Martin kept her in the dark about his dealings. All she needs to do is be educated in policy and introduced to our network. She will not be tainted by Joe Roscoe's arrest, and neither will dear Charlotte, even though she held an internship with the firm at my suggestion. Roscoe will keep his mouth shut, take his punishment for his behavior, and fade away.

Roscoe's rule over K Street has ended. I wonder which firm will become the lobbyists du jour? Whoever it is, I'm already connected to them. It's a win-win for the Smith Institute.

Spencer assures me all is well. For now, I will focus on Jody's campaign. I google *best luxury hotel in Columbus, Ohio*, and click on the top result. I book their most expensive suite beginning tomorrow through the evening of the special election.

The first step toward Jody's election is to win the sympathy of her constituents. A celebration of life, perhaps, saluting Martin's accomplishments and featuring the grieving widow, resilient and strong? He did a lot of good for the district, and we'll be sure to highlight that. We'll invite everyone in the district to attend. It will be a multimedia showcase of his legacy in the district. I'll present the idea to Jody, and I assume she'll love it.

Second step: destroy Harold Kestler's reputation and Jack Dobbs for good measure, despite the awkward and unfortunate fact he is now Charlotte's father-in-law. The politics of personal destruction know no bounds, not even family. Heck, Jack proved that himself at the rehearsal dinner. This is the fun part. Jody already gave me the URLs she registered, and I've added some more. We'll have plenty of attack websites and a myriad of misleading search results about the candidate and his biggest backer.

I place a call to my favorite cutthroat media consultant. I know he'll love this campaign. The American public is just so easy to persuade if you know what you're doing. And I do.

A Guide for New Members of Congress from Mimi Smith of the Smith Institute

Kick off your campaign as soon as possible, with the most media attention you can muster. The road to federal office is rocky, bureaucratic, and stressful. And until dark money is out of the system, you're going to need to raise cash. Be sure to hire a trustworthy, experienced team, including a compliance attorney to keep you out of trouble.

JODY

Asher Townhome

I touch the white leather cover of the photo album a courier handed me after I opened the front door. The note says "With compliments and condolences, from Vanessa and the wedding photographer, Rachel."

I don't know if I have the energy to flip through its pages, even though I know it won't include any photos of Martin's dire last few moments at the reception; nor will it include photos of the gourmet meal never served, the first dance never danced, the cake uncut.

Once Martin died, everything ended, of course. The wedding reception, the reporter's investigation, his affair, the ethics complaint by his lover, my daughter's golden and perfect vision of how life is supposed to be.

I take a seat on the living room couch and open the album. The first photo is of Martin and me flanking Charlotte. One happy family for one last photo. The bags under Martin's eyes are still visible despite the airbrushing and color correction the photographer must have done. He's thin, thinner than I noticed because I saw him all the time. The tricks of the photographer trade have made me flawless and thinner, too, my light-blue "mermaid" dress—as Martin called it—shimmering next to Charlotte's beautiful wedding gown. Her gown was adorned with tiny pearls hand-sewn by a team of women. The result was perfection, and jaw-droppingly expensive.

My heart hurts a bit for my daughter, but mostly it's filled with anger over Martin's blunder. It didn't have to end like this. Not for him or for us. I touch his smiling face in the photo and remember the anger, the humiliation, I felt that night, waiting for the story of the intern to come out: the societal shaming was already at a fever pitch over his connection to the Roscoe affair. What did he see in Sarah, anyway? And then I know. She was a younger version of me, taller and with a thinner build, but otherwise remarkably similar to how I looked in my thirties. Of course. That must be it.

Oh, Martin, why were you so weak?

I turn the page and find a wonderful photo of JJ and Charlotte surrounded by their wedding party, all young and full of promise. I turn the page again, and there are Jack Dobbs and his wife. The nerve of him, hijacking the rehearsal dinner to announce his candidate's run. Martin did us all a favor, dying as he did. He took the spotlight away from Harold Kestler, and now it's mine to step into.

I'm a natural. I am quite capable of seducing a large number of people, making them believe I am what I appear. That's a huge benefit for this office; trust me, I've been watching and taking notes. I'll conquer the district like I conquered DC society. I'll make big promises I can't keep, and I won't feel sorry about it, not in the least. In return, my constituents will love me and feel sorry for me, the poor widow.

Life has treated me so unfairly that only the voters can help me put the pieces back together. Helping them through my public service will help *me* heal. What a great win-win!

Mimi wants a celebration-of-life event to honor Martin. I like the idea, especially if we get media coverage. I'll be a media darling. Back when Martin was elected, candidates were judged by their leadership skills, education, and commitment. Those days are long gone. I'll just tell folks what's wrong with people like Harold Kestler. It's all about making him look terrible. And for fun, I'll throw Jack Dobbs under the bus as often as I can. I'll stare into the camera and tell voters that if Kestler is elected, they'll lose everything—their taxes will go up, they'll lose their jobs, everything will go terribly wrong. I'll insinuate he's a communist or socialist or something. We'll send out terrible photos of him, doctoring them and making him look like a monster. A beast.

I'll need to talk to Mimi about this. I flip another page of the photo album and find a gorgeous photo of Charlotte and me. I slip it out of the album. This photo will be an important part of the campaign story, I know: a devoted wife and a poor young woman, who was left devastated on her wedding day. Poignant.

I close the album and leave it on the coffee table. It's time to pack for campaign season in Ohio. Typically, since Martin was so well known, I could skip most of the Ohio district events and only fly back for Fourth of July, Christmas services, the annual art competition, and the Easter egg hunt. The constituents presumed I was there whenever Martin was; that's a common assumption about those of us who live in DC and not in their districts. It's a lie.

I'm fond of those.

I reach under the bed and pull out the suitcase containing the contents of Martin's office safe. I pop open the lock and finally give myself permission to read some of the contents. There is an official envelope with Martin's name embossed on it. He's written my name on the front and the words "Open if anything happens to me. I love you."

I swallow and open the envelope. It's a letter.

Dearest Jody,

If you are reading this, something has happened to me. I do want you to know I've only ever loved you and Charlotte.

Let me begin by saying I think Mimi is trying to ruin me, and I don't know why. I have done everything she has asked for all these years, but now it is not enough.

I am sorry about Sarah, and I can't believe I was that weak. I know Mimi was behind the leaked photo of us. It was taken by a Smith Institute tracker. I don't understand why she would do that to me—to us.

I hope someday you will find it in your heart to forgive me.

Love,
Martin

I touch my cheek and realize a tear has found its way there. Ridiculous. There is no time for pity or sorrow, both weak emotions. And while the photo of Martin and Sarah together was never published, I have seen a copy of it, their clandestine embrace in Sarah's apartment captured by a person lurking outside. Would Mimi actually do that? Send her tracker to take the photo and then leak it? I remember tearing the image into tiny bits when I discovered it slipped under my townhome door a week after Martin died. The note read "Thought you should know." Was that Mimi too?

I need to focus on winning and polishing the Asher name. I need to stay angry and keep moving forward. And I will.

I open the envelope with Martin's voting records. It's all a bunch of numbers: bills, dollar amounts, dates, times. I believe the government would be interested in all this, but I am not ready to share it.

I slide everything back into the suitcase, lock it, and tuck it away under the bed. I have a campaign to focus on.

My suitcase for the trip to Ohio is open on the bed. I've taken to sleeping upstairs in the guest bedroom so I don't see Martin's gruesome death face at night. My clothes are scattered about, but I'll get organized. Columbus is lovely in the spring but could have a spike of hot or cold weather by the time June twelfth rolls around. Layers, that's the key. Congressional-looking, conservative red, white, and blue layers.

As I grab my clothes from our bedroom closet, I glance at Martin's side of the closet, still filled with his navy, gray, and black suits. His ties hang in a color-coordinated array, mostly shades of blue. Poor Martin. He died of stress and secrets. He died from guilt. I didn't have anything to do with it, not really. My little punishment drops just made him feel as bad as he should have. I touch his congressional pin and take a deep breath. I can't help myself. My pity for Martin turns to excitement. If I play my cards right, I could be wearing one soon.

I remember not to get ahead of myself. This will take hard work, I know. I pick up a framed photo of the two of us seated at a lavishly set table—gold china plates and gold-rimmed crystal glasses, white linens—on the Great Wall of China during Martin's second term in office. It was an incredible setting, all the supplies—tables, chairs, decor, and food—carried up by hand, just for our delegation.

We sat in awe, amazed at the vastness of the Great Wall, the country, our good luck to experience it all. We even had a clear blue sky that day. "Jody, are you beginning to see why I love these people? Look at the ingenuity," Martin exclaimed as we waited for the first course.

I don't know if the people were ingenious or simply desperate to impress, but I was beginning to see why Martin loved them. "It's something," I agreed.

"This is why it's a win-win to be friends with this nation. They want a partner to help educate their population, pull them out of poverty. They will be a great friend to the United States if we help them now," Martin said.

As he spoke, Mimi slipped into the seat next to him. "Hear, hear," she said. "There is so much good to be done here, Congressman. Glad you could join us, both of you. This is just the beginning."

Mimi has been by our side since the beginning. Whispering in Martin's ear, helping us with Charlotte's schooling, opening doors, helping in whatever way we asked. But what did she get in return? Whatever she wanted, is the answer. I'm sure of it. But now what does she want? Why is she helping me? I suppose to keep things status quo, whatever that means. Mimi thinks she knows me. She thinks I'm as malleable or more so than Martin. She sees me as the supportive spouse. I will let her believe I am what she thinks I am until after the election. Because right now, I need her, no matter what she's done to Martin, to us.

I shake my head and focus on packing. I grab a sweater with the state bird, a red cardinal, embroidered on it and tuck it into my suitcase. I'll be sure to bring a buckeye necklace too. Optics are everything, Martin taught me. I can do this.

It will be interesting to be in Ohio for such a long period of time. I've never lived there, not really—only long enough for Martin to win his first campaign. And I've never liked it there either, but that's another little secret.

A GUIDE FOR NEW MEMBERS OF CONGRESS FROM MIMI SMITH OF THE SMITH INSTITUTE

Your yard signs are your most important advertising tactic. Don't let anyone tell you otherwise. Buy enough for everyone who wants one, and then some. At the end of the election cycle, there will be sign wars. They'll take yours in the middle of the night, and you'll do the same, although this activity is illegal, so do not officially condone it. ☺

Do not run out of this precious commodity. Name recognition is the most valuable asset when it comes to the ballot box. Your name should be in everyone's front yard.

MIMI

Glazed doughnuts. I hate them. Ohio folks love them. We have now entered what my husband, Spencer, calls the "round food" portion of the campaign: pizza, doughnuts, bagels, cookies. These are the carbs that fuel our staffers and our volunteers; these are the foods we present to tempt interested voters wherever Jody speaks. We are, thank goodness, at the end of the campaign. It's finally June.

Today, we're in a church basement in some small corner of the district. Jody's become a pro at this—a trouper, really. When we started out, she had to check her notes to keep on track with her speeches. But now she has them all memorized. I taught her retail politics—how to walk into a small business, introduce herself, and ask for support. It didn't take long for her to find her footing. In many cases, the shop owners already knew her or knew Martin. The Asher name has resonance here, and Jody is right about another thing: she will receive the sympathy vote.

I watch as she steps up to the podium. There are forty or so polite, vaguely interested church members in attendance. Just behind Jody, through the open door, I spot our campaign coffee truck. My idea.

We wrapped a food truck with her logo—the Asher name, huge, in red, white, and blue—and drive around the district, offering coffee and conversation and doughnuts. It's been a big hit; local newspapers can't get enough of it and of course, the photos of voters smiling as they enjoy a free cup of joe courtesy of Jody, their dead congressman's wife, are social media gold. #AsherCountry. #TheLegacyContinues. #VoteforJody. #CupofJody.

"Thank you all so much for coming here today," Jody begins. She's wearing a navy suit and a white T-shirt. The suit says she's honoring the importance of the office, while the T-shirt and white tennis shoes say she's approachable and sensible. She's also wearing her spouse pin because, well, why not and it looks important. "I want to say a few words about why this campaign is so important, why your vote for me and for my husband's legacy means more jobs and lower taxes for Central Ohioans."

As Jody continues her stump speech, I scan the crowd. They seem interested; some even lean forward. One guy is recording her on his mobile phone, and I make my way through the crowd. Once I'm next to him, I tap his shoulder. "No video. Thanks."

He slips his phone into his breast pocket, but I stay next to him. I know he's not a Republican tracker. Trackers have sinister smug faces and the ever-present video camera to try to catch politicians in embarrassing moments on camera. I know all of them by heart now, and he isn't a tracker. He could be harmless, or he could be a different sort of Republican operative, a plant mingling in the crowd, spreading rumors and looking for dirt. Any small slip of the tongue, any mistake by Jody, can instantly be made into a digital attack ad. Or worse.

I should know. It's what we've been doing to poor Harold Kestler. Or should I say #KestlertheCrook. We have an entire website devoted to making it appear as if Harold is a very bad guy. He isn't, but you would think he was if you looked at the site. That's the point.

We'll launch our so-called closing argument television commercial tonight. Voters will see a montage of photos of Jody and Martin through the years—Martin with presidents, Jody volunteering for various worthy causes—and then will hear, in Jody's own words, how she will continue to deliver for the district just like her husband did for all the years. "This is Asher country," she says to the camera. "The legacy continues with your vote on June twelfth. Thank you."

And we'll also launch our final attack on Harold Kestler. Turns out Harold, like Martin, partied a lot in high school and college, and we have a lot of photos of him doing it, thanks to his "friends" who happen to be Democrats today. I mean, who didn't party in college, but that is not the point. The point is to make Harold look terrible. The point is, in a state drowning in death because of opioids, Harold supports drug companies over families. He's one of them, maybe even a drug dealer. Who knows? Here he is smoking a joint. He doesn't care about your kids. Here he is bent over a mirror. Is he snorting cocaine? Who knows? Harold isn't fit to be your congressman—he's just looking for the next party. And the drug manufacturers love him for it. #CrookedKestler.

The moment he took campaign money from the prescription drug lobby, we had him. That he's also taken money from the NRA and other shady entities has been pointed out in previous advertising. Harold's a drug-abusing crook who doesn't pay his taxes. Oh, and he's a white guy. At least Jody is a woman. #YearoftheWoman.

As Jody wraps up her speech, I move away from the guy I've been watching and make my way out to the coffee truck. We have little Harold on the run. Our polls show we're up ten points. I'm tempted to have Jody call Jack Dobbs just to gloat and rub our success in his face. But she won't do it. She promised Charlotte she would have no communication with the Dobbses, except JJ, and she's kept her word. That doesn't mean attacks on Jack are off-limits, not at all. We ran great digital ads with Jack and Harold smoking cigars on a golf course. I mean, come on. White privilege at its finest, as we pointed out. Two rich guys, out of touch and probably hooked on drugs. It really makes me giddy. I'm almost ready to pop the champagne and head back to DC. Almost. But not quite yet.

"Great job," I tell Jody as she climbs inside, followed by our two staffers. Walker is former military; he's the body man who watches for trouble. Tammy is our communications director. She's done a great job, and she hopes to come to DC with us. Turns out, we have an opening, as Sarah has taken a job with a nonprofit. Everything is working out just fine. Media stories have a short shelf life these days. With Martin dead, the news cycle has moved on, thank goodness. Despite Martin being on the brink of arrest when he died, I think the rest of the Ashers are in the clear, at least for now.

My candidate is beaming.

"Thanks. I felt like I really connected with them," Jody says, settling into her preferred seat as Walker starts the engine. We served coffee before the speech, so now the goal is to get out of here before anyone asks for refills.

We have miles to go today, and tonight.

"Don't tell me you're actually enjoying the campaign trail now?" I tease. "Somebody's looking at home here in the heartland."

"I wouldn't go that far," Jody says and looks out the window at the green farm fields. "But I do like speaking in front of groups of people. Feeling the admiration. I really do."

For some reason, that makes me smile. Sure, it's all a game and I've got my own agenda, but it's nice she's worked out so well as a candidate. I appreciate the effort she's put into this race. She's come into her own on the campaign trail.

"That's great. Hopefully you'll like the legislating part of the job too," I say. "In my experience, you'll either love that part or hate it. Martin really loved it—crafting bills, the compromise, the debate, the work of it. I've brought some policy briefs, if you're interested in studying up?"

Jody looks at me. "There's plenty of time for that. Let's get through the next five days. Besides, I am familiar with Martin's positions, his votes. And I'll have positions of my own."

She thinks she is, but she doesn't really know anything. She's a spouse, not a legislative aide. "Sure, OK. We'll wait until after you win. And of course, I'll be beside you every step of the way, helping you vote the right way."

Jody doesn't answer me. Instead, she turns away and looks out the window.

A Guide for New Members of Congress from Mimi Smith of the Smith Institute

It was reportedly Mark Twain who said, "There is no distinctly native American criminal class except Congress." In fact, the requirements to be a member of Congress are not tough to meet: twenty-five years old, a US citizen for at least seven years, and a resident of the state you're running in. You don't need to live in the district—see tip above—but you should. These requirements set a rather low bar. I hope you are more qualified than this, for all our sakes.

JODY

The reporter and her cameraman are standing just outside the ballroom. Tammy waits with them, waits for me. I take a moment to enjoy the room, which has been decorated for our victory party after the votes are counted later tonight. I kick a blue balloon back into the sea of balloons filling the ballroom. I cannot wait to deliver my victory speech. A thought works its way into my head unbidden: if only my mom could see me now. Not that I'd invite her here, and not that she'd show up. But still, I can't help but smile because she'd never believe I could accomplish this. Win a congressional seat. Me. She discounted my ability to do anything. But Martin . . . Martin would be proud.

I think back to two nights ago. My debate with Harold was one for the ages, if I do say so myself. I was happy to see Charlotte in the front row of the audience; it was a surprise and the energy boost I needed for the final grueling event of the campaign.

Turns out I may not have Martin's natural charm, but I have something equally as valuable: I'm full of rage. I came that way, I suppose. Anger can be very persuasive when hidden inside a suburban wife's immaculate shell. The debate was a perfect example.

"Mr. Kestler, can you explain your eagerness to take money from the likes of Big Tobacco, Big Pharma, and the gun lobby, all the while not paying your own taxes?" I asked him. "Doesn't that make you against family values? Doesn't that make you, among other things, a crook?"

"Look, Mrs. Asher, you're telling lies up here, spreading rumors about me and my family," he said. He looked a little rattled and very sweaty. As he took a drink from his bottle, some water dribbled onto his suit. Classic. "Meanwhile, you and your husband literally were on the brink of an investigation. Your husband was having an affair with an intern in his office."

"How dare you try to tarnish the memory of my husband? Mr. Kestler, you are running against me, not my husband," I said, my voice firm, my rage just below the surface.

"You are running your campaign on the merits of your husband's legacy, so I do believe the audience here, and the voters in general, have a right to know just what that legacy entails," Harold said.

I stared out into the auditorium with a smile before delivering the final blow.

"This isn't about your family or mine—may my beloved husband rest in peace," I said. "It's about the people of Ohio's twelfth district. They deserve a Congress member who fights for lower taxes and more jobs, who doesn't condone illegal drugs, let alone partner with those who make them. This is my dear husband's district, and I intend to protect it from the likes of you or any corrupt politician who may come along. Remember, this is Asher country!"

The crowd went crazy. Harold looked like he might cry. I smiled at Charlotte, who could only mouth, "Wow." I don't think she knew what type of a candidate I'd become. But I assumed she wasn't surprised I'd risen to the challenge.

After the debate, she came up to me and gave me a big hug, her growing stomach a wonderful part of our future and great campaign material.

"Mom, wow, you're tough," she said. "And all those lies about the poor man."

"I'm a natural," I said.

"I know," she said. "But I had no idea how useful that would be in politics. That was amazing. Dad could never have lied like that."

"Thanks," I said, pulling her away from the microphones and the crowd of voters waiting to speak to me. The fact that I've always been open about my issues to my daughter is healthy, I'm sure. I want her to understand me and, in turn, become nothing like me.

"I know, Mom," she said. She cradled her stomach then, as if to protect her baby from me. Might be wise. I'm kidding. I'm harmless, unless you are a political opponent. I wondered if Charlotte was worried her baby could be like me. These types of so-called antisocial personality disorders can skip generations.

"How are you feeling?" I asked. That was the appropriate motherly question, I realized.

"Great. And JJ's great," Charlotte said. "I saw his dad in the back of the room tonight. He left before the debate was over. It's tough, all of this. I'll be glad when this race is over and things can sort of return to normal. Jack's not used to losing. JJ says he's taking it hard, and he's not even the candidate. I'm proud of you, Mom, I am."

"That makes me beyond happy," I said. I couldn't see the back of the auditorium thanks to the stage lighting. "Can you stay for the victory party?"

"I have to get back to DC. Work, JJ . . . you know, life," she said. "You'll be home soon. I'm proud of you, Mom, even though this campaign turned evil."

"Yes, well, that's the nature of things these days," I said and kissed her cheek. "I need to go shake hands. Those voters are waiting."

As Charlotte walked away, and before I could reach my adoring fans, I locked eyes with Mrs. Kestler, Harold's gorgeous young wife. I flashed her my spouse smile, and she promptly turned away, pretending to talk to one of her friends. I had to laugh.

"Jody. Can I have a minute?" Jack Dobbs appeared beside me.

I looked at my nemesis and realized, *I've won.* "Sure, Jack, since we're related and all. Charlotte said you left, snuck out before the debate ended."

"I was disgusted," he said. "But I have to give it to you: you're as corrupt as your husband. I guess that's how elections are won these days, but I'm out—out of politics. My life is great without all of this crap."

I wasn't sure what he wanted me to say, so I smiled. Sometimes silence is golden.

After a minute, he said, "Enjoy the swamp, Jody."

"I already do, Jack. My best to your lovely wife," I said and turned away to greet my adoring fans and voters, leaving Jack alone and defeated in the back of the room. So sad, Jack was.

And now, as I make my way across the ballroom, relishing my win and realizing just how far I've come, Tammy waves. She's standing with a gaggle of press people. "Here we are, Mrs. Asher."

The first reporter smiles and says, "Colleen Marco, NBC 4 News. How do you like the sound of 'Congresswoman-elect Asher'? Exit polls show you with a firm lead over Harold Kestler."

"I like the sound of it very much," I say. "But we need to wait until the polls close, until every last vote is counted, before we'll make any sort of victory announcement."

"Let's say you do win. What will be your priority as a new member of Congress? Should we expect a change from your husband's style or votes?" another reporter asks.

"Well, I'm looking forward to starting fresh. I'll of course uphold Martin's legacy. As I've noted on the campaign trail, he did so much good for so long. I want to make sure I'm held to an even-higher standard. I will make the people of Ohio's twelfth district proud they live in Asher country."

The reporter looks to the cameraman. He nods. "That's all we need. We're headed over to the Kestler campaign office to talk to him. They aren't even planning a party."

I can't help but smile. "Too bad. The voters can tell truth from lies. I guess Harold has learned that lesson. And so has Jack Dobbs. Come back for the party tonight. It's going to be fabulous."

I turn around, filled with the adrenaline rush that media hits provide. Mimi stands alone in the middle of the ballroom, in the sea of blue balloons. Tonight, the ballroom will be packed with supporters celebrating our victory. But at the moment, she's alone and frowning.

I make my way to her side. "What's wrong?"

"I just got a call from Max Brown, the reporter who was chasing Martin," Mimi says.

"I know who he is," I say. "What does he want now?"

"He says if you win, he's back on the story," Mimi says. "He thinks you were somehow involved with Roscoe. He says he never dropped the story but that he was waiting for a new development to pin another article to. And he has it: your victory."

"That's ridiculous. He's bored. Besides, it is bad form to go after a widow," I say. "He's just bluffing. Let's give him the Ashbrook story. Maybe he'll write a piece about how similar the Ashers and the Ashbrooks have become?"

"I don't even know what you're talking about," Mimi says, arms folded.

"Ohio Congressman John Ashbrook was in office for years. He was running for the Senate when he died of a peptic ulcer on the campaign trail. His wife, Jean, ran in a special election and won. She served out the last seven months of his term. Redistricting eliminated the seat the next cycle, so she was a member for only a few months," I say. "That's not going to happen to me. But otherwise, similar story, right?"

"Max won't care about this little story of yours, though. He's a Capitol Hill watchdog, a serious reporter," Mimi says, tucking her dark hair behind her ears. She's wearing a beautiful silk suit, the same bright blue as the balloons. "Not *People* magazine."

"Oh, oops, my mistake. I just thought it was a fun parallel. And you're right, I'll have Tammy pitch *People* magazine," I say. I suddenly seem to have become as quaint as one of my constituents in the church basement. At least, that is my image, and I'm sticking to it. Mimi is annoying me, staring at me like she can read my mind. She cannot, although I'm quite certain she believes she can. Meanwhile, as soon as I'm in office, I'm going to follow the money and find out all I can about Mimi Smith. I would like to ruin her, I've decided, the way she tried to ruin Martin. But for now I need her.

Mimi smiles. "*People* magazine? Really? Look, I'll handle Max. You focus on your victory speech."

"Sounds great," I say. "Thanks again for everything, buddy."

"Um, Jody," Mimi says. "There isn't anything to this, is there? You are squeaky clean, right?"

I reassuringly look her right in the eye. "You knew Martin as well as anyone. He would never involve me in anything unethical," I say. "He might have left me a letter detailing all of your unethical, treasonous behavior, though."

"What?" Mimi asks. Her face drains of color.

"Oh, I'm just kidding. You and I are both squeaky clean," I say. I love the look on her face. I love to keep her off-balance, questioning what I know. She wants to believe I'm an idiot. I will show her I'm not.

"Of course," Mimi says. I like the fact she looks rattled.

Spontaneously, I give Mimi a hug. We aren't demonstrative typically, so I know I've caught her off guard. "Isn't this all just so exciting? I'm about to be a member of Congress."

ANONYMOUS STAFFER'S TIPS FOR NEW MEMBERS

When setting up your office, don't hire anyone you can't fire. You'll be under pressure to hire supporters, friends, the mayor's daughter, or your cousin's nephew by marriage. Resist the urge with all your strength. And remember, hire your chief of staff first if possible and pay what he or she is worth. If you ignore this piece of advice, you will be sorry. The Hill will eat an inexperienced chief for lunch.

JODY

As I stand next to Charlotte in one of the gilded, history-filled rooms of the Capitol, my left hand on the Constitution and my right hand raised in the air, I'm filled with energy. It's the week after the election, and I've been walking on clouds. The pomp and circumstance of the swearing-in, knowing that it is me this time. I'm in the spotlight. This is the drug that makes people politicians, makes them keep coming back.

"Congratulations, Jody. Welcome to Congress—this time as a member," the Speaker says.

A photographer tells us to smile.

"Jody, may I have a word with you in private?" the Speaker asks. I follow her outside to the Speaker's Balcony and enjoy the vast view. Today is the best day ever.

"I want you to enjoy the rest of Martin's term," she says. "You've earned that right. Don't make waves. Make memories."

"That's my plan," I say. The sun is so bright I shield my face with my hand.

"Good. I will expect you to vote with the caucus, including any legislation regarding China. Understood? If you do the right thing with your votes, you will be known as more than a placeholder, I assure you that," the Speaker says.

"A 'placeholder'? I don't think so. I worked hard to win the special election," I say. "My district loves me."

The Speaker smiles and leans closer to me. "Your district loved Martin and felt sorry for you, but it is ready for change. You did a wonderful job damaging Harold Kestler. We won't forget that. Good luck, Congresswoman."

I watch as she walks back inside and disappears into her suite of offices. I take a moment to process what she's said, what she's implied. She believes I'm a placeholder, a poor widow just holding the office for the next seventeen months until Frankie Dawson can take it all away.

That's not going to happen. I see Charlotte, Mimi, and Spencer waiting in the hallway just inside. I wave to them and invite them outside on the balcony.

"This view never gets old," Charlotte says. "Mom, I've got to get back to work. It was so exciting being here with you. JJ is looking forward to dinner tonight. So am I."

"Can you find your way from here?" I ask my daughter, even though I know the answer. She's spent her entire life visiting the Capitol and her father, exploring tunnels, soaking in the history, playing with the other congressional children. She likely knows this place better than I do.

"Of course. See you later, Mom."

"So now the real work begins, Congresswoman," Spencer says, shaking my hand.

Beside him, Mimi grins. "She's ready. Don't you worry. We've got the new staff in place. We'll hit the ground running."

Mimi is temporarily acting as my chief of staff, just until a suitable candidate is put in place. David still wants to come back and work for me. He has arranged a sit-down for this afternoon.

The new scheduler, Jackson, is a people pleaser who knows his number one job is to make me look good and keep me happy. As Mimi delivered those lines, I made note. Isn't that how everyone in life should treat me? Ha! Tammy from the campaign has joined the DC staff, and I have kept the legislative team in place. Despite the Speaker's warning, I will be continuing my husband's legacy, not abandoning it.

As his letter hints to and the supporting documents indicate, he was bought and paid for during most of his time in office. I take a deep breath and look up at the cloudless blue sky. My husband was a criminal. But his positions have been quite rewarding for both of us. The question now is, do I continue his corruption or do I take what I know, the documentation Martin left, and use it to bring others down? Or can I use what I have to up the price? Am I more valuable than Martin was? Can I make myself appear so?

I feel Mimi watching me. I give her my best obedient "member of Congress" smile.

ANONYMOUS STAFFER'S TIPS FOR NEW MEMBERS

Tip O'Neill once said, "It's easier to run for office than to run the office." Running a campaign and creating a congressional office are vastly different tasks. Setting up a House or Senate office includes all the challenges of starting a small business, with all the red tape of bureaucracy. It's completely overwhelming at first, and for some, it will stay that way. Those people don't last.

MIMI

I hang up my phone and lean back in the desk chair. I've taken over David's desk and sent him on a mini vacation. I haven't taken the time to remove all his personal effects, so a framed photo of him and his not-very-attractive wife standing on the deck of some cheesy cruise ship mocks me. I push it over onto its face.

Jody will not step onto Martin's committees, nor will she receive the classified intelligence briefings, according to the member of leadership staff I just spoke with. Martin served on the Foreign Relations and Intelligence Committees. Jody will be shoved onto the Education Committee. No power, no clout. No influence for my clients.

Before I break the news, I call Spencer.

"What did you expect? She doesn't have any experience. She's simply there to fill a seat. We all know that," my husband says. "Focus on what we discussed. Get the visa program approved. Invite Jody to Beijing in August."

"That sounds horrible. Beijing in August is miserable," I say. "I hear you, though. I talked to the Academy of Social Sciences. They'll meet us anywhere during recess."

I look around, reminding myself I'm speaking from inside an official congressional office building. Are there bugs? Who knows.

"I need to go," I say.

"Good. OK, well, keep going," Spencer says. "Oh, and Roscoe is talking."

I swallow and let that sink in. "He wouldn't."

"No, I suspect he'll give the feds a few low-level staffers, a freshman congressman or two," Spencer says. "He's a smart man. Sloppy, but smart."

A migraine begins working its way up the back of my neck. I hang up, then yank open David's desk drawer and rummage around for an aspirin. No luck. I open my office door and make eye contact with the intern manning the welcome desk.

"Hi. Do you have an Excedrin or Tylenol? Anything?" I ask. Before she can answer, I see him.

Max Brown.

"Hello, Mrs. Smith. Congratulations on the successful campaign." He stands up.

"He's been waiting to speak to the congresswoman, but I told him she was too busy," the intern says. "I'll go grab you an aspirin, ma'am."

"Thanks for the congratulations. Look, Mr. Brown, your story died with Martin Asher. This is a new congressional office, with big plans and a fresh orientation," I say.

Max shakes his head. "I'm not so sure she's not just an extension of her husband. They've been here, together, in the swamp for more than thirty years. She must know some things. You've been beside them all the way too. Why don't you let her talk to me?"

"Out!" I point toward the door.

"You sent this photo to me, the one of the congressman making out with his intern, didn't you?" He holds a photo in his hand. It's of Martin and Sarah.

"Put that away. Don't be ridiculous," I say. I feel a bead of sweat drip down the back of my neck. "That, whatever happened, doesn't have anything to do with Mrs. Asher. It will only upset her. Don't you have any class?"

"I happen to know it was you. Maybe trying to get me off the real story here? The man was totally going down, likely to prison. But look, now that he's gone, here she is, sitting pretty in his huge office. I hear she's even been invited to the President's Women and Power Group."

I didn't know about that. "Fabulous. She should be there. And you should leave."

"I'm not so sure she should be part of anything," Max says. "I think she's compromised, just like her husband was."

The intern returns and hands me a packet of Tylenol and a bottle of water. I retreat to David's office and slam the door. I take the pills and compose myself. I knock on the door that connects this office directly to Jody's, without the need to walk through the reception area, where Max is circling like a shark.

"Come in," Jody says, and I do.

Jody, Jackson, and Tammy sit on the two couches, a monthly calendar on the coffee table between them.

"We're going over all of the events I've been invited to," Jody says, her eyes glistening with excitement. "I had no idea Martin could attend all of this."

Could but didn't because it's draining and showy and mostly not important. "Yes, there will be plenty of things vying for your attention, but you need to focus on legislation, keeping out of the spotlight," I say. "Martin's scandal wasn't that long ago. In political circles, it's still on people's minds. We need to keep your reputation spotless, your work ethic without compare. Other scandals have already come along; his is almost forgotten. Let's just not do anything to draw attention to you."

Jody looks wounded. "That's Martin's scandal, not mine. I'm a new congresswoman. That's noteworthy. And I like the spotlight. The TV interviews are my favorite."

Tammy nods and says, "Congresswoman Asher is appearing on all the Sunday-morning shows this weekend. She's in high demand. She'll also be the keynote speaker at the National Museum of Women's monthly meeting tonight. Oh, and this just came in. The Congressional Club wants you to come and speak next month on what it's like being a member of Congress after being a spouse all those years."

"Are you finished?" I ask. My tone is a bit harsher than I mean it to be.

"Yes, ma'am," Tammy says. Her face matches the scarlet in the Ohio state flag behind her on the wall.

"None of this has anything to do with real power," I say. "Max Brown, the reporter, is outside your door right now, looking for something on you, anything on you, to keep his story alive. The more you're out and about, talking and schmoozing, the more likely he'll get what he's looking for." I fold my hands across my chest.

"Give us a moment," Jody says to the staffers. Once they've fled, she continues. "Do not tell me what to do. Do not tell me where to be, what to attend. I've had thirty years in this town, too, Mimi. I know what I'm doing."

No, she really doesn't.

If I say those words, though, she'll kick me out. I'm sure of that now. I can see the resolve in her face, the fracture in our relationship. She doesn't trust me anymore, not really. I need to kill her with kindness.

Spencer would tell me to focus on the larger mission. That requires backing down, for now.

"Of course you know what you're doing. I'm sorry. I'm used to counseling newbies to Congress, ones without any experience. I will stay out of your way, and I'll send them back in," I say.

"Good." Jody returns her attention to her social calendar. "Oh, and Mimi: when David arrives, please send him in. You don't need to join us. I know you have more pressing things to attend to."

And with that, I'm dismissed. I want to ask her if she's bringing David back as chief of staff, but I can't. I want to tell her what a mistake that would be. I want to explain how much she needs me.

Now more than ever. But I suppose she'll find out the hard way, like her idiot husband did. They think they are so important. It's a delusion. The real power in Washington belongs to the people behind the scenes. The people with money and real influence. The people who have a clear long-term mission.

People just like me. And we always win.

ANONYMOUS STAFFER'S TIPS FOR NEW MEMBERS

Despite what you've been told, Congress is staffed by some smart, dedicated public servants. While you may have campaigned "against Washington," hiring veterans of Capitol Hill offices will increase your likelihood of success in your first term. We've been here in the trenches while our bosses change, lose elections, or retire. We are the swamp. And we're good at what we do. At least, most of us are.

JODY

David walks into my office, proverbial hat literally in his hand. In addition to the straw hat, he's sporting a tan and a smile, all things out of character for Martin's dour chief of staff.

"What? Why are you looking like that?" I ask.

"The tan? We went on a cruise," he says.

"No, why are you looking at me like that?"

"Well, it's just amazing, that's all," he says. "May I?"

"Yes, sit," I say. "Oh, you're amazed I pulled off the win, is that it?"

"Actually, I'm shocked at how natural you look sitting behind that desk. As if it was you who'd been elected for sixteen terms," he says, taking a seat across the desk from me.

"I *have* been here for sixteen terms," I say. "Anyway, what would you like to discuss? I don't have much time." I watch the smile fade from his face as he realizes I'm not going to chat with him. I'm much too important for that. And, now that I'm no longer just a spouse, I'm far too busy.

"I want to apologize for not believing in your campaign. I know I let you down," he says.

"That's putting it mildly. But we did fine without you," I say. I feel the anger firing up in my stomach, and I don't try to tamp it down. "And here I am. Anything else?"

David looks at the hat in his hands and then up at me. "Martin was on the take. The K Street firms had him in their grip—several of them, not just Roscoe. He told some of them he'd pay them back. He was in too deep, with the wedding, with everything," he says.

"Do you really believe your pathetic attempts to tarnish Martin's memory are somehow going to endear you to me? Out!" I stand and point toward the door.

"Ma'am, there's some sort of video of the congressman picking up a package in a park. They're trying to say it was filled with unmarked bills, although there is no proof of what was inside," he says. "And in addition to the K Street money, Martin was in deep with the Chinese Communist Party."

"Of course he was. He had many friends in China. He always believed our two nations could work together. They are a poor rural country; they need our help," I say, knowing that may have been true in the past.

"Martin facilitated Chinese Communist Party officials gaining access to leadership, including the vice president. The People's Republic of China, PRC, had access through Martin to strategy meetings and who knows what else. Max Brown's story just scratched the surface before everyone's focus became his affair with the intern. I wouldn't be surprised if the PRC was behind the story breaking about the affair. They would like nothing better than to shift the focus away from them. But this story will come back around. The investigations never stopped into any of this. Only the headlines have. For now."

I'm about to grab him by his suntanned arm and physically escort him from my office. I wish I still had my body man from the campaign. "I need you to leave and never come back. Do you understand?" I ask.

"That's not a good move, Congresswoman," David says.

The annoying little man hasn't moved, and now he's smiling. What is going on? I again point to the door. "I knew Martin better than you, better than anyone. All of this is a lie. You are a liar, and I demand your resignation."

"Here are your two choices. Keep me on, and I'll keep my mouth closed. Turn me loose, and I give Max Brown a call. I hear he was just in your lobby out there a few minutes ago. I bet he's not far away. Your choice," David says. And finally he stands.

I cannot believe I'm stuck with him. I will figure out a work-around, but until then, he wins. Besides, Mimi is gone. I need someone in that desk. Chiefs of staff are hard to find, I hear. "Fine. I don't understand why you even want to work in this office, but you may stay for now," I say. "Mimi needs to get back to her think tank anyway. And, well, you do know your way around this place."

"Glad you agree. I'm going to get back to it. Let me know if you need anything," David says. "Um, I'll need my desk back."

I push the button on my phone. Mimi is going to be furious to be evicted this way, but I don't have any other choice. I need to keep David happy, and quiet. I'll figure out how to use him to my advantage. Mimi will just need to deal with it and go back to her think tank. I need to think, and scheme. I must keep everyone in check.

I take a deep breath and try to remember to smile. I buzz Mimi's desk. "Can I see you for a moment?"

"Be right there," she says over the phone.

David stands by the door between our two offices. When Mimi comes in, he nods.

"Wait in the chief's office, please, David," I say. He smiles and leaves through the door Mimi entered, closing it behind him.

"What's going on?" Mimi asks.

"I'm keeping David as my chief for now," I say.

"Even though he was going to leave you for Frankie Dawson's campaign?" she asks.

"Yes, but he does know his way around this place. He's a seasoned chief, and he knows what Martin and I stand for. Besides, you should go back to your real job. I've got this from here," I say. "Thanks for everything. I do appreciate it."

"Fine, that's just fine with me." Mimi does not look happy as she stomps out of my office, but really, she's been unhappy since we returned from Ohio. It's not my fault. As much as she's told me to stay out of the spotlight, I can't help myself. I love being on television. I love the makeup, the lighting, the deference of the anchors, the celebrity it is helping me to achieve. I'm recognized on the street here in DC. It's fabulous. I love it. Mimi does not. I think she's jealous of my newfound fame. The thought makes me smile.

She won't stay angry for long, I know that much. She and Spencer need Martin and me—well, now just me. And as I think about our codependence, I know there are others like Martin. Other Congress members she has cultivated. To polish the Asher family name, I need to figure out the network, figure out who is on the take and release that information with the records Martin has supplied. That way, Mimi goes down and Martin is a hero who saved democracy from his fellow Congress members. I sit at my desk and begin to make a list of possibilities. Mimi is friendly with dozens of politicians. Which ones has she paid off? Who is in too deep like Martin was?

The vote clock above me on the wall buzzes. I never paid much attention to it as a spouse, but now I suppose I should. I step into my private bathroom and check the placement of my member pin. Perfect. My phone lights up with a text. It's from my legislation director.

Congresswoman: There are four votes tonight. You should vote yes on the first three, no on the final vote. See me with questions.

This text makes me wonder again how hard Martin really worked. Did he read all the bills and know what he was voting on, or did he just take direction from his team? And since Martin was in the pocket of lobbyists, and was Mimi's client, then would he be receiving texts from them too?

My phone lights up with a text from an unknown number.

Your votes tonight: Yes. No. Yes. Yes.

And then another text. NNYY

I stare at my own reflection in the mirror. Of course I knew most of what Martin was doing. I didn't know all the specifics, but I did know we wouldn't be able to afford the life we lived without his special friends and their special donations, legal and otherwise. And now, with his letters and records from the safe, I know exactly what transpired.

I think of our townhome, Charlotte's first-class education, our vacation home in Florida, and so much more. Martin did a good job of playing it down, of pretending most of what we had was inherited, that he came from a trust fund family. But any sort of digging would reveal some, if not all, of the lie.

The wedding pushed him too far; paying for it made him desperate. I do feel guilty about that. But then I remember Sarah, her dark-brown eyes, her disdain for me. And then I go back to feeling nothing at all.

There's a knock on the door.

"Congresswoman, it's time to vote," David says.

I touch the strand of pearls around my neck as I check my makeup. I look good—congressional, powerful.

"I'm ready," I say, then join him in the office.

"Shall I escort you to the floor? I can wait for you outside the cloak-room, just in case you have any questions," he says. We walk out the private door and hurry onto the members-only elevator. My staff can only ride on this elevator if I am present. Two of my colleagues join us.

"Welcome," one of the men says to me.

"Marty would be proud," the other says. "You going to vote like him or vote like a Democrat?"

David jumps in. "You'll have to wait and see, sir."

The doors open and I step off first, David hurrying beside me as we make our way to the subway car. I can't believe I get to sit in the members-only car of the subway too. As the driver closes the doors, I take a moment to enjoy the short ride between Raymond and the Capitol building. Everything is starting to be so real. So what if my committee assignments are a big step down from Martin's? I'll work my way up in ranking and stature. I've thought this all through. The Speaker thinks I'm just serving out Martin's term. But I've made a different decision. I love this. I am here to stay.

At least until I exact my revenge on Mimi. And I will. I can forgive her for compromising my husband, for seeing his weakness, our need for money, and exploiting it. But I will never forgive her for leaking the photo, the proof of Martin's affair. The one she made possible. For that, there must be a reckoning. But for now I will focus on making history.

We ride the elevator up from the subway, and David escorts me to the hallway outside the House floor.

"I'll wait for you outside the cloakroom. Text me if you need anything. You have your votes? Any questions?"

"Thanks," I say. "I've got this." I step onto the House floor and immediately look up to the galley—my normal seat in this hallowed hall.

But not anymore.

A senior congresswoman rushes to my side. She is a whip, of course, making sure I vote with the party. Martin always made fun of them because he usually didn't listen to the party's wishes. They always threatened to primary him but never did. His seat was safe. Asher country, after all.

The congresswoman touches my shoulder and leans in close. "Welcome! We're so glad you're here. All set on votes tonight?"

"I am!" I hold up my electronic voting card. I know I slide it into the slot on the back of the bench and press green for *yea*, red for *nay*, or yellow for *present*. Voting *present* means you don't have the guts to take a real vote, in my opinion. We're here to vote yes or no. Nobody elects a Congress member to just be present.

My row begins to fill with Democratic members of the House. I spot Martin's friend from Minnesota, and he waves to me. When it's time, I slip my card into the reader and vote yes. I vote yes all four times, including the last. I can't believe the heady sense of power I feel pressing these important buttons, seeing my votes reflected up on the big electronic board.

The whip is on me immediately. "Was that a mistake? The vote should be no. We don't want to remove the tariffs on Chinese goods. Right? You can fix the vote manually up at the podium."

I flash my spouse smile at her—correction, my *member's* smile. "It wasn't a mistake. Have a good evening."

Whoever sent me the texts didn't get everything they wanted and neither did the party. That should keep them all guessing. I know what I'm doing, and I skimmed the bills. You can please some of the people some of the time, am I right? I check my watch. I'm late for the president's cocktail party for women members of Congress. I've discovered all I really enjoy is the social side of this new job. I couldn't care less about legislation, about voting the way my staff wants me to. I wanted to take over this seat to feel some of the power and prestige Martin enjoyed.

As I take the elevator down to the parking garage, a realization dawns on me: I don't feel more powerful now that I'm a member of Congress. If anything, I have less freedom, less control. Not what I expected at all. My days are scheduled down to the minute, filled with people I don't want to talk to coming to my office, and having long, dry conversations with the legislative staff. Unless you care about policy, it's just a dull day. Day after day.

It may sound shallow, but it requires too much energy for me to compete and care here. I can only take so much. When Martin was in office and I reviewed legislation, it was only to pretend to be informed. Am I an impostor? Not really. I did want to hold this office. I like giving speeches now, and I like people calling me *Honorable*. But the sitting around and waiting, eating horrible cafeteria food at my desk in between the constant stream of people coming into my office and shaking hands—well, my hand sanitizer can barely keep up. It's a wonder Martin wasn't sick all the time, what with all the people who come to lobby me. It's overwhelming. And none of these types of constituents bring cash or presents.

And then there's the threat of Joe Roscoe, languishing in prison, biting his tongue. Would he ever say anything about me, Martin, or Charlotte? No, of course not, but the reality that he could hangs over me like a dark cloud. I don't like that at all. Obviously, with Martin's death, the focus has moved elsewhere—to others, I remind myself.

The House of Representatives is a club, and I'm a new member without any real friends. Some of the members have been kind, have asked me to lunch once or twice. But mostly, I'm alone when I'm not surrounded by strangers. David and I coexist. I think Mimi is still mad at me because I essentially fired her from the chief of staff position, and since then, unlike Martin, I don't do exactly what she tells me to do. I don't want to. I want to do things my way. I know I need to confront her soon or maybe expose her and Spencer for what they truly are. But the timing hasn't been right.

It's hard for me not to completely rebel against her and her control, but I have to remember I have enjoyed the benefits of our relationship for decades. So I do placate her in small ways—with votes that align, with meetings I take—but not in everything she suggests. Same for the party. They're always telling me what to do. I don't listen all the time. Too bad.

I am my own person. I'm an enigma, much like my husband was. The Ashers are special; I need everyone to understand that, and eventually they will. Oh, and I need the money we're used to. I really need it. With Roscoe behind bars, that source has gone dry. I will find another option, and I know it likely won't be Mimi.

I'm excited for tonight's reception, though, and the opportunities it may present. These are the things I like to attend. As I drive down Pennsylvania Avenue, I wonder if the vice president will make an appearance tonight. It would be good to say hello, remind him his favorite Asher is still around.

Although I'm sure he already knows that and is dreading our first encounter. Too bad, Eugene. I'm your nightmare. A lovely one, of course, who just keeps haunting you no matter how high you soar.

Anonymous Staffer's Tips for New Members

Staffers work long hours. Period. We all come here with shiny idealism in our eyes and end up with dark circles under them. Over time, if we last, we tend to be a little jaded. But we're smart, and we usually have your back. Try to appreciate this sacrifice and treat your staff well. Try.

MIMI

Pepito's Casa Restaurant

I picked the window table, tucked into the corner, to assure our privacy. And I drove here, to Jody's neighborhood, to make her believe she's the one in control of things. Actually, I don't need to make her believe anything. She has become a power-hungry monster—ask anyone—and she's been in office only a month. I've heard through the grapevine that her staff hates working for her. I've also heard the party is shocked by her erratic votes. All in all, she's a mess, it seems.

This is all my fault. I talked the Speaker into supporting Jody instead of Frankie Dawson, shooting her a text before Jody even had the call with her. And I got her elected. I made the powers that be believe that she would be a loyal placeholder, an easy pawn for all of us to manipulate. I convinced my client of the same.

That has proved to be a wrong assumption. She will not listen to me.

I created the monster, and now I'm going to have to eliminate her.

She's late. Almost half an hour late, so far. I motion to the waiter. I'll order a tapas or two to tide me over. I hear she was drunk at the White House during the president's reception for women members of Congress. Something is troubling her, perhaps. Maybe it's just all a little too much for a simple spouse to handle?

I wonder if I should remind Jody of all I know about her and her husband's dealings. Would she be shocked by my stories, my intelligence? Would she be amazed by all I know, the secrets she thinks nobody can uncover? How exposed would she feel if it all were to come out?

She has no way of knowing who I really am, of course, and likely, she'll never know. For my part, I know everything there is to know about Jody and Martin Asher. Even spent a little time with a certain drunk Mrs. Prescott in Palm Beach once upon a time, sharing stories about Jody's youth. It did make me feel sorry for her, just a bit, I'll admit. And Charlotte—the apple of Jody's eye, if there really is one. Charlotte always seemed to be a prop for Jody. But don't feel sorry for the girl; she's got me and, now, a loving husband to provide all the love she never received from her mom. And a baby on the way.

Charlotte and I had a chance to spend some quality godmother time together just after Jody decided to run for office. We went to lunch. I wanted to make sure Charlotte was handling things all right, what with her father-in-law supporting Harold and her mom taking him on. And of course her father's shocking death. She's a strong young woman, with a solid head on her gorgeous shoulders. She told me her mom often apologized to her for her inability to show emotion and feel true love. Charlotte told me Jody tries hard and that she seemed genuinely upset when her dad died. That, to Charlotte, was a good sign. Poor girl. I guess I should commend Jody for her self-awareness, but her daughter's childhood must have been tough.

"Everything is fine with me, Mimi," Charlotte assured me as we finished up lunch. "JJ is the best thing that ever happened to me, and the baby is due in a couple months. We're creating our own family, our own future. What my mom does is her business. I'll always support her and love her, but I also know who she really is."

What an interesting upbringing the girl had.

"OK, well, you know I'm here for you, no matter what. You just call me. Anytime. Any favor, big or small," I told her. She is such a sweet young woman, the opposite of her mom. And she has political aspirations. We will have a long and mutually beneficial relationship, I predict.

As for Jody, she will fall in line, or she will fall from power. I am ready to deliver the message. Frankie Dawson is waiting, and she'll be a wonderful addition to my congressional roster.

It doesn't matter that Jody is late tonight. I know she'll show up.

She doesn't have a choice.

ANONYMOUS STAFFER'S TIPS FOR NEW MEMBERS

It's the little things that are most important. Be sure you stock your office with something inexpensive that's made in your district, and offer it as a gift when important donors and constituents visit. One of my bosses handed out hot sauce made in his district, while another gave visitors a small bag of peanuts grown in her district. Folks treasure these small gestures, trust me. Another tip is to offer constituents the gift of a US flag that has been flown over the Capitol building. It is a popular gift that often becomes part of the family legacy, passed down for generations.

JODY

I check the time. I'm going to be late for dinner with Mimi. I know she'll understand. She knows how things work.

"Madam, the Russian ambassador's envoy is here," David says. He escorts a rather rotund white-haired man into my office.

"Congratulations on your successful campaign, Congresswoman. We sent our condolences about your husband earlier. He was a great congressman. I know you will be the same," he says. His accent is thick, but his bright-blue eyes are charming. We shake hands.

"Thank you. Please come in," I say and grab a small bag of buckeye tree nuts I give as a gift to visitors for good luck. "Here. Buckeye nuts. They're poisonous but quite beautiful."

Breshefski chuckles and seems to consider a response, but instead slips my gift into his pocket.

"Please, have a seat," I say. I'll admit I was surprised to learn that Martin had been friendly with the Russians too. "What can I do for you?"

"Oh, nothing right now. We just wanted to visit, to let you know your husband was a great friend to us, and us to him. You and I have met before, of course, many times, Mrs. Asher," Breshefski says.

"No, I don't believe we have," I say. I'm lying. I don't like this man's tone, his presumption of a close relationship between us, although clearly, we have taken advantage of his generosity. Oh, Martin.

"Regardless, we will get to know each other. We will expect likewise from you." He smiles through his threat.

"I'll be sure to remember your kind visit," I say. "And now I must ask you to leave. I have another meeting."

He bows, says, "Thank you for the nuts," and walks out of my office.

David reappears. "What was that about?"

"Did he have an appointment? I didn't see it on the daily run-down," I say.

"No, he just appeared. He and Martin were friends. He dropped by pretty regularly, so when he said you wanted to see him, I thought you did," David says.

"Well, it's fine," I say. I did want to have the meeting and had been expecting it. I need to follow the money, remember, and keep it flowing. Our lifestyle wasn't all funded through Mimi and Joe Roscoe, it seems. I look at David. "I need to get going."

"Ma'am, I know you don't want to hear this, but the staff is upset. You're completely ignoring their legislative direction on a lot of your votes. As you know, the scheduler quit this morning based on your tirade. The whip's office called and wants an explanation of your latest vote. She said, and I quote, 'What is wrong with the Ashers? Are they on China's payroll or something?' As of now, I don't really have a good answer for them. Do you? Are you compromised?"

I stand and pack up my briefcase. I can feel David's stare. I hate that I need to justify my decisions. I'm trying to keep everyone off-balance until I decide my next move. Because there is one thing I've discovered: I am not meant to be a member of Congress. This is a horrible job. David continues to stare. I take a deep breath.

"Martin and I both consider China an important partner. As for the party, I'll vote with the caucus tomorrow. I like some of the legislation, like the infrastructure bill. I like that."

"That's not the point. You don't want the Speaker to pull her support after only a month in office, but that's what's going to happen. She's told the DCCC you will not be an endorsed candidate next cycle, even if you change your ways. Do you understand what that means?" David exhales. "They can take you down, you know. Your own party can come after you. Is this just about money and power? Do you even care about this country? This job?"

I smile. No, I don't. "Of course I do. It's just that . . . well, I don't know, this member-of-Congress job isn't what I thought it would be. But I'll call the Speaker, ask her to lunch," I say. Of course she'll refuse, but it will be fun to ask.

"She's not going to go to lunch with you, Congresswoman," David says. "You dodged a bullet when Roscoe didn't implicate Martin in his plea deal. He gave the feds unimportant members, a couple two-term congressmen."

I stare at David. Of course Joe wouldn't squeal. We all go way back. "It was a good development."

"For you. And Martin. But what about the country? The thing is, somewhere along the way, Martin changed. He started doing ethically questionable activities. Everyone knows that now because of Max Brown's reporting," David says. "And just because Roscoe didn't implicate Martin in his plea deal last week doesn't mean he still won't."

I'm being attacked by my own staffer. Accused of wrongdoing. I close my briefcase and head for my private exit. I don't have to listen to these sorts of accusations. I mean, it simply doesn't look good. "I don't know what you are implying, but I don't like it. I'm not my husband. I'm my own person. I'm honorable."

I walk out of the office in a huff and down the empty hall to the elevator bank. I'm not especially honorable, I know. But who is in this place? It's a town based on compromise and hidden agendas. Mine included. I'll hold this seat until I'm ready to vacate it. Even though I would love to vacate it now, I will bide my time.

I still have some sleuthing to do. Joe Roscoe is under control, and it seems the Russians are too. Mimi is lurking around in the shadows, unhappy with me and my votes. She must know things will come to a head between us; that's why she invited me to dinner, I suppose. But I'm not ready to reveal my hand yet. I've started my list of compromised congressmen, the ones Mimi controls. I will confront her but only when the time is right.

As I wait for the members-only elevator, I think about Breshefski's visit. Of course I know the man. I'm glad he stopped by, although a heads-up would have been nice. We met at the World Economic Forum in Davos, Switzerland, many years ago. He was acting as Russia's envoy on the environment back then, and Martin was invited to present at the important conference for the first time, thus beginning Martin's fondness for China, our misunderstood global partner.

Apparently, Martin was well liked and well connected with the Russians too.

I admire the glorious new Swiss watch adorning my wrist and smile. A gift from the Kremlin that landed in my hand when I shook Breshefski's. It sparkles with diamonds and is quite stunning. There are rules for everything here, of course. You can only accept gifts under twenty-five dollars of value, or something ridiculous. You can't even receive a good bottle of wine for that price. As for the Swiss watch, it's not a gift from the Russians. It's from Martin, with love. It says so on the engraving on the back.

There really are two sides to every story; you just have to be open to them and repeat them convincingly.

Things were so simple back then during our first trip to Switzerland, when Martin spoke at Davos. I was thrilled to be there in the audience, the wife so proud of her husband.

The elevator doors open and I step inside. Maybe it's worth finishing out Martin's term if only to get an invitation to Davos. I know I'll be invited as Martin's successor. This year, maybe I'll be the one they celebrate. The parties at Davos are great, the best I've been to, actually. I smile at the thought as the elevator carries me down. I've decided. I will finish this term in style and then blow this whole place up.

Anonymous Staffer's Tips for New Members

Are you married? Your spouse's role in your congressional activities is up to you and should fit you and your family. Some are involved in weekly calls, hiring decisions, and strategy sessions. Others prefer to return to their normal lives once the campaign is over, barely setting foot in DC. Whatever you decide, decide it together and make your staff aware. Most of us will tell you to keep the spouse out of the office as much as possible, for all our sakes.

MIMI

Pepito's Casa Restaurant

I watch as Jody walks in the front door of the restaurant, slowly, as if she hasn't a care in the world. Her blonde hair is professionally done, shiny and shoulder length, and her sensible khaki pantsuit is fitted, designer, and obviously expensive. Gold jewelry glistens from both wrists and her neck. She looks wealthy and powerful. I made her both of those things.

She smiles at me and waves like she isn't forty-five minutes late for dinner.

Like she is the boss.

"So sorry I'm late," she says, slipping into the seat across from me. "I hope you understand. Votes and all."

"Votes ended almost two hours ago," I say. We lock eyes.

"Well, things at the office are just crazy. The staff, well, there's always a crisis, you know." Jody picks up the menu. "I've never been here, but I hear great things."

"It's great for date nights and privacy. Lobbyists and media haven't found it yet. Not that I can tell, at least," I say somewhat ironically. "Why don't you figure out what you want for dinner. I'll wait."

I've learned over the years that silence is a powerful tool. Most people are uncomfortable sitting in silence. I'm not one of those people.

Jody reviews the menu quickly and places it on the table. "So what's up?"

"That's a rather broad question. Many things are happening, but mostly, you are causing quite a stir," I say. Jody looks at me a moment, perhaps considering whether this is a compliment. It is not. It is time for Jody to learn who is boss. As Confucius wrote, *There cannot be two suns in the sky, nor two emperors on the earth.*

"When your husband and I started working together, we had a mutually beneficial orientation. A team spirit aligned with a common purpose to help Americans understand China and China's modest goals of restoring our proper place in the world. It was a beautiful partnership, for all of us," I say. "And then Martin became sloppy. As you know, he began hustling money from others, not just through our think tank. Joe Roscoe was the biggest mistake. I hear Martin was making inroads with Russia too."

"Why are you rehashing what I already know? And don't you think Martin's affair with the intern he hired based on your recommendation was the biggest mistake?" Jody waves to the waiter. "I need to order. I'm in a hurry."

As soon as the waiter departs, I say, "It was the final mistake, that affair. He would have been removed from office. That's why it was important to expose it. He was finished in this town anyway. And it needed to be because of that young woman, not because of his ties to China or my think tank."

"I heard you were the one who leaked the photo," Jody says, eyes narrowed. "How could you do something like that? It's despicable."

"Oh, so you know. Fine, I'm glad you do," I say. "How could I not leak it? It had to happen. Martin was careless, and so many people were trailing him. If it wasn't me, someone else would have. You know that as well as I do."

"All I know is that you placed that girl in his office, and then you framed him. The stress killed him. *You* killed him," Jody says. Her eyes flash with hatred.

"Are you accusing me of something?" I ask. "Are you saying Martin was a poor victim here? Are you trying to say *you* are?"

Jody leans back. "I don't know what really happened with the intern, and I don't want to. I just know he was stressed, the media started buzzing about a photo—about proof—and then he died."

"If stress killed him, then you're responsible. Your constant demands for more money, living beyond your means. You are never satisfied," I say. "That is what led to Martin's demise: greed."

"There's nothing wrong with ambition, but there is something wrong with taking advantage of a man who has done everything for you," Jody says. The waiter places a red wine in front of her, and she takes a large sip. "Even when he's been compromised. Even when you're the one who compromised him."

"As if," I say.

"You're ambitious and clever. We're the same, in a way," Jody says.

"We are very different," I say. "I have a moral compass." And a clear long-term goal. The one-hundred-year plan. Something most Americans just don't understand but we Chinese are born knowing. This is why, in the end, we will emerge as the global superpower.

"That's rich. 'A moral compass'? You're nothing more than a lobbyist disguised as a think tank," Jody says. "We both know it."

"You know what else we both know? That our think tank paid for Charlotte's education and your townhome. That she never would have been admitted to Sidwell Friends without our help and a falsified pedigree, which you approved. Your vacation home in Florida was a gift from me, my people."

Jody stares at me. "So what? Nobody cares."

I chuckle. "Oh, they would care if they knew. You and Martin were savvy and created a backstory of wealth that never existed on either side. And, Jody, what about your own sad childhood? I'm sure your mom would love to do an interview or two, for the right price," I say.

"Why are you doing this?" she asks. She takes a big sip of her wine.

"Doing what?" I tuck my hair behind my ears. My innocent look.

"Bringing up the past. Charlotte is grown and married; no one will care about that nonsense. And as for my mom, I've not spoken to her for a decade, or longer, as you know," Jody says.

"Doesn't matter. Max will care," I say. "And there's so much more to tell him about."

"There's a lot I can tell him about you too; don't forget. It seems to me like we should reach some sort of détente," she says.

"Maybe, but with conditions," I say.

"What do you want?" Jody asks. She leans forward.

"You will not run for office again. You will announce that filling your husband's seat has been the privilege of a lifetime but that you're stepping aside to make way for the next generation, and you will back Frankie Dawson," I say.

Jody finishes the wine in her glass. "Sure, I'll consider stepping aside, but I have a few conditions of my own."

"I'm afraid you don't have any choice," I say. It's amusing to see that she thinks she is the one in control here. Amusing and sad.

She studies me for a moment. "Look, maybe just let me stay in office, keep the seat, I'll toe the line. I'll vote your way. Let's just not ruin a good thing. I'm just getting started. It's only been a month. Besides, you don't know if Frankie Dawson will be your friend. You know who I am. It's the Asher seat," Jody says. "And remember, I know all about you too."

How silly of Jody to threaten me. It's pathetic, really. She only knows what I've allowed her to see, nothing more. Meanwhile, I know exactly who and what you are, Mrs. Asher. It is my job. And now I need her to step aside and get out of my way. I lean forward, elbows on the table, candlelight dancing between us on the table.

"You're wrong. I do know all about Frankie. I am always playing the long game. You are not as important as you think, Jody. You've always been expendable; all of you have been. And my clients want you to know the retainer we paid to Martin all those years will not be reinstated. You have proven to be unreliable and untrustworthy. My clients only reward those who are consistent and true. You are not. In a short time, you've become a joke on the Hill."

Jody crosses her arms in front of her. Apparently, she didn't like the joke comment. Truth hurts. I watch as she motions for the waiter, and he brings her another glass of wine. She takes a big sip before responding.

"Martin left me a record of everything he has done for you and your clients. I can bring you down, Mimi." Her blue eyes flash with anger.

"I don't believe you. That would be political suicide for you and would ruin your entire family. Even if Martin kept records, you won't turn them over. You're bluffing, and it's rather pathetic," I say. "Try to finish out the Widow's Mandate with grace, Jody. And then go away."

"Fine, I can do that. I don't even like the job, but I need your help to—" Jody says.

I stand up, ignoring her groveling. "Oh, look, dinner is served. Enjoy."

"Wait, where are you going?" she asks.

I turn and walk out of the restaurant, leaving her with what must be a million questions and the check.

She can afford it. I happen to know that. She's been spoiled and coddled—all the Ashers have been. But that's over. We have moved on. Jody is irrelevant. And quite frankly, that saddens me a bit. I had high hopes for her after the successful campaign. I was afraid the job would be over her head. And I was right. It's unfortunate, but it's time to forge ahead.

I walk by the restaurant window and feel her stare. I turn, smile, and wave goodbye.

ANONYMOUS STAFFER'S TIPS FOR NEW MEMBERS

Committee assignments are an important aspect of your term in office. The more prestigious the committee, the more powerful you'll become. Think it through and then make your case to leadership in writing. Don't even think about asking for Appropriations or Ways and Means. That's for senior members. Be humble. Even though you just got elected to Congress, you do still remember what it was like to show humility, don't you? You can't be that jaded. Not yet.

JODY

Asher Townhome

My anger has subsided enough so that I can finally sit. I've been pacing around the couch for a good hour since arriving home from that ridiculous dinner.

How dare she just walk away after I kindly offered to step aside as a truce? I take a deep breath. I know—my rational self realizes she has been helpful to Martin and me in many ways. She's opened doors, funneled funds, taken us on trips. She's spoiled Charlotte and helped me win Martin's seat in the special election.

But now, apparently, she's finished with me. She'll simply direct her clients' money elsewhere. My mind flashes on the face of Representative Bob Dyer of Washington State. I recall seeing Mimi and Bob sitting together at a variety of functions over the years. I remember their easy banter, his pricey sports car. I walk to the kitchen and write his name down. He is just another congressman on Mimi's payroll. He's just like Martin: Consistent. Pro-China. A workhorse for Mimi's interests. It's obvious, when you think about it.

I think of starting up a campaign again, without Mimi's support. I imagine the fight with Frankie in the primary. I don't have it in me, I don't. But I'm not finished in DC.

I look at my new watch and smile. Mimi might think she can ruin me, but we have other friends, Martin and I. Sure, Roscoe & Partners won't be sending money my way, not with Joe in federal custody. Nor will Mimi and the Chinese. Fine, but I don't like how she handled it. Like she can simply dismiss me and I'll fade away. The Honorable Congresswoman Jody Asher doesn't just disappear. Not until she wants to. And believe it or not, Mimi and I want the same thing: I won't seek reelection, but that's my choice, not hers.

The result is the same. We are on the same page. But she will think she won. I don't like this feeling—the losing feeling.

I vacillate between calling Mimi or showing up at their estate in Kalorama and telling her that I'm not going to run for another term, and demanding her help in return. I don't have anybody on my side.

That's it. I don't have anyone, not really. All the people in our lives were present because of Martin. He was the magnet; I was popular because he was. I was important because he was. I was liked, tolerated, because everyone loved Martin. I know that, of course. And most of the time, it doesn't bother me. But just now, as I realize I've been abandoned—kicked to the curb by my supposed best friend and the entire party—well, it hurts. I'm human. I am.

My mind flashes back to the elegant cocktail reception at the White House, the president greeting me at the door with a warm hug, giving me his condolences for Martin and congratulations for holding the Asher seat. The president of the United States welcomed me into his home. I couldn't believe my good fortune. The first few days in office were heady, with ceremony and firsts. But it is clear I will be forced to serve out the term and go away, as Mimi said.

I need something else, something more.

I've put myself in this corner, I realize. Mimi has made it clear that if I expose her, she'll ruin the Asher name forever. I think of Charlotte, working her way up in DC. I must make a plan. In this moment, as I turn off the living room lights, I have a sense of Martin's terror, his fear.

That everything he'd done over the course of his career in the House of Representatives would be mocked, criminalized, stained by the Roscoe mess and his ties to China. And then, when the intern story began to emerge, it was all too much to take.

When Mimi leaked the intern story, she knew it would be the end of his career.

If I don't go along with her demands, what will she do to me? Will she start leaking stories to ruin my reputation, to drive me out of office? What is she capable of?

I don't put anything past her. I dial her number and it rolls over to voice mail. "It's me, Jody. I agree with you. I am not cut out for this job, and I'll step aside after I finish this term. In return, I hope you will help with my next step, for old times' sake. Thank you and please call me back."

I climb the stairs to our bedroom and realize I miss Martin. He was my only friend. In our bedroom, I pick up the framed photo of the two of us on one of the swearing-in days long ago. In this photo, Martin's face is unlined, his jaw square and his look sure. There is none of the sagginess that comes with age, none of the tension that comes with the job itself. This was pure happiness.

"Martin, what should I do?" I ask his photo. "What would you do?"

He'd use everything in his toolbox—that's what he'd do.

I swallow as I review my new plan. I think of the contents of Martin's safe, now stored in the suitcase under my bed. In addition to the letter and the paper trail leading to Mimi, he's left me things to assure my future. He'd want me to be happy. He'd know that I'd hate the actual work of being a member of Congress. He told me so every time I complained about him getting all the attention, all the praise.

"You'd hate this job, Jody. There are so many people telling you what to do. Your every minute is scheduled," Martin said more than once. "You're much better suited to being the spouse. The partner with the real power."

As with many things, he was right. I need to plan my graceful exit to a better position, something worthy of my status as a DC mover and shaker. I need to move up to something much more prestigious than a lowly member of Congress. And all these people owe me that. It's up to me to decide what I want and tell them.

I finally take a moment to relax. I look up to the ceiling. I touch the glistening gold watch on my wrist, and I have the answer. "Thank you, Martin."

PART THREE

October

Anonymous Staffer's Tips for New Members

It's a free-for-all every four years after the presidential election. The Plum Book is updated then and contains facts on more than nine thousand federal civil service leadership and support positions to be filled. You read that right: nine thousand. This is just a fun fact for you to know in case one of your constituents is looking for a job. Or maybe after one term, you'd like to make a change?

JODY

Rayburn House Office Building

October is such a lovely time of year in DC. The tourist flock has gone back to their home nests, the air is still pleasant, and the grass still green. I cross the room to the bookshelf and admire the latest photos on display.

I pick up one of fellow new members and me in Israel over our August recess. In this photo, I'm admiring the Dead Sea and trying very hard to make new friends. At the Wailing Wall, the representative from Florida and I hit it off. I think he may have even had some sort of crush on me. We shall see.

With that trip, and my new focus on pretending to follow the party's legislative agenda, I hope I'm back in most of leadership's good graces. I'm a team player. I have friends, sort of. I am worthy. I'm low profile these days, and no one calls out to me as I walk the streets of the Hill. My fundraising has dried up. It's almost as if the big donors all know I've been sidelined by Frankie Dawson, even though it hasn't been announced. It doesn't need to be. All the big donors talk, and the grapevine is tightly controlled from the top. I haven't been told anything, not officially at least. Mimi never returned my call, but she also hasn't threatened me with exposure, so I suppose we are in some sort of truce.

Every night, my dreams turn to nightmares of being alone, old, and powerless, sitting in a rocking chair in my townhome when the police knock on the door and take me to prison. But in the morning, when I wake up, the reality sets in. It's up to me to choose my next step, and I have. I have pivoted as well, although none of them know it. And so far, the pivot plan seems to be working, my new job coming into focus. And it's huge.

"Madam, do you have a moment?" David asks, popping his head in from his office. "We should go over your ask for the vice president just one more time."

David and I have come to an agreement: he will help me rise to a new position, and in turn, I will support his jumping ship and working for Frankie Dawson. It's a relief of sorts to one day say goodbye to him and not have to see his dreary face every day. And the feeling must be mutual. He even smiles on occasion now.

I am pleased I've decided what I want even though my hand is being forced by the powers that be—all of them. "Sure, let's go over the ask. To me, it's simple. I'd make a capable and effective member of the cabinet. I am a known quantity. Give me Education or Transportation, perhaps? And in turn, I'll endorse Frankie Dawson for the Asher seat."

"Yes, that's good. It turns out, though, only Secretary of Education is open right now, so focus there. Talk about your love of public education. These things take time, so go for the open spot. Remind him you have the perfect credentials for a cabinet position. Be firm," he says. "The party will look pretty bad forcing a poor widow out of office without giving her a new role; remind him of that."

"I will. Don't worry. Will I also be speaking with the president? Or should I wait and bring it up at our next Women in Power cocktail reception?"

I notice the shift on his face. "What?"

He clears his throat. "You've been removed from that group, unfortunately."

"Removed?" I'm stunned. They really are all against me, even though I've been playing nice lately. It's frustrating how mean these people can be. How shortsighted and cliquey.

"Your best bet for a cabinet spot is the vice president. He is the only one still willing to take your call. I don't really understand why he does," David says. "For old times' sake, for Martin, he says."

Whatever. That's not the reason. "For Martin, of course. I'm ready. I'll leave for his office shortly."

"Oh, Congresswoman?" David says, stopping in the doorway. "Just so you aren't blindsided, the Speaker is announcing your retirement today at her press conference."

I'm speechless. That is not in my plan. I am in charge of my next step, not her. Man, I really hate this job. You can't trust anybody. So much for trying to get along these past few months. They were going to get rid of me no matter what I did. Fine. They can have this thankless seat, but only if they give me what I want. I take a deep breath and shake my head.

"There really is no loyalty in Washington, is there? After I worked so hard to save Martin's seat, this is how I'm thanked? I mean, I'm still here for another year of my term. Why now?" I ask. I do realize my voting record put me in the doghouse and is responsible for my premature lame-duck status. I had no idea it would happen so quickly, so publicly. "They need to give me some time."

"They can't. Frankie Dawson needs to fundraise," David says. "Simple as that."

David turns up the volume on the television mounted on my wall, the one that is always on, muted, and tuned to headline news. We watch the Speaker walk to the podium. She gives her usual update, and my shoulders begin to relax. David is wrong, it seems.

"And now I'll take a few questions. Max Brown from the *Times*," she says.

"Thank you, Madam Speaker. My question is regarding Ohio's twelfth district. I heard rumors there is change in the air," he says. I glare at his image on the screen. I hate Max Brown. Why won't he leave the Ashers alone?

"You always find out before I'm ready to tell you, but yes, Congresswoman Asher has made a decision to retire the seat after she completes her husband's final term in office. She has been a fine representative, and we thank her. You know, we all appreciate the thirty-two years of combined service Martin and Jody Asher will have given to our country and their constituents when Jody finishes the term, but it is time for change. I'm excited by the fabulous young woman candidate who has stepped forward to run for the seat. She's already working hard and will be on the ticket in the March primary. Frankie Dawson will be an excellent member of Congress."

As the Speaker takes another question, I drop into Martin's desk chair. I remind myself I have a plan. For a moment, I want to send a donation to Harold Kestler. For a moment, I want to send him an apology and erase all the negative attack ads we ran against him and tell him I'll campaign for him this time around. I think about Jack Dobbs. Charlotte and JJ would probably be glad if their respective parents were on the same side for once.

But that doesn't help me. Not now. I need to focus on my next act—my preservation, my rise to the cabinet. And I need to stay one step ahead of Max Brown or figure out how to get him on my side.

ANONYMOUS STAFFER'S TIPS FOR NEW MEMBERS

The offices of the vice president of the United States are stunning. In the formal ceremonial office in the executive office buildings, next to the White House, the VP sits behind a desk used since Theodore Roosevelt in 1902. And if you pull the drawer open, you'll see the signature of every VP since the 1940s. That little factoid and the thickness of the bulletproof-glass windows—thick, really thick—are my favorites on this tour. Even if you're not a fan of the party in power at the top, go over for a tour.

JODY

Eugene sits behind his historic desk. I know he's reluctant to stand when I enter the room, but he must. I am a woman—a congresswoman, no less.

"Jody, so lovely to see you," he says. "Ah, I should say 'Congresswoman.'"

I wait until his staffer leaves the room and we're alone. "Cut the crap, Eugene. We both know you'd rather see anyone but me."

"Interesting and crude. Have a seat, Jody," he says. He motions to the chair opposite the ceremonial desk.

"Have you signed your name in the drawer yet, or is that for at the end of your time in office?" I ask.

"I have another three years to get around to that. Well, if the president's popularity remains this high, we'll have another term . . . so seven years." He smiles. Eugene Acton is a tall, slender man who reminds me of a serial killer. I don't know why, but he's lost all his former appeal. He was something to look at back in our undergrad days, I'll tell you.

"Yes, the president is popular. You, not as much," I say. "Look, I need a favor."

"I figured. I need to stay away from you, so I doubt I can help. That article by Brown. Well, he got close to me. I don't think I should formalize our connection by helping you in any way."

"Yes, that was quite close to you. And you are guilty of taking all that dark Chinese money. But Martin died. The story went away. You're lucky. But you owe me. I need you to put in a good word for me. I'd like to be Secretary of Education. In return, please tell the president and the powers that be I will support Frankie Dawson's run. I think this is a good deal for all of us."

"I'm supposed to stick my neck out for you?" Eugene asks. He leans back in his chair, steeples his long fingers.

I take a moment to look around the room and take in the huge chandeliers, the ceiling and walls decorated with allegorical symbols of the navy, the mahogany floors, the black-marble fireplaces. This room exudes history and importance. Eugene does not.

"Yes. For Martin. For his memory. You guys were friends," I say. It's true; they were. "I'm assuming that changed only because of the story."

"Martin introduced me to the wrong people," Eugene says.

"You asked him to. You wanted new donors, additional campaign-funding streams," I say.

His eyes widen. "How would you know anything about that?"

I take a deep breath and shrug my shoulders. "I have a great résumé." I pull it out of my briefcase and slide it across the desk. "I love public education."

"Didn't your daughter go to a private school?" he asks with a smirk.

"I will be a loyal member of the cabinet."

"You haven't even voted with the party most of the time since you got here," he says.

"But here, in the cabinet, I will follow the president's lead. I will. I admire him very much. Please tell him that," I say.

"Why don't you tell him yourself?" he asks. He likely knows the answer but wants to hear me admit I've been kicked off his committee. I won't give him the pleasure.

"Well, he's busy, and you have his ear. I've asked to leave the Women in Power group. I just don't have the time. Anyway, as soon as you formally submit my name for a cabinet position, I'll hold a press conference and wholeheartedly support Frankie Dawson. I'll say glowing things about you and the president. You'll never have a bigger fan. Just like the good times long ago." I stand and extend my hand. I hope he doesn't make me threaten him further. "Do we have a deal?"

Eugene stands, hands on his hips. "I'll try. That's all I can promise."

"That's not enough. Think about everything Martin did for you," I say. "He shared everything with me, you know. Everything. And of course, there's the little secret between you and me."

Finally, he extends his hand. "You have a deal."

"Great. I'll see myself out. Oh, and Eugene, how long do these things take to fill, these positions?" I ask.

"Cabinet? Months, usually," he says. "The president won't want to appoint a sitting member of Congress. Our majority is too tight. If he decides to appoint you, it won't be until after the November election."

"Well, I suppose I can wait a year," I say. "Time flies when you're having fun."

As I walk out the door, my phone rings. It's Charlotte.

"Mom, I'm at the hospital."

"Oh my God, are you OK?"

"Yes, I'm in labor. Are you coming?" she asks.

Great—just what I needed to make me feel even older. I'm going to be a grandma. I remember Charlotte is on the line. "I'm on my way."

"Oh, and Mom, if it's a boy, we're going to name him Martin Asher Dobbs but call him Asher," she says. "In Dad's memory."

"I'm surprised you didn't have to name him after his other grandfather, Jack," I say. I'm smugly pleased that she isn't adding in Jack's name.

I've barely thought of him since the election, and thankfully, Charlotte and JJ never entertain me when Jack and Margaret are visiting. JJ says his dad is back to playing golf and ignoring politics. Likely a good outcome for him, as he wasn't successful at backing a candidate.

"We have enough Dobbs men with J names," she says. "Hurry. The contractions are coming closer together."

"And if it's a girl? Will you name her Jody in my honor?" I ask.

"No, Mom, that's not on the table," she says. "Got to go!"

"Good luck," I say before we end the call.

OK, fine, I'll go by the hospital. I know it's the "right" thing to do, but since when have I cared about that?

Babies are great for social media, though. I smile at that thought. Grandma's on her way, baby. This baby may be just the thing I need to soften my image and get back in the party's good graces. My appointment is a shoo-in now with Eugene's backing and a cute little grandchild. I've been reading up. Cabinet secretaries have so much freedom. They can travel the world for fact-finding and to learn diverse best practices to implement back home. And they are invited to all types of events, including Davos. This is all going to be so wonderful.

ANONYMOUS STAFFER'S TIPS FOR
NEW MEMBERS

Now that you're in Congress, you'll need a district office (at least one) and a DC office. These both need to be staffed, and your budget is tight, so pick well. If you pay too much to the district director, for example, your chief of staff will know and be mad. And vice versa. It's a juggling act. Who holds the most power? You'll have to decide. Good luck. Very few offices achieve a healthy working relationship between district and DC. That's just a fact. You'll see on your calendar that you have assigned district workweeks. Those are the times you are to be in your district, working for your constituents. In reality, most of that time will be spent working on your own reelection, but you'll do some ribbon cuttings and the like and call it district work.

JODY

It has been at least six months since I've been back in the district. Flying into Columbus reminded me of working together with Mimi to win this seat. It seems like such a long time ago now. Back when we had a common purpose, a common enemy. We haven't spoken since the night she left me to pick up the tab at the restaurant in Eastern Market.

Sometimes I'm saddened by our estrangement. Some nights, I wake up in a panic, imagining Mimi holding a press conference and revealing all the Ashers have done to undermine democracy. But mostly I'm grateful for our détente of sorts. It has given me time to pick my next job in the cabinet, time to vote with my caucus and not with Mimi's client. I've had space to breathe and not worry about other people's expectations. That's all Frankie Dawson's problem now, thank God. I'm sure Mimi is intimately involved in Frankie's future. And all I can think is *good riddance*.

Besides, I've had grandma duties to attend to—at least that's what all the people who follow me on social media think. Including my district director, Peggy, who is the kindest person on earth. If I told her I could never leave DC because of my grandson, she's sappy enough to believe me.

I just used little baby Asher as an excuse to delay the in-person Frankie lovefest for as long as possible. I also didn't want to announce my retirement from Congress before my name was attached to the cabinet position. But I'm under a lot of pressure. The March primary is in three weeks. Frankie will win the primary—no other Democrat is running, and my name isn't on the ballot, but the party wants me to campaign with her, to transfer whatever goodwill is left from the Ashers to her. It's frustrating, but here I am.

I smile at Peggy, who's waiting like a well-trained dog next to the door. Our district office is in a drab, cheap retail strip mall. I've never liked it, but Martin said the price of the lease was right.

"Hi, Peggy, good to see you," I say.

"Welcome, Congresswoman. So good to have you in the district finally. How's the grandbaby doing?" she asks.

"He's just great. I'm sure you've seen his photos on my social media," I say. The baby is photogenic, I'll give him that. He takes after Martin, and me a bit. There is very little Dobbs in that tiny person. I like visiting him every Sunday, when my schedule permits. I hold him. Charlotte takes a photo. We post it on my socials, and my fans love it. And my daughter, well, she's head over heels for the little guy. She's a kind, devoted mother. That's nature over nurture for you.

I look around now and wonder why the office is so empty. Shouldn't they all be dying to see me? "Where is the rest of the staff?"

"Oh, they're setting up for the press conference," Peggy says. "We are so excited to have an event here. It's been so long. And of course, we rented the space next door for the afternoon so we don't mix official business with the campaign. We need to be careful."

"Of course," I say and follow her through our dingy office space, which is decorated with yard signs from over the years; government-issued, beat-up office furniture; and one plant, through a door and into another dismal, empty space. It's all quite homey; that's what it is. Peggy and her team were with Martin for years and joyfully carried on when I was elected. They're capable and efficient, performing constituent services with glee. I can't even imagine the mundane duties, but it gives these public servants all such pleasure.

"Say, what will happen to all of you if Frankie Dawson wins?" I ask. I haven't thought about their futures—only my own, of course. It's survival of the fittest, it really is.

"Miss Dawson came here and met with me. Asked me to work for her," Peggy says. A big smile crosses her plain face. "Of course, since you're retiring, I said yes!"

Without asking me first. Charming. I paste on my biggest fake member-of-Congress smile. "Great!"

The empty room now turned press conference site is pathetic. They've taped a yard sign from the special election to a beat-up half podium that sits on top of a beat-up desk. This is not what you'd call going out in a blaze of glory. But, I remind myself, I will elevate my status soon as a member of the cabinet.

"Hi, Congresswoman," says someone I don't know. "We're so honored to have you here."

I make a note that I should have come to the district more often. If I had wanted to run again, I'm sure I would have. Right?

"Thank you, dear," I tell the eager young woman. "Lovely job with the podium."

"Tammy says all three TV stations will be here. Isn't that something?" she says.

There's a buzz in the back of the room. I turn around and watch as Frankie Dawson, wearing a white pantsuit, blows into the room. Her red hair catches the eye, that's for sure.

I stand and wait for her to come to me. That's how it's done. She takes huge strides, and she's next to me in a moment.

"Frankie Dawson. Congresswoman, it's so nice to meet you finally," she says. I stare at the American flag pin on her lapel.

Instinctively, I touch the member pin on mine. "Well, here we are. When do we start this thing?"

Peggy says, "They'll be here in ten minutes. This will give you two a moment to catch up, strategize."

Frankie Dawson has the support of the party leadership, the Democratic fundraising machine, and the president. I'm simply an obligation at this point, someone to be patted on the head and placed in the trash. Until I join the cabinet. I can't wait for that moment. I stare at Frankie.

"Harold Kestler is a pretty formidable opponent, I'll tell you that much," I say. "And he did build up some good name recognition during our campaign. And he's got money."

"You really beat him up last cycle. I plan to continue to hit him where you wounded him," she says. "Your campaign was run so well. That's why I'm so excited to have Mimi Smith helping me."

"She's helping you? That's strange," I say. "I didn't realize she intended to be so regularly involved in congressional campaigns. I thought when she came on board my campaign, it was just a favor for a friend. We go way back. We went to law school together; our husbands were friends."

"Oh, I know. We go way back too. She's my godmother, if you can believe it," Frankie says. "She and my mom came to the States to study at the same time."

"From China?" I ask.

"Yes. They grew up in the same village. And don't say it: I know I got all of my dad's Irish features, unfortunately," she says. "I don't look half-Chinese, but I am."

Mimi strikes again. She's surprising. I knew she had Chinese heritage, but I had no idea she'd grown up there. She never mentioned her early years. It was as if she were fully American by the time we met in law school. I make a mental note to investigate Mimi's family—her village, her past—and have my team do a deep dive on Frankie while they're at it. "You fooled me, that's for sure."

Frankie smiles.

Peggy says, "Oh, the camera crews are here. Are you ready? Miss Dawson, do you have any signage with you?"

Frankie says, "I thought you'd never ask. Bring the sign in!"

A staffer hurries in, struggling to carry a huge rolled-up banner. I watch, bemused, as they hang the DAWSON FOR CONGRESS sign on the wall. It dominates the room.

"Well played. Likely Mimi's suggestion?" I ask.

"Of course. She's involved in everything," Frankie says.

"Of course she is," I say. "Let's get this over with."

We step up to the podium, and I don't waste any time. "Thank you for being here. On behalf of my husband, Martin, and me, thank you for allowing us to serve you for thirty-two years. We hope to have helped all who needed it, and we hope we made you proud. This isn't the last you'll hear of Jody Asher. I have been tapped to help at the cabinet level in the new history-making administration. But today isn't about me, so please join me in welcoming the next congresswoman representing the twelfth district, Frankie Dawson!"

I step aside as Frankie rambles on about her campaign promises, the same ones we always made. My mind drifts to Mimi, and I wonder why she never mentioned knowing Frankie's mom. She never told me about that close personal connection. But why would she? Neither of us has any use for the other, not anymore. I have my plans, and she is passionately implementing hers as we speak.

I spot her now, standing in the back of the room, her expensive black designer suit a stark contrast to the shabby surroundings.

We do not smile when we make eye contact. I find something interesting in Frankie's words and look away.

I don't need Mimi anymore. And obviously, the feeling is mutual. As long as she stays out of my way, I'll stay out of hers for now. I have been adding to my list of other congressmen on her payroll, building my case against her. If Frankie wins, I'll add her name.

Mimi should know I could ruin her just as easily as she could ruin me. Martin told me everything. I intimated that much at dinner. I watched her blink. So we have a mutual standoff, one she thinks she's winning. But at any moment, I could expose her for what she really is.

She must know that. I hope she's worried. Because when the time is right, when I'm more powerful than she is, I will destroy her.

MIMI LEUNG SMITH'S FAVORITE CHINESE PROVERBS:

Don't try to prove what people suspect, or you'll make your guilt still more obvious.

The player is lost; the watcher is lucid.

Soldiers don't hate deceit.

MIMI

And there she is at the press conference, tucked into the corner on a folding chair, nervous and jittery, like she's sitting on a carpet of needles. And now she's staring at me. Oh, I see you, Jody; don't worry. I am enjoying watching you shrink in the face of the new congressional candidate, fading under her bright light. I know it's hard. She's young and beautiful and has a real—albeit embellished—résumé behind her.

I see you, Jody, and your rice is cooked. While I'd like to eliminate you, my team has decided surveillance is warranted for now. If you do happen to be granted a position in the cabinet, then and only then will we become cordial again. I saved your sad little voice mail, the one begging me to be your friend again.

How ridiculous.

I turn my attention to the ugly podium as Frankie finishes her speech. I remind myself to smile and applaud. This will be my only visit to this district for this campaign, although Frankie believes I will be hands-on. No, I did that once, and we saved the seat, but I will not be wasting my valuable time here. Frankie is quite capable, and Harold is wounded. We will win this seat again. My work here is done.

In the meantime, Spencer and I have turned some of our focus to matters back home. The client has asked us to assist with the social credit–system rollout. The system digitally pulls every aspect of your life together and provides a score, so to speak. Like a credit rating. If your score is high, you are considered a good person and can move freely in society. Bad people, criminals and the like, will be contained. I love the social order of my home country. The chaos that is this country cannot last. And neither can our jobs here.

Most of what I have done these past thirty years is now possible to accomplish virtually. I'm one of the last noncyber consultants, as we're called, a physical presence who infiltrated the highest echelons of power. My success is well known, and my rewards will be vast.

I smile at the thought as I meet Jody's stare. We've made a good team of sorts, all these years. And now it's only a matter of time before I disappear. I'll wait until Frankie Dawson is sworn in and tie up a couple of other loose ends. I am not in any hurry. Jody won't appreciate it, but when I do decide to leave, it will be a spectacular, eye-opening exit that will destroy everyone in my network here.

It's just the way these things are done. As Sun Tzu wrote, "The opportunity to secure ourselves against defeat lies in our own hands, but the opportunity of defeating the enemy is provided by the enemy himself."

ANONYMOUS STAFFER'S TIPS FOR NEW MEMBERS

Every once in a while, try to plan something fun for your team. A baseball game together, dinner or drinks out. They'll appreciate it, if they like you and respect you. If they don't, they'll think it's a chore. That's when you'll see who is loyal and who needs to go. Get rid of the ones who complain about having fun.

JODY

I sit on the couch in my office and watch TV. I don't have much of anything else to do. Truth be told, I am a little sad today, despite the pleasant May weather. Of course I still haven't heard a peep about the cabinet position, but I'm trying to be patient. The reason for my sadness, aside from the abject boredom associated with being a lame-duck member of Congress, is that today is the day of my favorite event: the First Lady's Luncheon.

As a spouse, this event was the highlight of my year. I would think about my outfit for months. I sparkled in the VIP party room before the event and made sure I was one of the clicks—or photos—with the First Lady, no matter the party. Each First Lady tells the committee how many clicks she'll do before the event starts. It's a special thanks to big donors and the committee members. Only one First Lady has ever limited clicks in recent history. But even then, I was one of them.

I always volunteered to be on the planning committee and worked my way up so that this year, if I hadn't been elected to Congress, I would have been the chairwoman of the entire event. I would have picked the theme, selected all the flower arrangements and the dresses for the Junior Hostesses, who are presented each year at the event. I'll never forget how proud I was when Charlotte walked the red-carpet runway in front of the thousands of guests in attendance.

As a member of Congress, I'm invited to attend, but I'm no longer on the committee. Truth be told, I'm no longer relevant in that social circle. I can't take this much longer. I need an answer from Eugene. I need to know my next steps.

"David, come in here," I yell. I know he can hear me in his office on the other side of the door.

"What is it, ma'am?" he asks, swooping in the door like a frightened owl. "What's wrong now?"

"Nothing. I'm bored," I say.

"Apologies, but that's what happens when you announce you're retiring. Everything evaporates," he says. "Though with your cabinet play, you have garnered some attention."

"What do you mean?" I ask.

"Max Brown called this morning. Wants to interview you," he says. "I told him to fuck off."

"Good," I say.

"He's so annoying. You'd think he'd move on. In fact, I thought he had. Haven't heard from him since he asked the Speaker that question and she fired you," David says.

"She didn't fire me. I wanted to move on, move up," I say.

"Max said he doesn't think you're qualified to be a cabinet member," David says.

"He's not qualified to be a journalist," I say. "Maybe I will speak to him. Try to convince him he's wrong about me. I'm perfect for the job."

"Not a good idea, Congresswoman. I'd leave it alone," David says.

"Call him back. Tell him I'll talk to him. Today," I say. "Don't worry. I can handle this."

Once David leaves the room, I place a call to Eugene. I'm sure his wife, Betty Ann, is enjoying herself at the grand luncheon. I picture her, fat and happy, up on the riser at the head table as a guest of honor. She will be the one to introduce the First Lady. Yes, I'm jealous.

"The vice president's office," a staffer says, answering what I thought was Eugene's private line.

"I'd like to speak to Eugene, please. It's Congresswoman Asher. It's important," I say.

"One moment," she says. "Oh, I'm sorry, Congresswoman Asher, but the vice president has stepped out to a meeting. He will return your call."

Funny. He seems to run from the office every time I phone. "Tell the vice president that I expect his call this afternoon, at the latest. Thank you."

I mean, how dare he stonewall me like this?

David pops his head through the door. "Max Brown is here."

"Here? In the office?" I ask. "Wow, that was fast."

"He's eager to speak to you," he says. "Shall I send him in?"

I take a deep breath. At least this won't be boring. "Yes, thank you."

Max Brown shuffles through the door from the reception area. I stand and point to the couch across the coffee table from the one I've been sitting on all day.

"Thank you for seeing me, Congresswoman Asher," he says. He's such a stereotypical print reporter. Disheveled hair, too long and messy; wrinkled shirt. If he's trying to make me think he's harmless, he's mistaken. I'll never forget the damage he did to Martin, to me, to our reputation.

"What do you want?" I ask and sit.

"Here's the thing: I don't know what you know about all of your husband's dealings, but you certainly were the beneficiary of a lifestyle beyond a congressman's means for almost thirty years," he says.

"My husband had family money, not that it's your business," I say. I can feel the anger rising, but I must keep my cool.

"No, he didn't. Neither did you. You see, I thought the story was just his shady dealings with Joe Roscoe. Literally got a tip that your husband picked up an envelope of cash from a drop site on the Friday of your daughter's wedding. That's gutsy, especially since he knew I was onto this," Max says.

"I don't know what you're talking about," I say.

"Fine. But there's more, isn't there? Your campaign manager, Mimi Smith . . . you all go way back. In fact, she and her husband went to law school with the two of you, and now they run the Smith Institute, a lobbying firm disguised as a think tank with close ties to China. There's no difference, is there?" he says.

"I wouldn't know," I say. I examine my manicure and decide I'm in need of a touch-up.

"The Smith Institute is an official partner of the Chinese Academy of Social Sciences in Beijing. That academy is a front for the Communist government," he says.

Ah yes, Max, you're correct. I make sure to keep my expression neutral as I ponder my response. Martin and I were guests of the academy on many trips to Beijing. Max must know that. They were just innocent cultural exchanges. Of course that's all it was. There is an excuse for everything, a cover for every move. I take a deep breath. Martin would be proud.

I look up at Max and meet his gaze. "I don't know what you're asking me. None of this is relevant to me. Go after Mimi and Spencer; I'm fine with that. I've got another appointment, so if you'll excuse me . . ."

"Are you a foreign agent?" he asks, standing up.

"Don't be ridiculous," I say. "I am a member of the United States Congress. You have done enough damage to my family. Get out!"

Max Brown smirks. He seems pleased. "I'm going. But this story isn't over. By the way, I hear there's about to be an announcement about the Secretary of Education."

"For once, you've heard something correctly," I say with a smile. "I'm looking forward to serving."

He shakes his head and opens the door. "You're not the one being nominated, I'm afraid, Congresswoman Asher."

"You're wrong," I call after him. My heart beats wildly in my chest. Eugene better not let me down. My hands clench into fists. "I will be Secretary of Education."

I hear him chuckle as he walks out the door. "No. It's Adele Wise. The announcement is imminent."

After he leaves my office, I realize I'm shaking. He seems to know more than I do about the cabinet. He also knows a lot about Mimi. Perhaps the enemy of my enemy will be my friend again.

I pull out my burner phone and call Mimi's private number. She answers, which is a surprise.

"What do you want?" she asks.

Charming. "How's the Dawson campaign going?" I ask. Pleasantries aside, she's caught me off guard with her tone, so I pretend to care about Frankie Dawson.

"She's likely going to win. Not by a large margin, though. Kestler's doing a good job," she says. "I don't have time to talk."

"Oh, how am I? Thanks for asking. I'm not so good. I haven't heard about the cabinet position. You promised to help if I stepped aside for Frankie Dawson," I say.

"I've done all I can. I've got to go," Mimi says. She hangs up.

I pitch my phone across the room, enjoying the sound of impact.

David opens the door without knocking. "I'm so sorry, Mrs. Asher."

"What?"

"You didn't get the cabinet position," he says. "The president just announced it in the press briefing. He selected the wife of former senator Wise. They are big donors. Adele Wise will be the new Education Secretary."

I turn around so he cannot see the rage in my eyes. I have been set up. I have been played, by all of them. And they think I will just go away; the widow will retreat to her townhome, spend time with her grandson.

How dare they? I trusted Eugene to come through. I did everything the party asked. Mimi, too, for that matter. I even had that ridiculous press event with Frankie Dawson. I fell prey to their deception.

They have all pushed me too far. It is time for revenge.

I leave my office through the back door, not bothering to tell David where I've gone. For all I know, he's been part of this big lie. From now on, I will trust no one, no one except Martin.

The art of the campaign is much like the art of war. There will be casualties. Make sure you get them before they get you, no matter what it takes. You must stay one step ahead and document everything. You never know when you'll need it. But when you need it, you'll have it. Use it.

—Congressman Martin Asher

JODY

As I pull the suitcase out from under the bed, my heart skips a beat for a moment. What if it's empty? But as I enter our code and the lock pops open, I see everything is as I left it. I take a deep breath of relief.

"Dearest Jody," Martin had written on a Post-it note attached to the foreign bank accounts. "As we've always discussed, if anything ever happens to me, this is all you need. Use it. Enjoy life. It's over too soon. I love you."

A ping of sadness works its way through me, but I chase it away. We were a good team, Martin and I.

Before I pull out the folders Martin left for me, I grab the one I created. It is labeled FRANKIE DAWSON. After I discovered Mimi was her godmother, after I found out she would be stealing the Asher seat, I had our opposition research team go to work.

I enjoy rereading what the researcher discovered: Frankie Dawson is not who she seems. Her résumé is fake. Check references. She never worked at Facebook; she worked for a nonprofit. Everything about her is manufactured. The party likes her because she's a young woman, biracial, and supposedly tech savvy. She's fooled them. She also has ties to Mimi and Spencer deeper than ours. Do not endorse her. She is not suitable to be a member of Congress. Here is a list of alternate candidates. All the information you need to prove she is a fraud is detailed in the attached.

I close the folder. I wonder if Martin would agree to sabotaging our party's candidate if it meant Jack Dobbs's candidate would win the Asher seat?

I smile. Of course he would, if he knew what Mimi and the rest have done to me.

I put the Dawson research folder aside. I pull out an accordion file labeled VP. Inside are a small recorder and more documents clipped together behind a cover page, which is again written in Martin's hand. I'm already familiar with the contents of this folder. I listened to the recording the night I brought the contents of the safe home.

Eugene has been foolish to cross me. He really has. I decide it's time to call him again. At home. I'm sure he's listening to his wife drone on about the First Lady's Luncheon. He'll enjoy the distraction. Ha.

I dial the number, and my call is forwarded to voice mail.

"Hello, Eugene. This is Congresswoman Asher. Look, I'm a bit upset here because I am supposed to be the Secretary of Education. You promised me. Others promised me. That's why I agreed to give up my seat, the Asher seat," I say. I keep a smile on my face to keep my tone sounding friendly.

"Thing is, Martin left me with something that's yours. I know you'd love to have it, but so would others. If you don't want it to fall into the wrong hands, you'll do the right thing and get me in the cabinet. I don't know what's left—the Interior, maybe—but I don't care. Surprise me! And please give my regards to Betty Ann. I was so sorry to miss the First Lady's Luncheon. I'll call her soon to catch up, maybe talk about old times. That would be fun, wouldn't it? Bye!"

I hang up and reflect on Eugene Acton, my college boyfriend. I thought we'd be together forever because I was young and desperate to get away from my mom and my life, and leave everything behind.

Eugene said he felt the same, about everything. Until he met Betty Ann, the heir to a mustard fortune. I was everything Eugene ever wanted, except rich. Sweet Betty Ann Lowery came into the picture after we'd been together a year. Virginal, pure as the driven snow, and driving the newest-model BMW—white, of course. Eugene wasn't the only one whose head she turned, but he was the only one for her.

I couldn't compete, not with that sweet southern drawl, the fancy restaurant meals, the swirl of specialness. When he broke up with me, Eugene said he'd love me forever, but he had to move on. He was so sorry but hoped I'd understand. We stood on the lawn outside my dorm room. I could feel the prying eyes of other students watching us from their windows.

"And, Jody," Eugene said, his voice calm—loving, even. "Betty Ann doesn't know we slept together. I mean, sure, she knows we went on dates and all. But she doesn't believe in that before marriage. So, well, can we keep that as our little secret, please?"

I laughed. "You are ridiculous. You're starting a relationship on a lie? Pretending you've never had sex? In college?" I was disgusted, angry. I knew this was coming; I'd heard the rumors. And of course, I'd scoped out her dorm room, even took a few rings she'd never miss. I saw the photo of the two of them pinned to her bulletin board. I read his love note to her. In fact, it was in my pocket as he broke up with me.

"I'm in love. I hope you'll respect that and that you'll find someone too. You're—well, very special, Jody," Eugene said. His words felt like a slap across my face. *Special?* What did that mean?

"Please. We are so good together, we are. I know you love me," I said, begging him like a fool.

"It's over. I'm in love with someone else. Just accept that," Eugene said. His voice grew angrier; the pity was fading into hate.

"It's the money, isn't it? That's what I don't have," I said.

His patience was gone. "It's not that. She has everything you're lacking." He touched his chest. "She has a heart."

272

I didn't tell him he was probably right. I didn't say anything more. I pulled the note out of my pocket and tossed it at his face. As I walked away, he called after me.

"This is what I'm talking about, Jody. This is wrong. How did you get this?"

I opened the door to the dorm and turned around. "I guess we all have our secrets, don't we? Good night, Eugene."

Had I hoped he'd come back to me? Of course. He was my first real boyfriend, although he is correct that I don't love well, especially not back then. Not now, either, truth be told.

I stand up and stretch. The past is just that, except now I need Eugene to come through for me, and I suspect, now that I've reminded him of all he can lose, he'll do the right thing.

It's four o'clock: the perfect time to pitch the assignment editor at the local television station in Columbus. I wonder which one will do the best job with the Frankie Dawson takedown. Channel 4, the NBC affiliate, always treated Martin well. Channel 10, the CBS affiliate, once ran a story on me, interviewing so-called experts about whether a widow would be qualified to be a candidate for Congress.

I call Channel 4's assignment desk from my burner phone. As I suspected, they are eager to run the story after I promise to forward the details of Frankie Dawson's big con. I don't divulge her ties to Mimi and Spencer and the Smith Institute. Doing so would likely reveal too much about me. Besides, I want to take Mimi down more directly, more spectacularly.

There soon will be a perfect opportunity to reveal exactly who Mr. and Mrs. Smith really are.

My phone lights up with a call. "Why, Eugene, what a pleasant surprise."

"Knock it off, Jody," he says. "I don't appreciate being threatened by you."

"I don't know what you mean. I am not threatening you. I'm asking you to keep your promise. I was to be Secretary of Education," I say. I walk to the window and watch a group of high school kids hurrying down the street. The energy, the potential, their futures filled with major disappointment because their dreams won't come true.

"I tried. I did. What do you have? Tell me," he says. I can feel his panic through the phone. His breathing is short, ragged.

"Calm down, Eugene. It's just a little recording of you and Martin talking about money, that's all," I say.

"Oh my God." He exhales. "He recorded me?"

"Insurance. Smart, right?" I ask. "I need an important position in the administration, Eugene. Or Max Brown will get an interesting tip with audio proof. There's so much I can tell him."

"It will bring you down too," he says.

"Nope. Just you. And Martin, but Martin is OK with that now," I say. He would be. He's the one who left it for me.

"You're going to need to give me some time," Eugene says. "Just . . . don't do anything rash, please. And leave Betty Ann out of this."

Oh, so gallant. So pathetic. "You never told her about us, did you? About everything that happened? You are so pathetic."

"Jody, just give me a couple months. Please. I beg you," he says.

"Sure, Mr. Vice President. I'll give you a couple of months. But I'm out of office January third. I'd like to know what the future holds," I say.

"Why don't you just enjoy your grandchild? Enjoy the nest egg Martin left for you," he says.

"What nest egg? Martin was a public servant throughout our marriage. You're the one with the rich wife, Eugene," I say.

"I have as much on Martin as he has on me. Both of you are corrupt. I know it. I could help everyone see it. You've been on the take for years. Roscoe is just the tip of the iceberg," he says. "China, Russia. There's no end to the Ashers' greed."

I turn away from the window and walk to the bar cart. It's time for a cocktail.

"Only matched by your own. I know you won't say a word about any of that, Eugene. Remember, I have the proof. You have nothing. Get me a position. Oh, by the way, I would be open to an ambassadorship. I've always been fond of Switzerland," I say. "I've always been a natural diplomat, don't you agree? And the cheese fondue, the crisp air, the mountains. Yes, I'm well suited for Switzerland."

"Give me some time." Eugene hangs up.

I pour myself a drink. I think about the other manila folder from Martin's safe and the note written in his stiff handwriting on the cover.

> Dearest Jody,
>
> Remember when I promised we'd be rich someday? Inside this folder, you'll find the treasure—an insurance policy, so to speak, for you and our daughter. Our annual trips to Davos provided a perfect cover for me to set these things up. Unfortunately, since you're reading this, I am dead or incapacitated. Since I am gone, you also will receive a visit from a Russian friend. Accept his gift when offered, my dear. Imagine it is from me as a final farewell.
>
> Please don't forget Charlotte. She loves you. I know she has JJ and his family's money, but sharing is caring. I think you'll find you have more than enough for your lifetime and hers. I love you, as well as anyone could, and I apologize for my mistakes.
>
> Yours truly,
> Martin

I glance at my watch, my gift from Martin via the Russians, and miss him more. I am not certain how much money is in the accounts I found listed inside the folder or why he didn't access any of them to pay for the wedding. Likely, it would have been flagged internationally. I hear it's tough to set them up, tough to cash them out. Truth is, I didn't know any of them existed. I heard Martin's promises about a light at the end of the tunnel, a golden future when we were ready. I thought it was hyperbole and appeasement. Turns out, it was a fact. I slip off the watch. A sequence of numbers is engraved on the back. I imagine they are the code to another Swiss account in addition to the ones in the folder.

Oh, Martin.

Sometimes you can believe promises politicians make. Not often. But sometimes.

The State Department's Guide for New Ambassadors

The Residence of the Ambassador of the United States in Bern, Switzerland

The residence of the Ambassador of the United States in Bern is situated on the grounds of what was once a nineteenth-century cottage called "Blumenrain," and it has been expanded and upgraded over the years. This is a spectacular assignment, should you be chosen. The staff is seasoned and professional; the house, magnificent. The country, well, perfection. And Bern is a short five-minute walk away. Enjoy!

JODY

Rayburn House Office Building

It's finally November, and I'm scrolling through the US Embassy site for the hundredth time. I've become enchanted by Blumenrain, the US Ambassador to Switzerland's residence. Its history and elegance intrigue me, as does the fact I am rumored to be in line for this appointment. And, of course, easy access to the bank accounts makes my heart thump with excitement.

Eugene says he has been "working hard," whatever that means.

I look at my watch and realize it's time. It's David's last day. Too bad, David. He bet on the wrong horse, again. With Frankie Dawson's defeat and Harold Kestler's win, David is out of a future job with Frankie, and I'm tired of seeing his drawn face around here. Besides, it's not like there is much to do now that the party is ignoring me. I have no committee assignments, and I basically just attend the paltry number of events that still land in my in-box. I need to keep my profile up in DC. But the truth is, I'm bored. DC has become boring. Maybe it always was?

My legislative staffers mostly have abandoned ship for other offices, and those who haven't will jump into new congressional offices once the next class is sworn in. There will be plenty of freshman Democrats to choose from. We swept the midterms, except for Ohio's twelfth. A shocking upset. Ha.

David sticks his head through the door. "I guess this is goodbye."

More like good riddance. "Yes. It is."

"I hope you get another position in the administration," he says.

"And I hope you find another chief of staff job," I say.

We're both lying.

"Oh, Harold Kestler is in the lobby. Do you want to see him?" he asks.

Interesting. "Sure, why not," I say. We shake hands. "Goodbye, David."

David exits for the last time as the intern shows Harold Kestler in the door. It seems like forever since I first saw him at the rehearsal dinner where he humiliated me, forever since I humiliated him in our debate and defeated him in the special election. And now here he is, the next representative of Ohio's twelfth district. I haven't run into Jack Dobbs yet, but I'll find a way to let them know I made this win of Harold's possible. They owe me.

"Thank you for seeing me, Congresswoman," Harold says. The spring is back in his step, and his eyes gleam as he takes in my office. "Wow. This is stunning."

"Yes, it's what thirty-two years in office will do for you," I say. "Have a seat."

"I'll be in a basement office somewhere," he says. "But I'll work my way up."

I don't care either way. I shrug. "What can I do for you?"

"Oh, nothing. I just wanted to thank you for helping me be a better campaigner the second time around. And to thank you for leaking the dirt—I mean, facts—about Frankie Dawson." He leans forward. "I know it was you."

Ah, that was such a sweet defeat. The news media pounced on all the juicy tidbits I provided and even found more of their own. By the time the election rolled around, even the DCCC had pulled their funding of her campaign, diverting it to other winnable seats. Poor Frankie. Poor Mimi. Too bad, Madam Speaker.

I smile at Harold because I can't help myself. "Don't be ridiculous. Why would I help you? You're a Republican. You embarrassed me and my husband at our daughter's wedding," I say, folding my arms in front of me.

"All true, Congresswoman. But you were more upset that the party forced you out, angry about Dawson and her lack of respect for you. You hated her more than you hate me," he says. He stands up and takes in my office some more. "Look at that view of the Capitol. I cannot believe I will be working inside that amazing building. Anyway, thank you. And good luck on your next appointment. I hope you get what you deserve."

"Likewise," I tell him. "Oh, and Harold? You do know it will be tough for you to keep the Asher seat. The party will do everything possible to take it back."

"Well, we'll see. I suspect the constituents will welcome a congressman who actually does the work. I mean, your husband's measly three bills in thirty years is a pretty low bar. I'm confident I can deliver results. It won't be hard to look better than the Ashers," he says. "Good afternoon, Congresswoman."

I come close to throwing a brass American eagle–shaped paperweight at his retreating figure, but I don't. I'm beyond caring about Harold Kestler. But I do make a note to donate to his opponent next cycle.

It's the least I can do to help make sure he's a one-term wonder.

It's time to check in with Eugene, something that has become a weekly ritual. He is running out of time.

"Vice President Acton here," he says. Someone must be in the room for him to use the formal title.

"Congresswoman Asher here," I say.

"Good to hear from you. Say, I have my chief here with me, and you're on speakerphone. And your ears must have been burning, because we have some good news."

I take a deep breath. "What a coincidence. I'm always game to hear good news."

"Congresswoman Asher," the other man says, "on behalf of the president and vice president, we are pleased to offer you the position of Ambassador to Switzerland."

Oh, what a surprise! I'm glad they cannot see me or the huge grin spreading across my face. "What about a position in the cabinet? Isn't that more impressive?"

"I'll take it from here," Eugene says to his chief and then picks up the phone. "Look, Jody, I put my neck out on the line for you with this. You mentioned Switzerland and I got it for you, and now you're complaining? Certain ambassadorships are quite prestigious, and actually, this one is more suitable for your background. I can't believe you're acting like this."

"Calm down, Eugene, I'm just kidding," I say. "I'll take it. Thank you. When do I start?"

I hear a big sigh. "You'll need Senate confirmation, but if all goes well, and it should, January fifteenth. So it's a yes?"

"Yes," I say. I'm already dreaming of cheese fondue and so much more. I'll need to tell Charlotte.

"Your term will be two years—or six, if we manage to get reelected," Eugene says. He drops his voice to a whisper. "Which brings up my final point: I cannot be a part of any scandals, do you understand? I need your word that you'll destroy whatever it is Martin left you."

"Oh, of course, Eugene," I say.

"And you will leave me, and my wife, alone," he says.

"Oh, how sad. No more lunches with Betty Ann, but we did so enjoy our catch-up session. She seems a bit lonely, just a heads-up." I'd invited the Second Lady to lunch a month or so ago to light a fire under

Eugene and remind him I was still waiting for an appointment. I didn't tell Betty Ann about the extent of our college relationship, Eugene and I. That's for another time, perhaps.

"You have a lot of nerve, you know that?" Eugene says.

He should stop talking now. He is the one with everything to lose.

"Well, that's a good quality for an ambassador to have, don't you think? Thanks again," I say.

"The State Department will contact you about the process. Good luck and goodbye."

He means good riddance. I know that. I stand and walk to the window, look out over the Capitol dome. I've been here and done all I could. It's time for a change.

Madam Ambassador. I like it, I really do. I'll keep our townhome for my triumphant return from my European adventure.

More than anything, though, I cannot wait to get my hands on those Swiss bank accounts.

THE STATE DEPARTMENT'S GUIDE FOR NEW AMBASSADORS

You represent our nation to everyone you meet. You are like a walking, talking American flag, spreading goodwill across the world. If you know the local language, please use it. Your host nation will consider it a courtesy. If you don't know the history of the country, please read about it before taking residence to avoid any international embarrassment for yourself and the president.

JODY

Turns out, my only real job as ambassador is to host parties, and that is something I can do with gusto. Unfortunately, they don't need anything from me but my fake ambassador smile and a handshake when I greet guests at the door. The staff is led by the Charge d'Affaires, who is efficient and plans every event to perfection. He seems completely unconcerned about who happens to hold the title of ambassador.

In fact, I could leave right now to travel the world and things would run as smoothly as, perhaps more smoothly than, when I'm in residence. Let's face it: the Swiss don't need me for anything, and Lichtenstein, well, who even knows about them? I didn't. It's a beautiful little slice of the Alps where everyone speaks German and looks at you suspiciously. And even though it's March, it's still cold here, much to my chagrin.

I'd rather be stationed in the Caribbean, but Martin stockpiled our fortune here, not Grand Cayman, so here I will stay. Very rich and quite bored, but happy. As happy as I can be when I've been marginalized. Marginalized and safe. Charlotte and the baby will be here in April.

We will eat fondue. I will practice being a good grandma. The thought makes me cringe.

In the meantime, I do have a few loose ends to tie up.

I have summoned Max Brown for a visit, and he should be here at any moment. I'll receive him here, in the music room. The fireplace is cozy, the furnishings are impressive antiques upholstered in muted grays, and the view of the Alps out the window is breathtaking. This room wows even the snobbiest of my guests.

But I suspect the only things Max will care about are the items in the folder.

I've been torn, I must admit, as to which folder to give to Max. I worry it is too soon to bring Eugene down.

Isn't it better to have him in office and compromised? He takes my calls and so far, has tried to help me.

I decided it was too soon for that little piece of revenge. I will wait until Eugene is out of office, and then I'll forward the recording of him, Martin, and Mimi discussing the donations from leaders of the Chinese Communist Party and what they will expect in return. Eugene is complicit despite his denials and proclamations of innocence, of course, and has done his part, quietly pushing China's interests during his term in office.

He knows what I have on him.

I walk to the corner of the music room and pull on an oil painting, revealing a safe. I punch in the code and slip the VP folder in for safe-keeping, just until I can take it to the bank's safety-deposit box. I pull out the other final folder Martin left for me.

MIMI is written on the tab in his familiar handwriting.

Inside is this letter, the one I just finished crafting.

To Whom it May Concern:
Mimi Leung Smith is the daughter of high-level Chinese Party Members and wealthy factory owners

and intellectuals. She came to the US on a student visa and became an American citizen after marrying Spencer Smith. Together with her husband, she created the Smith Institute, one of the leading think tanks in DC. Mimi Smith is a Chinese Communist spy. She skillfully recruits members of Congress, including my husband. Once you are ensnared by her, it is hard to break free. Martin accepted hundreds of thousands of dollars in cash from her, from the People's Republic of China, over the years. In return, he voted favorably when requested to do so. He blocked legislation that would have hurt China and adamantly defended them as our allies, even as facts to the contrary began to emerge in recent years.

I, Jody Prescott Asher, was not involved in these matters and knew nothing of this until opening the files left for me by Martin in a safe in his congressional office. He was worried about his safety and should have come forward while he was still alive. But he was in too deep.

Although the cash has been spent, I do hope the enclosed documents and records of their interactions and her expectations of Martin through the years will help with your investigation. The People's Republic of China has a skilled operative in Mimi Smith. And it had a completely compromised congressman in my husband. Other members I suspect she has on her payroll include Bob Dyer of Washington, Dan Immel of California, and Tom Carson of Iowa.

Mimi and Spencer Smith are a danger to our democracy. While they appear to be successful business owners and Washington socialites, they are in effect Chinese operatives, some of the last noncyber spies around. You should be able to bring them to justice with the attached.

Sincerely,

Honorable Ambassador Jody Prescott Asher

I close the safe and carry the MIMI folder to the coffee table. I'm ready for my visitor.

"Hello, Ambassador Asher. Nice place you've got here." Max Brown walks into the room, looking as disheveled as usual and as equally out of place here as in my DC office.

"Thank you for coming, Mr. Brown. Have a seat." I point to the couch, a seat next to the fireplace.

"You seem like a natural here," he says. "The environment suits you."

"Oh, you know that's not true. You know I grew up poor as dirt; you told me you researched it all, talked to my mom," I say. My stomach clenches. The hate I feel for this man is tempered only by the knowledge he can help me.

"Well, you've come a long way since then. I mean it. You seem calm, settled," he says.

Looks can be deceiving, young man.

"Thank you, I guess. I have a proposition for you," I say.

"I know. That's why I'm here. On my own dime, as promised. My editors don't know a thing," Max says. "No one knows I'm here. Your staff thinks I'm Winston Able, as instructed. I hope you aren't planning on murdering me."

In my mind, I imagine picking up a gun and shooting him in the forehead, dumping his body in a cold alpine lake. But I digress.

"If I give you a big story, with all the proof and documentation you need, will you leave me and my daughter alone?" I ask.

"Your file is still open. You know the focus of the story was always your husband, his decades of corruption," Max says.

"Poor Martin. He did the best he could. He is not *the* story," I say. Although I must throw Martin under the proverbial bus to implicate Mimi, and to save myself, I know he would understand.

"Your husband was a crook; we both know it," Max says. "Now that you're out of office, I think you're less of a threat, less of a story. I could let it go for something bigger."

I imagine being joined on the couch just now by Eugene Acton on one side and Mimi Smith on the other. Eugene is terrified; Mimi smiles.

"I'm going to need more than your word on that. I'm going to need you to write a story that exonerates me," I say. "I'll need it to run before I give you the contents of this folder."

"I can file something this afternoon, from here. You got lucky. Joe Roscoe does seem to be keeping his mouth shut about the Ashers," Max says. He stands up and walks to the window. The view gets them every time. "You know what? Sure. I'll do it. As long as the scoop you have for me is bigger than a dead congressman's corrupt dealings that his wife *must have* known about all along."

He turns and looks at me. I shrug.

"Can you give me a hint about what's in the folder?"

As Max watches with interest, I pull Martin's notes and records and my letter from the folder. "My husband wrote this all down before he died. It's almost as though he knew he'd need protection someday. Sometimes I wonder if he was murdered. I can't prove that Mimi Smith had anything to do with his death, but we both know she's the one who leaked the photo of Martin and the intern, and then he died," I say.

"True," Max says. "If you knew about all that, why did you make her your campaign manager for your special election?"

"You've heard of keeping your friends close, your enemies closer," I say. I hand him the letter and watch as he reads my words. I think about the path Mimi and I have traveled in the few years since Martin's death:

from friends to partners with the same goal during my campaign to a standoff of sorts while I was in office to now. Now all I want is to ruin her before she ruins me.

He finishes reading and leans back on the couch. "And your husband left all the proof?"

"He did. Dates. Times. Votes. Notes. Cash payment records. Receipts." Of course, I don't add that he didn't make a record of the largest payments. Those were sent here, to my Swiss accounts.

"Why are you doing this? She will come after you, I'd suspect," Max says.

I've considered that, but I don't think she will. If she knows the game is up, she'll return to China. If she doesn't and tries to take me down, well, Max's story will exonerate me. I'm the grieving widow, forced out of her husband's seat. I'm harmless, a lonely ambassador spreading American goodwill across the land. I am the American flag.

"I'm not worried," I say. Besides, I have all the money in the world, and I will use it to hide from Mimi if I need to. "Her value and power evaporate once she is exposed. Once you publish this story, it's all over."

"Let's do this," Max says. "I'll come back tomorrow to pick up the file, after my glowing story about you runs."

I watch Max walk out of the room and take in my new surroundings.

This is a wonderful place to hide. Ask anyone. I think Switzerland is the original hiding place. I'll be content here for as long as Eugene is in office. I'll enjoy the fresh mountain air, as much cheese and chocolate fondue as I can eat. And I'll host parties I don't have to plan or execute. You can never get too much of that.

And then I'll make my move. I already have an idea for my next act.

TWO YEARS LATER

MIMI LEUNG SMITH'S FAVORITE CHINESE PROVERB:

As distance tests a horse's strength, time reveals a person's character.

MIMI

Villa Spencer
Hangzhou, China

Our home on the shore of West Lake is like paradise to me, and Spencer is learning to adjust. He can work anywhere—that's really all he likes to do—and he's happy as long as he enjoys the view from his office. And he does here. The only disruptions to our complete bliss are the mosquitoes that attack me while I stroll through our lush gardens, but I assume the Party will find a solution to them soon enough. We are good at conquering nature here.

My phone lights up with a text from my new employer and neighbor, Joe Wu, a billionaire and cofounder of a global tech venture. So far, he has been pleased with our work, and we have been well rewarded. We have become something like friends. Joe enjoys a good scandal and often asks for detailed descriptions of what happened before I left the United States, stories from inside the Beltway. He especially likes the part about the vice president, and I must agree. It was a well-deserved fall.

Sometimes, on quiet mornings like these, I think about Jody. I tell myself she didn't win when she placed the story about us and our think tank with Max Brown. But she did win. She escalated my departure timeline and left us scrambling to close shop and flee. We made it out, though, because the US government is slow and ineffective against us. I'm heartened when I focus on what will happen when China's dream comes true. I like to think I was a small part of the plan. The hundredth anniversary of the founding of the People's Republic is in 2049, and I hope to live long enough to revel in our victory as we step into the role of the world's superpower.

I take a sip of green tea and smile. Jody may have won our little battle, but China will win the war.

A Guide for New Members of Congress from Mimi Smith of the Smith Institute

Don't take it personally if you don't win reelection, but don't expect to be treated the same either. This town is fickle, and tough. Hold your head high. And if you get caught up in a scandal of your own making, deny, deny, deny; then lie low for a bit. The swamp loves a comeback, almost as much as it loves celebrities, so be patient, and be ready for a triumphant return.

As the Chinese proverb says, "When the winds of change blow, some build walls, while others build windmills."

JODY

Turns out, you can have too much of a good thing. In this case, fondue. And once you do, it's hard to zip up your favorite dresses. I check my reflection in the mirror. I've still got it, but I need to cut out the cheese. As the ambassador, I've been extended an invitation to Davos, my last official duty before the new administration selects their appointee. It's a shame, really, that Eugene brought the president down with him. But that's what happens when you are an unfaithful liar: the truth catches up to you no matter how much you hide it from Betty Ann and the world.

Our daughter—the one Eugene and I gave up for adoption all those years ago when I got pregnant during our undergrad days, the one whose private adoption paid for my college tuition—made quite a splash in the news.

I never suspected Sarah was my daughter. I didn't have any idea, not until I read about it online. I don't know how Mimi found her, but I suspect my mother must have let something slip. I had moved back home during the pregnancy and handled the adoption as quietly as I could, without any help from Eugene. It was so long ago I'd almost put her out of my mind. Almost.

Once Max's story on the Smith Institute ran, Mimi leaked the story of who Sarah's birth parents were to the press. It was her last big salvo before slipping away to China with Spencer. It was shocking, but at least it marked the end of our hold over each other.

Just when I thought I held all the cards, Mimi trumped me with my daughter. I still can't believe she figured out who Sarah was and convinced her to take a job in Martin's office. All to compromise Martin, me, and the vice president. Mimi couldn't have known Martin would flirt with the intern, but that must have played into her plans perfectly. That took a lot of nerve. When I think of Mimi now, how low she would go, I'm disgusted. I'm glad she's exiled to her poor country. Every time I visited Beijing, I was choked by the dirty air. I can't imagine living there, and I'm glad that's her fate. I picture her in some gray-aired agrarian village, her days long and boring.

Despite its importance, the Smith Institute story faded fast in the white-hot light of the vice president's secret love child. Even Max Brown wrote about it. Eugene had always presented a religious, holier-than-thou front. No-sex-before-marriage sort of thing. Ha. And now this. He was the talk of the town.

As for me, for the most part, the press was discreet and sympathetic. I'd been through enough with my husband having an illicit affair with my long-lost biological daughter. Besides, I was in Switzerland, far outside the Beltway. Sorry, Mimi, but your last move didn't hurt me much.

Not like mine hurt you. I chased you out of town, out of the country.

When the press did ask me about Sarah, I kept my comments supportive, saying things like of course it was her right to find her parents and that I wished her well. I was surprised to learn of her identity and stunned by her untoward relationship with my husband. I don't have any interest in a mother-daughter reunification with Sarah, of course, and neither does she. Not with me. Not with anyone, really. Turns out, she is just like her mom, inside and out.

Sarah did pursue a father-daughter relationship with Eugene. I'm assuming it was for the fame his spotlight could provide, and it worked. She's some sort of celebrity with a big social media following now. She has a whole clothing line of love-child items, with a wink and a nod to the vice president as a part of each design. They even appeared on a daytime talk show together. I guess Sarah's appearance by his side softens the blow of his Chinese connections—the recording I gave to Max of Eugene and Martin was damning. Who knows? It works for them, although I cannot imagine what Betty Ann is thinking.

Well, I can. But I don't feel sorry for her. She stole Eugene all those years ago. Karma is . . . well, you know.

Charlotte is trying to understand too. All she said when she called was, "Why didn't you tell me?"

"You know she means nothing to me. I gave her up so long ago," I said. "And I had no idea who she was when she worked for your father, when all that nonsense happened. Of course I didn't, or I would have warned Martin."

"But she is my half sister," she said. "Maybe I'll reach out?"

"That's entirely up to you. But I wouldn't, honey. I'd leave her alone. She seems to be a lot like me, if you get my drift. Your decision, but I'd steer clear. Oh, and I'm coming back to DC," I told her.

"I know, Mom. I can't wait to see you," she said.

Charlotte had decided she was interested in a career in politics. She'd been working her way up via campaign-staff field positions. I must admit, she'd make a great congresswoman someday. I imagine her beating Harold Kestler next cycle and smile.

I turn to the task at hand: making myself alluring. I smile at my reflection in the mirror; a new diamond necklace sparkles in the light.

I have my own personal reasons for attending Davos this year. I happen to know that Senator Jeb Tucker of Oklahoma will be here. He just lost his beloved wife, Lucy, after a long bout with cancer.

Senator Tucker and I have been flirting for years.

Just as I hoped, I see him across the room at the opening night's reception. He smiles, a smile that reminds me a bit of Martin's. Martin would have made a great senator; everyone told us that. He just didn't have it in him to keep pushing forward, keep growing. But I do. I watch as the senator makes his way to me.

"Hello, Jeb," I say as he takes my hand. "I'm so sorry to hear about Lucy."

"Thank you. It was a battle," he says. His silver hair is thick, his grip is strong, his blue eyes damp with sorrow. "She held on for as long as she could."

Sudden death does seem a bit easier by comparison, I suppose. I push Martin's death face out of my head.

"Well, she's in a better place," I say, still holding on to his hand. I hate that line, but it comes in handy, I suppose.

"Walk with me?" he says and leads me through the crowd. We have a natural ease, Jeb and I. I've been part of the club, so to speak. I'm familiar and safe.

And hopefully somewhat attractive, despite my recent cheese-weight gain. "What a lovely night," I say once we reach a private balcony. The who's who mill about all around us, but I came here for only one person. And here we are.

I haven't dated since Martin's death, and I'm ready.

"Such a shame about Eugene," he says. "What a way to end a career."

"Yes, such a shame," I agree. "China is dangerous, we all know that."

Jeb discreetly doesn't bring up our love child, Sarah, or her dalliance with Martin. Or Martin's ties to China. I'm glad he will overlook those uncomfortable little facts. It was a long time ago, Eugene and I. And Martin is dead.

"Amen," Jeb says. "Your maiden name is Prescott?"

"Yes," I say, thrilled he has done a little research.

"As in, the Bush family?" he asks with a big smile.

"One and the same." There must be a common ancestor somewhere along the line.

"Say, Jody Prescott Asher, would you consider joining me for dinner tonight?"

"I can't think of anything more lovely, Senator," I say. Just a couple of lonely widowers finding comfort in each other's arms. I've always thought being the spouse of a senator would be fun. I'll rejoin all my clubs, but this time I'll be even more powerful.

"Good. You're moving back to DC now that the administration is changing?" he asks as I slip my arm through his.

"Yes, of course." I have done my research too. Jeb Tucker lives in a grand home in Kalorama. Oil money will do that for you. My Swiss money will fund the redecorating I'm certain it needs. "I can't wait to get back into the DC social scene. Switzerland is wonderful, but there's nothing like the Hill."

"You must be feeling sort of isolated in Switzerland after all those years inside the Beltway," he says. "You're very good at all of that social stuff. Lucy hated every minute of it."

"Oh, I love it. I can't wait to jump back in. Although some of the clubs won't have me, because I'm no longer married to a member of Congress," I say.

Jeb holds the door open for me, and we step into the relative quiet of the hotel lobby. I feel his arm wrap around my waist, and I lean into him.

"Well, things change, don't they? This feels right," he says. "All of it. I'm so glad I spotted you here. It's like fate."

As I smile and look into his sad blue eyes, I see the spark of lust.

"Yes, it is," I agree.

And now, just like that, I've found my next job. I will woo this man and return to DC as a senator's wife. Watch out, society. I'm coming back, stronger than ever. And I'll finally live in Kalorama. Be still my heart.

Speaking of that, I wonder how strong Jeb's heart is? From what I've read, he's had his issues. And he's old, at least in his midseventies. What a shame. We'll make the most of it for as long as we can. The Tucker name is to Oklahoma like the Asher name is to Ohio's twelfth.

"Shall we?" he asks. He means for us to go find a dinner spot. But I have much more planned.

The rest of his life, actually. And beyond. I suppose I could invoke the Widow's Mandate in the Senate. It's much easier; typically, a governor just appoints the spouse. No nasty campaigns, none of that—just the governor hugging the grieving widow at the press conference. How civilized. I wonder if being a senator is as boring day to day as being a member of Congress was? We'll see.

"Jody?" Jeb says, pulling me back to the present. "Ready?"

Well, I was getting ahead of myself.

I give him my biggest spouse-widow-member-of-Congress-ambassador-and-soon-to-be-senator's-wife smile. "Oh yes. I'm coming, Senator."

You know what they say: behind every successful senator is the next wife who will keep him in office until his last breath.

ACKNOWLEDGMENTS

Wow. This is my ninth novel. And if you've read this far, thank you for being here. I've dreamed of becoming an author since the third grade, and because of readers like you, my dreams have come true. Many thanks, too, to the book world of authors, reviewers, bloggers, librarians, bookstores, and bookstagrammers. What a vibrant and supportive community we are lucky to share.

What fun working with brilliant developmental editor Charlotte Herscher again, our third book together. Thank you for all your insights, your quick wit, and your fast turnaround. It's a pleasure working with you. And to the rest of my fabulous team at Thomas & Mercer—including Megha Parekh, Gracie Doyle, Sarah Shaw, and so many more—you guys are the best team an author could wish for, and I hope we can continue together long into the future. Thank you to my literary agents, Meg Ruley and Annelise Robey. I am so lucky to have you by my side. Special shout-out to Andrea Peskind Katz for coming up with some fabulous wedding hashtags. We all know that's not easy. Thanks to the book-to-film team at the Gotham Group, especially Ellen Goldsmith-Vein.

This novel is special to me for many reasons. It is my first set in Washington, DC, and hopefully, it's not my last. Although this is a work of fiction, the DC setting and some of the social events contained in *The Widow* were inspired by the time my husband served in the United States Congress and the people we met there. What a wonderful, magical, historical, and stressful world our House and Senate members and their families inhabit. It's quite unique and, of course, a spectacular setting for works of fiction.

Thank you to Christine Anderson for helping me navigate it all. I couldn't have done it without you.

I'd like to give special thanks to some special congressional spouses who are the ones making things happen, with heart, behind the scenes in DC and who welcomed me with open arms. I'll inadvertently forget someone, I'm certain, and I apologize in advance, but special thanks to Patti Garamendi, Lisa McGovern, Betty Ann Tanner, Julie Dann, Debbie Lowenthal, and April Delaney. My deepest, sincerest gratitude to you all. And to my "classmates" and friends from the whirlwind 2018 election, especially Annalise Phillips, Leigh Byrne Rose, June Trone, Chrissy Levin, Jacki Cisneros, Lacey Schwartz Delgado, Andrea Neguse, Pam Harder, Deserai Crow, and Christine Riggleman: it all was better because you were there too. I'm so grateful for our friendship.

As always, thanks and love to my husband, Congressman Harley Rouda. I'm so proud of all you have accomplished during your time in politics so far. What an honor to be by your side through it all, in DC and in life.

Thank you for reading. I hope you enjoyed *The Widow*.

ABOUT THE AUTHOR

Photo © 2018 Kristin Karkoska

Kaira Rouda is a multiple award–winning, Amazon Charts and *USA Today* bestselling author of contemporary fiction that explores what goes on beneath the surface of seemingly perfect lives. Her novels of domestic suspense include *Somebody's Home, The Next Wife, The Favorite Daughter, Best Day Ever*, and *All the Difference*. To date, Kaira's work has been translated into more than ten languages. She lives in Southern California with her family. For more information, visit www.kairarouda.com.